# DECEPTION *So* DARK

# DECEPTION SO DARK

DECEPTION SO · BOOK TWO

## Clara Kensie

*To J:*
I. D. W. T. M. A. T.

# CHAPTER ONE

THE HEARTLESS THING about the past is our inability to change it. It's too late to make any alterations. Too late to warn those you love that something horrible is going to happen to them. Too late to tell them that the people they trust the most are actually the bad guys.

The past does not have an Undo command.

As the early January wind howled outside, I shivered in the foyer of my old house in Twelve Lakes, Illinois. Only the thrift-store furniture that had come with the rental house, along with a thin layer of dust on the surfaces, remained. Before they fled, my parents and siblings had destroyed everything we brought into the house, leaving nothing personal behind. No clothing. No books. No half-empty bottles of shampoo. Not even any fingerprints.

My family was gone, and they were never coming back. My parents, because they were now incarcerated in the Underground prison of the Agency for Psionic Research. My brother and sister, because they believed they were on the run from a killer named Dennis Connelly, and because they believed he'd already killed our parents and me.

A vise clamped around my chest, making my breath hitch.

Behind me, my boyfriend Tristan wrapped his arms around my middle, drawing me to him, and instantly opening my lungs again. It had been three weeks since my siblings disappeared, and the APR still had no leads in their search for them. Tristan and I had woken before dawn this morning to make the five-hour drive here from his home in Lilybrook, Wisconsin, hoping to find something the APR had missed. "You can wait in the car if this is too hard," he murmured. "I'll look around on my own."

It *was* hard to be here, in this house, this place of lies and betrayal and pain. But I needed to be here. "Two people looking are better than one," I said. "Besides, this is the only way I can see Jillian and Logan again." And I needed to see them again as much as I needed oxygen.

Even if the only way I could see them was through a vision.

"You're lifting the fog?" Tristan asked, stiffening.

I nodded, already lifting the fog that kept the visions away. Just a little, then a little more.

My newly-discovered psychic ability allowed me to see the past. Suppressed by a mental fog until recently, my retrocognition showed me the history of an item, a place, or a person. I was going to use my retrocognition now, to see my brother and sister.

I kept my breath slow. Even. Steady. I adjusted the fog again, lowering it this time, then nudging it a tiny bit higher. I needed to keep it balanced just right. Too much, the fog would overwhelm me. Too little, the visions would crush me.

There. In the thinning fog. A vision of Jillian from three weeks ago, our last night in Twelve Lakes, right after my family realized that I'd been kidnapped. Her long blond hair was disheveled, and her usual tall, ballerina grace was eviscerated by slumped shoulders as she sobbed into her hands.

I tried to keep the swelling grief and shame at bay, tried to push the despair and guilt deep into the fog.

"Careful, Tessa." Tristan's voice cut through the fog. "You're about to lose control. I can see it happening."

Whereas I could see the past, Tristan could see the future. His precognition took the form of warning premonitions—visions of something about to go wrong. He used to have premonitions only about himself, but once he fell in love with me, he started getting them about me, too.

Heeding his warning, I adjusted the fog before I lost control. I lowered it, raised it, made it thicker, then thinner. Once it was perfectly balanced, I looked for my brother.

There he was. Logan. Standing tall and lean, his chin thrust out in a display of feigned courage as our parents, eyes wild with panic, instructed him and Jillian to run, to run and never stop.

The fog danced and swirled around me, carrying Jillian's sobs and Logan's fear with it.

I breathed in fog instead of air.

"Tessa," Tristan said, sharper this time. "Too much."

I adjusted the fog again. Took a deep breath. Went back in.

Just in time to see Jillian and Logan dash out the front door, lugging several getaway bags each, into the snowy night.

"Wait! Don't go!" I cried, running after them. "Mom and Dad lied to us! *They're* the killers, not Dennis Connelly!"

The sound of my own desperate voice shattered the vision like glass. I'd shouted to an apparition, an illusion, a mirage. Jillian and Logan couldn't hear me, would never hear me. They were gone.

The most heartless thing about having psychic visions of past events is watching the people you love run straight into disaster, and being unable to stop them.

*Is it over?* Tristan asked silently, though his voice was clear in my head.

Unable to speak around the lump in my throat, I replied in the same manner. *The visions are gone. It's over.*

But it wasn't really over. It wouldn't be over until I found my brother and sister, and told them the truth about our parents.

The APR had been searching for my siblings since the night they ran off, but they had no leads. Not a single one. They'd even followed up on my theory that Jillian and Logan would go to our former hideout in Union, Nebraska to seek help from Jillian's old boyfriend, Gavin. But so far, my brother and sister hadn't gone to Nebraska, probably because they were following our parents' rule to never return to one of our previous hideouts. On the slim chance that they did go to Union, the APR left instructions with Gavin's parents to call the agency right away.

A small part of me hoped they wouldn't go to Union, where they would only learn that Gavin had died of a brain aneurysm two years ago, the same night our family fled that hideout. They would not learn, however, that our mother had planted that aneurysm with her psychokinesis, to keep Jillian from contacting him.

Poor Gavin. Killed simply because Jillian loved him.

I swallowed my grief. There would be time for that later, after I found my brother and sister and we could mourn for Gavin together.

Hoping for more visions of my siblings, I took Tristan's hand and led him upstairs to the second floor. The dust on the railing would have driven my mother mad. She was probably keeping her Underground prison cell immaculate. My comatose father would have no idea if his prison cell was dusty or not.

Logan's bedroom was first off the top of the stairs. "Just one thing," I said. "I just want to find one thing." One thing we could bring back to the investigators to help them with their search. But like the rest of the house, Logan's room was empty except for the dented and scratched secondhand furniture. No sheets on the bed. No books on the shelves or posters on the wall. No clothes in the closet. No hints that this room's most recent occupant was a lanky fourteen-year-old boy. Even the air in here was stale and hollow.

Almost filling the door frame with his height and broad shoulders, Tristan stepped into Logan's room. A single sunbeam streaming from the window illuminated Tristan's blue eyes and made his sandy brown hair turn gold. "Let's get started," he said.

Knowing the probability of finding anything was next to zero, I searched in each dresser drawer while Tristan looked under the bed and between the mattresses. Even if Logan had accidentally left something behind, the APR would have found it. They'd scoured the house and hadn't found anything.

We didn't either.

Disappointment draining the strength from my legs, I sank to the bed. Tristan slid the dresser from the wall, then gave a little gasp. "Tessa. Look."

Behind the dresser, against the wall, on the floor, lay a piece of paper.

I pounced on it, then held it between my fingers, careful not to wrinkle it.

Composition paper, torn down the left side. The kind printed with treble clefs and staff and bar lines. The kind Logan used to write music. He'd even jotted a few notes on the bars.

This was more than a piece of paper. This was a piece of Logan.

I lifted the fog to see my brother, his dark hair neatly combed, playing his saxophone. As I watched, he jotted a few musical notes onto a page in his composition book. Then with a frown and a quick shake of his head, he ripped the page from the binding and used his psychokinesis to float it toward the garbage can. While he wrote new notes on a fresh page, the paper slipped under his dresser instead.

"I can't believe Kellan didn't find this," I said. John Kellan. With his red beard, scowling lips, and cunning, ruthless ambition, he was the APR investigator who'd finally captured my parents.

"I'm not surprised at all." Tristan moved the dresser back in place. "All he cared about was apprehending your parents. Finding your brother and sister is far from his top priority. He didn't even come back here himself. He sent an untrained security guard. Said it was all he could spare."

Another vision appeared in the fog, of a short, bored guard dressed in the standard-issue black APR jacket, giving a cursory glance into Logan's bedroom, then leaving.

"How can Kellan not care about finding them?" I said, dismayed. "They're out there, somewhere, scared and alone. They think I'm dead. They think our parents are dead. They think there's a killer after them."

"We don't need Kellan. I'll find them for you," Tristan said. "I promise." He pressed my hand to his chest, right over his heart. He'd done this same thing just yesterday, our last day in the Underground cell, when I was about to leave him forever. *"I will never forgive myself for failing you in Twelve Lakes,"* he'd said then. *"And I will spend the rest of my life making it up to you."*

He'd failed me by lying about his true identity as a junior agent on Kellan's mission to capture my parents. He betrayed me by telling Kellan my family's secrets. He failed to keep me safe from Kellan's plan to kidnap me and hold me as bait. He failed to stop Kellan from punching me, an act of vengeance because one of my parents' victims was his brother-in-law. He deceived me about his true identity as

Dennis Connelly's son.

I'd tried to leave Tristan. I'd gotten as far as the elevator that would lead me up to the ground floor of the APR and away from him forever. But I couldn't get on the elevator. I couldn't leave him. So I ran back to him. Tristan had betrayed me because he loved me. I forgave him, fully and completely. I accepted him back into my heart, and I would never let him go.

I forgave him, but he would never forgive himself.

He raised my hand to his lips and kissed it. "Come on. Let's see what else we can find."

My bedroom was across the hall. I gave it a quick glance as we passed it. My family had destroyed my things too. Closet empty, bed stripped of pillows and blankets. No sign that I had never, not even once, slept in that bed without waking up from a nightmare, biting back my screams.

I passed my parents' bedroom without looking at it. I did not want any visions of them.

Next was Jillian's room, where cosmetics and hair supplies should have been flip-flopping through the air, her bed unmade, her socks and sweaters dangling from half-open drawers. But like my younger brother's, my big sister's room was empty. Stripped and stale and still. The only movement was specks of dust drifting in a sunbeam.

We found nothing in her dresser drawers or between her mattresses. Lips tight with determination, Tristan pushed each piece of furniture from the wall. He moved the sheetless bed, and—

"Her pointe shoe," I exclaimed. In the far back corner under the bed frame was Jillian's battered ivory ballet shoe. Dirty and worn, the ribbon frayed, she must have forgotten to destroy it when she got a new pair.

I slipped the shoe in my bag, along with Logan's composition paper.

Sheet music and a shoe. All I had left of my siblings. But it was two items more than I had just an hour ago. They would have to do, until we found my brother and sister.

The bright afternoon sun was powerless against the frigid wind that swirled and howled around us as we rushed to Tristan's car in the driveway. I was wearing the only clothes I had: Tristan's blue hoodie from his old high school tennis team, his sister's jeans that she'd decorated with five sequined butterflies down one leg, and a pair of laceless sneakers from the APR. Tristan shielded me from the cold as best he could, tucking me under his arm. "First thing we need to do when we get home," he shouted over the wind, "is get you new clothes and a winter coat."

I nodded, miserable. Not because of the cold, but because finding my siblings would be almost impossible. It had taken the Agency for Psionic Research eight years to find my family. But now the APR wasn't putting much effort into finding Jillian and Logan. It could take them twice as long to find two psychic, powerful, terrified teenagers with an almost unlimited amount of cash and eight years' experience in running, hiding, and aliases.

A heavy, panicked sob tore through the wind, but it hadn't come from me. It came from two shadows, running into the night, heavy bags slung over their shoulders. Then a low, faint shout, just an echo: "…train to Union Station…"

Jillian and Logan. In a vision that had escaped from the fog. It vanished as quickly as it had appeared, but it was all I needed.

"I know where they went from here," I said, elation blooming in my chest. "They took a train to Chicago. Union Station."

"How do you know?" Tristan asked.

I pointed into the sunny, snowy yard, where my siblings had been running in the dark night just moments ago. "I heard Logan say it. In a vision."

Tristan squinted into the wind, down the road. "It makes sense. The train depot's only a mile from here in the town square."

I twirled, the frigid air becoming refreshing and crisp. "We can find them. Us. You and me. With my retrocognition. We'll follow their path. They're three weeks ahead of us, but by now they should have settled somewhere, living under new names. It might take us a few days, but we'll catch up to them."

"I promised my parents that we'd be back in Lilybrook in time for dinner tonight," Tristan said. But his protest had no strength; he was already convinced. Kellan had fired Tristan from his job as a junior agent, but finding Jillian and Logan on his own would prove to the APR that he would be a good investigator after all.

Finding Jillian and Logan would make up for failing me.

He lit up from the inside out: first his eyes, then his smile. "Union Station, here we come."

I laughed, and the wind carried it away with the snowflakes. As early as tomorrow, next week at the latest, Jillian and Logan could return with us to Lilybrook. No more lies. No more aliases. No more paralyzing fear that each day would be our last. Just happy, stable, peaceful, normal lives.

Finding Jillian and Logan was my top priority, and therefore it was Tristan's. We didn't need the APR. We had my power of retrocognition and Tristan's warning premonitions. We had each other.

Together, we would find my siblings.

# CHAPTER TWO

RISTAN DROVE US straight down the road, just over a mile, to the little train depot in Twelve Lakes' town square. Today was a Saturday, and the faded schedule mounted on the door informed us the next train was arriving at one o'clock, only five minutes from now. We'd made it just in time. From here, it would take almost an hour and a half to get to Union Station.

Too cold to wait outside, we entered the tiny depot. A wall of plate glass windows faced out toward the train tracks. One window had been replaced by plywood, slightly dimming the interior. Only one other person was in the depot, a college-aged girl in a red wool coat and brown fur-trimmed boots, sitting on a bench and scrolling through her cell phone. On her way to see a friend, perhaps, or to meet a guy for a date. Just a normal girl, with a normal life, with normal problems. Certainly not a girl whose parents had used their powers of remote vision and psychokinesis to blackmail and murder people.

The normal girl gave Tristan and me a disinterested glance, then returned to her phone.

Tristan sent a quick text to his parents to tell them what we were doing. Too anxious to wait patiently for the train, I paced the perimeter of the depot.

Five minutes until the train arrived. Then another ninety to Union Station. How much farther away could Jillian and Logan get in that amount of time?

Ninety-five minutes too far.

But they had been *here*, at this train station in Twelve Lakes, just three weeks ago. If I lifted the fog, I should be able to see them. Maybe they'd made a plan and decided where to go after Union Station.

Concentrating, keeping my breath even and steady, adjusting the fog increments at a time, I filtered through the histories of all the passengers who'd been here in the past—

"I see them!" I cried. Wispy, flickering in and out and surrounded by fog, but it was definitely them. Huddled together on the wooden bench in the far shadowed corner. Sneakers wet from their mile-long trek through the snowy night. Snow dusting their hair and shoulders. Logan on guard, gaze darting from door to each corner and back to the door. Jillian crying into her hands and shivering from cold.

*Shh,* Tristan said silently, with a nod at the girl in the red coat before pulling me to sit next to him. *What do you see? What are they saying?*

I returned my focus to the bench in the corner, then lifted the fog a bit more to reveal Jillian heaving a great sob, the plate glass window shattering behind her, and Logan admonishing her to control her PK. Then the images flickered and faded away, disappearing like vapor.

*Jillian was so scared that she broke the window,* I told Tristan. *But now the visions are gone.*

*At least we're on their trail,* he said as the train whistle blew outside. *We'll pick it up again at Union Station.*

Shadowed, chilly, echoey. Dirty, gray, and underground. Chicago's massive Union Station platform was much too similar to the Underground prison of the APR. I'd lived in an Underground cell for three weeks, hiding the truth about my parents' crimes in the fog, insisting that Dennis Connelly was the real killer, insisting that Tristan had only pretended to love me so he could help capture my family. Until yesterday. That was the day my retrocognition, suppressed by the fog my entire life, finally gave me all the proof I'd ever need, or want, that I had been wrong.

Tristan kept me close under his arm as we walked down the platform, then through the concourse and up to the lively and noisy Great Hall. From gloomy and dim to bright and bustling in an instant. I had to squint against the sunlight streaming from the windows and reflecting off the shiny marble floors.

Businessmen and women rushed past, some shouting into cell phones. Mothers tugged their children behind them and pushed screaming toddlers in strollers. Everyone hurrying, chatting. "So many people," I breathed.

Tristan called my name, but I could barely hear him over the crowd. It was just so *loud* in here. So many people, and the number grew by the second. Women wearing pillbox hats. Men with narrow ties. Teens wearing fringed vests.

"Tessa!"

A rowdy group of guys in blue Cubs jerseys pushed past on their way to a game, hooting and high-fiving each other.

*Bring in the fog, Clockwise.*

Hearing Tristan's nickname for me, the first word he'd ever spoken to me, snapped me back, and I brought in the fog.

The *loud* shut off like someone had pressed a mute button.

The slick floor of the station shone like glass. There were a few dozen people in winter coats waiting on benches and hustling to the escalators or out the doors, but compared to how crowded it was just a few seconds ago, the enormous station was now almost empty.

Those Cubs fans were not on their way to a game. It was January. It wasn't even baseball season.

I blinked up at Tristan. "All those people. They were just visions. The fog lifted and I didn't even know it."

"You're still learning to control it," he said. "But we have to go."

"Why? I haven't even started looking for Jillian and Logan."

He tapped his head—a warning premonition. "You're going to lose control and pass out." He started to turn around, pulling me with him.

I shook his arm off me. "But I'm good now. I have the fog back under control."

"Not for long. I'm still seeing it happen."

"I'll be fine."

"No, Tessa, you won't. It's going to happen unless I get you out of here." He tapped his head again. He believed I was going to pass out, and there was no convincing him otherwise.

"Then I'll find them before I pass out," I said. "How long do I have?"

Tristan frowned, anxiety and doubt chasing each other behind his eyes. "You have one minute before we go back to the train. Sixty seconds."

I nodded as visions began solidifying, although I hadn't lifted the fog yet. Carefully, cautiously, I raised it. Jillian and Logan could have gone in any direction from here. I concentrated on finding them, peering through the dense crowd. Even standing on my tiptoes, I was too short to see above anyone. So many people had been in Union Station that a sense of any individual, even my own brother and sister, had become impossible to distinguish.

"I don't see them, Tristan."

"Then don't look," he said, his voice echoing from far away. "Think. Quickly. We're at Union Station, downtown Chicago. What do you think Jillian and Logan would do next? Would they stay and hide somewhere in the city, or would they go somewhere else?"

I tried to think. I wanted so badly for Jillian and Logan to be here, in Chicago. So close. Just one city to look in, instead of a whole country. A whole planet. But I knew they'd never stay in Chicago or anywhere near Twelve Lakes. They believed a killer was after them—they'd run as far as they could get. "I'm sure they left the city."

"Okay, good. We can eliminate all the local routes and concentrate on transportation that leaves Chicago." Guiding me through the fog, he rushed me over to a map of Union Station mounted on the wall. "There's an Amtrak station in this building, and a Greyhound station a few blocks away. Or they could have taken a city bus to the airport. Which one would they pick?"

Dizzy, woozy, heart pounding in my ears, I labored to keep the fog close. Visions of all the people who had ever been in this station were threatening to break free. My mind was swimming in a sea of fog, in an ocean of visions.

"Time to go," Tristan said. He took my arm, but I shook him off. With a huge effort, I pushed the visions away. The exertion made me weak, but the visions were gone again.

"No. I'm still feeling fine," I said. "I can do this."

With an impatient sigh, Tristan took my arm again, but only to support me rather than to take me away. "Bus, train, or plane, Tessa?"

I took a deep breath and licked my lips. My mouth was so dry. I had to think, but the thick fog made it difficult. I forced myself to focus. Bus, train, or plane.

My family had never taken a plane while we were on the run because security was so tight. We paid cash for everything so we didn't have to use credit cards or show identification, and that was impossible when purchasing a plane ticket. I was positive they didn't go to the airport. That left buses or trains.

Buses made lots of stops. It would be easy for Jillian and Logan to get off at any of the stops if they felt threatened or unsafe. But it would also be easy for someone to get on. They would wonder if every man boarding the bus at every stop was Dennis Connelly, or someone working for him.

Jillian and Logan had lots of money. Bags of cash. They could easily afford two tickets on an Amtrak train. A cross-country train wouldn't make as many stops as a cross-country bus, but it would be easier to hide on a train. Trains had dining cars. They'd have food. Trains had private sleeper cars. Privacy meant safety.

But they could also have walked out of the station and onto the streets, and taken a cab somewhere. Or walked to a used car lot and bought a car. Or bought a car from someone who was selling it privately. They didn't have licenses, but that wouldn't stop them from driving.

Too many options. It would take hours, days, to track each one, and I only had seconds to leave before Tristan's premonition happened. If I picked the wrong option…

"A train," I heard myself say from far away. It was only a guess, a wish, a hope. "They might have taken the train somewhere. We have to go to the Amtrak station."

"The Amtrak lobby is all the way across this huge build—" Tristan said, then his eyes opened wide. "It's going to happen, now, if we don't leave."

I took a few shaky steps. I had to get to the Amtrak lobby before the visions came back, and they were already pushing their way out of the fog. The effort to contain them was making me weak, making my heart pound, closing up my throat. I forced myself to keep walking. "I just need another minute."

Breath gaspy. Legs shaky. Head dizzy. I stumbled into Tristan, then forced myself upright again.

"Tessa, stop!" he demanded. "We have to go. Now."

"Help me get there," I said. "If I close my eyes, maybe I can keep the visions away."

I closed my eyes, but it didn't help. Whirling around me were people and names and facts and stories I didn't want to know or need to know but I *did* know, I knew it all, and everything spiraled deeper and deeper and I couldn't think couldn't breathe—

The visions blasted through the fog like an explosion.

Millions of visions. Surrounding me. Burying me. Suffocating me. Solid, unbreakable, impenetrable. I crumpled to the floor with a stifled scream—never ever *ever* scream—clutching my head, certain the visions would force my skull to burst.

The fog. The fog, the fog, I need the fog, where is the fog? I called it but it wouldn't come. It wouldn't come it wouldn't come. I called it, reached for it, tried to grab it and pull it in but my fingers just slipped through it.

*Tristan the visions they won't let me go so many visions hundreds thousands millions billions—*

The long silver knife pivots on its point, the blade reflecting the light. It glitters and glimmers, sparkles and glows.

A binder, thick and heavy with paper, opens with a screech. On each page is a photo of my parents' victims. The pages turn themselves, each page featuring a different victim, and another, and another. Endless pages, endless victims.

My parents are their killers, and the blood that pumps through my veins is my parents' blood. Tainted blood. Tarnished blood. Killers' blood.

From the pages of the binder, the victims stare at me. Accuse me. Loathe me. Despise me. Their eyes morph, meld, blend together, and become a single pair of eyes, dark as a starless night and black as a cavern of coal. Infinite black, forever black, impossible black, glowering at me with vengeful fury.

They want revenge. They want me to atone. They want me to bleed. They want me to pay with my tainted, tarnished blood.

The eyes grow, bigger and darker, rumbling and growling, louder and louder, then with a thunderous roar they explode, detonate, flashing silver, bright and blinding.

And the knife glitters and glimmers, sparkles and glows, and slices through the air.

I woke up on the cold shiny floor of Union Station to Tristan squeezing my hand. "She gets panic attacks," he half-lied to an emotionless EMT as she checked my pulse. He scraped his free hand through his hair. "I couldn't stop it from happening in time." Under his breath, he swore at himself.

Like a soft gray blanket, fog had settled over everything.

Murmuring with shock and pity, a crowd had gathered around me. A crowd of real people. People of the present, not of the past.

They stared down at me, their eyes wide with curiosity and soft with sympathy. Except for a hunched-over old man with a cane. He glowered at me with grief and shame, despair and rage, his eyes dark as a starless night and black as a cavern of coal.

I blinked, and his eyes lightened, becoming a watery, unfocused blue.

"Grandpa, this way," cooed the young woman next to him, who then gently took his arm and led him away.

I tried to raise the fog again, just a tiny bit, but it wouldn't budge. I couldn't see a single vision of the millions of people who'd been here in the past. The visions were gone.

Which meant Jillian and Logan were gone, too. I'd lost their trail.

Tristan and I would have to go back to Lilybrook without them.

# CHAPTER THREE

USHING HIS WIRE-RIMMED glasses up his nose, Tristan's father, Dennis, paced back and forth in the Connellys' family room. His mom, Deirdre, sat next to me on the couch, her curtain of frizzy copper hair not quite hiding her disapproving expression.

Tristan sat on my other side, elbows on his knees. "So that's what happened," he said. It had taken us almost an hour to explain the day's events to his parents, and now he hung his head in disappointment.

Dennis was disappointed too—in Tristan. "You took a girl with a brand new psionic ability to Union Station in Chicago. *Union Station.* That place has got to be a hundred years old. Millions of people have passed through it. She's retrocognitive, Tristan, and she hasn't learned to control it yet. You can't bring her to a place like Union Station."

Dennis Connelly. The man my family had run from for eight years. The man I'd believed was trying to kill us, to slice us open right down the middle. The man who had invaded my nightmares every single night. The man whose name I'd refused to say aloud.

But the whole time, he had only been trying to rescue me.

Now, under my breath, I whispered, "Dennis Connelly." Just

because I could. *Dennis Connelly* had no power over me anymore.

Now he was just Dennis. Tristan's father. And I was living in his home, which meant he was responsible for my welfare. He spent eight years of his life trying to bring me to safety; no wonder he was so upset with Tristan and me tonight.

"Didn't you think something like this would happen?" he asked.

"I *knew* it would happen," Tristan said. "I should have taken her out of there the second I had that premonition." Mac, his gigantic golden-furred mutt, whined and put his chin on Tristan's knee.

"Please don't be mad at Tristan, Dennis," I said. "He warned me. I ignored him."

Dennis scrubbed his balding head. "Tessa, I understand how important it is to find your brother and sister," he said. "The APR does too. That's why John Kellan is on the case."

Tristan's hands curled into fists.

"Kellan may not be our favorite person," Dennis said, "but he is the best investigator in the agency. And remember, Jillian and Logan may be frightened, but there's not really a killer after them. No one is going to hurt them."

True. My siblings were safer than they'd ever been, now that our mother wasn't around to use her psychokinesis to give anyone heart attacks or brain aneurysms, or fly anyone into a wall, or slice anyone open from a hundred feet away with a swipe of her clawed hand.

My hands fluttered to my belly. My parents told me that Dennis Connelly had sliced me open that day eight years ago. Now the five twisted scars stretching from my sternum to my pelvis were a permanent reminder of my parents' lies and deception.

At Dennis's concerned frown, I thickened the fog in an attempt to block my thoughts from him. Tristan and I could communicate telepathically, but only to each other, and only if we pushed. Dennis was a true telepath and could hear anyone's thoughts at any time.

Now, perhaps realizing I'd thickened the fog to keep him out of my head, he raised his palm. "Sorry, Tessa. I don't listen in on my family's thoughts unless I feel it's necessary. I won't do that to you again."

"Tessa, you can*not* ignore Tristan's warnings." Deirdre placed her hand on mine and gave it a tentative squeeze. "His premonitions are always on target, just like my dreams."

Unlike Tristan's premonitions that happened only minutes or seconds before the event, Deirdre had precognitive dreams about events that would happen days or even years in the future. She dreamed about Tristan bringing me to his home over two years ago, before she even knew who I was.

"I wish you'd have a dream that we found Jillian and Logan," I said.

I wasn't joking, but Deirdre gave a nervous little laugh. "Oh, honey. I wish so, too."

I glanced around the Connellys' family room. Stacks of magazines and papers on the coffee table. A collection of stuffed snowmen—a quick vision showed me that Deirdre over-decorated the house for each season and holiday—lined the hearth on either side of the fireplace, with a giant snowman propped in the corner. Scrapbooks and board games piled on an end table. A jumble of electronics on the desk: an eReader, a couple of iPads, a laptop. At least four remotes for the television and all its devices. A forgotten sweater slung over the armrest of the leather recliner. Knickknacks and mementos on every spare inch of shelf.

The Connellys' house wasn't dirty, but it was unorganized and cluttered. My mother would hate this place.

Deirdre rose and gave Tristan a kiss on his head. "Night, kids. Tessa, you can't go around wearing Tristan and Ember's clothes forever. We'll go shopping tomorrow."

"Be careful with that fog of yours," Dennis said to me. He patted

Tristan's shoulder, then put his arm around Deirdre. As they left, she gave his cheek a peck.

My mom and dad were like that. Even in our family's most stressful moments, they'd always been affectionate and tender with each other. But now, though they were incarcerated in the same Underground prison, they'd probably never even get to see each other again, let alone kiss.

As soon as we were alone, Tristan took my hand and played with the promise ring on my finger. A band of pearls set in gold, it was a replica of the ring from *Anne of Green Gables*, my favorite book. Tristan had given both the book and the ring to me in Twelve Lakes. The book was gone now, but I still had the ring, and I would never take it off.

"Kellan may be the best investigator," he said, "but he doesn't care about finding Jillian and Logan. I do. We'll find them, Tessa. Us. You and me. But you need to let me keep you safe. No more ignoring my warnings, okay?"

I nodded, then leaned my head on his shoulder and breathed in his scent of soap and strength and safety. I looked around the Connellys' family room, this room with worn crocheted afghans on the couches and a menagerie of childhood art projects on the mantle and framed photos of happy family moments on the wall. Moments my own family never had, and never would.

I wanted happy moments for Jillian and Logan. I wanted them to be safe, like I was now. I wanted them to be surrounded by love, like I was, right now.

# CHAPTER FOUR

LOCKWISE. WAKE UP. You're having another nightmare."

Rigid muscles, burning lungs, staccato heartbeat, suppressed scream. My nightmare of sparkling silver knives and glowering black eyes faded as I tried to remember where I was.

My parents were in prison. My siblings were on the run. But I was in the guest bedroom of my boyfriend's house, in Lilybrook, Wisconsin.

My muscles unwound, my lungs filled with air, and my heart rate pumped its way back to normal. I pried my eyelids open. The first orange-pink rays of the early morning sun shone through the windows, and Tristan was standing beside the bed in sweatpants and a Green Bay Packers T-shirt. Tousled hair, sleepy eyes, frowning with concern. "I thought you'd stop having nightmares now that you're safe."

Safe. I was *safe*. I blinked the last of the nightmare away. "Me too. But I'm fine now. Thanks."

After a quick kiss, Tristan slipped back to his own room before his parents overheard and assumed he'd spent the night in here. They were already upset with us for going to Union Station.

Instead of going back to sleep, I sat up and checked on Jillian's ballet shoe and Logan's sheet music, just to make sure they were still there. They were right where I'd placed them last night: on the dresser in front of the giant mirror, where I could see them from any point in the room.

I hugged my knees to my chest. This guest room, painted a cheery celery-green, would be mine for as long as I stayed here. A thick white comforter with tiny yellow flowers on the bed, plump pillows inside soft cotton cases. A plush green area rug. An overstuffed easy chair under the window, next to a sturdy bookshelf with vases and framed photos and books of all genres, invited everyone to curl up and stay as long as they wanted. Cozy. Welcoming.

Visions of the other guests who'd slept in this room over the years pestered me to set them free. Curious, I raised the fog.

All of the guests who'd stayed in this room were young, friends of Tristan and his younger sister, Ember. A teenage boy with blond dreadlocks and a straight nose and an easy, deep laugh. A group of three middle school girls in pajamas, giggling and imitating a new dance move they'd seen on the VMAs.

One guest stood out from the rest. A girl with wavy black hair with thick bangs. Pale skin and big wistful eyes, so blue they were almost violet.

She'd cried here, in this room.

Melanie. That was her name. Melanie Brunswick. Her last name was familiar, somehow, but I couldn't place it. She'd been here often, my visions showed me, from the time she was around eight until she was my age now, sixteen. Then her presence cut off abruptly, like someone had taken scissors to the visions and snipped her away.

When I felt that it was late enough, I slipped out of bed, tucked in the sheets and straightened the covers, then went to take a shower. The hall bathroom was shared by Tristan and Ember, but Ember took it over while Tristan was gone, and she'd completely girl-ified it. Bath rug, shower curtain, and waste basket in hot pink. Nail polishes, boxes of hair dye in pinks, purples, blues, and greens were tossed on the counter, along with headbands, lotions, and cosmetics.

I grabbed a couple of hot pink towels from the overstuffed linen closet and started the shower. Like the rest of the bathroom, the tub was cluttered with a hodgepodge of shampoos, conditioners, loofahs, and body soaps.

My mother would have been horrified by this bathroom. I disliked the mess too, but there was a sense of comfort to it. A hominess. A permanence. The Connellys could collect bottles of shampoo, and display family photos and art projects, and fill their closets with clothes and their bookshelves with books. The Connellys had no need to gather everything up at a moment's notice to destroy all evidence of their existence before fleeing town.

I'd lived in thirteen houses over the past eight years, and none of them had felt like home.

I turned the water hotter and stepped under the stream. How long would this house be my home? How long before the Connellys stopped being so generous with the daughter of the people who'd tried to kill both Dennis and Tristan?

Something tiny glittered in the corner of the shower. Just enough to catch my eye.

A pink razor. Or rather, the silver blade of a pink razor.

It glittered and glimmered, sparkled and glowed.

Glittered and glimmered.

Sparkled and glowed.

The steam from the shower grew thick, surrounding me in a cloud. Yet the blade continued to shine through the mist.

Glittered and glimmered, sparkled and glowed.

A hollow knock at the bathroom door made me gasp. Startle. Blink.

"Hey, Clockwise," Tristan called from the hall. "You doing okay in there?"

Did he have a premonition? Was I about to press that razor blade to my wrist again, like I had in the Underground? But I'd done that during one of the darkest moments of my life, when I was lost in the fog, lost in denial.

"Just checking to see if you need anything," Tristan said from behind the door.

"I'm good." My voice wobbled, so I cleared my throat. "Thanks."

No. No premonition. If he'd had a premonition, he would have busted through the door like he had in the Underground. And his tone was light. He was just being Tristan, taking care of me.

Not wanting to look straight at it, I peeked at the razor peripherally.

Nothing. No shine. No glimmer or glow.

I was fine.

After my shower, I used Ember's hairbrush to comb through my hair. I'd worn her jeans for the past two days. I was grateful that Deirdre was taking me shopping for my own things today, but I didn't know how I'd pay her back. I had no money. Any money my family had was never really ours, because my parents had stolen it all through blackmail.

In the bathroom's linen closet, I found a rag and a bottle of bathroom cleaner. I also found, in the way back, an electric rotary shaver still in its original packaging. Perfect. I wouldn't have to worry about that glittering, glimmering razor blade anymore. I tucked the rotary shaver neatly in the cabinet drawer, then straightened the clutter on the counter and cleaned the sink. Until I found a way to pay the

Connellys back, cleaning was all I could do.

As I sprayed the mirror with Windex, something rough and wet scraped across my ankle. I yelped, and a white ball of fur darted from the bathroom.

"You don't like cats?" a feminine voice said from the doorway. Ember, gathering her long purple hair into a bun and wearing fleece pajamas decorated with guitar-playing penguins.

"He just surprised me," I said. "I've never had a cat." Having a pet would have been impossible while my family was on the run. "But I've always wanted one."

When Ember didn't reply, just continued to stare at me warily, I added, "What's your cat's name?"

"Lyric," she said, "And this is Aria." With her big toe, painted lime green with a pink daisy, she pointed to the tiny brown dog panting next to her.

Aria yipped and wagged her tail so hard her entire back half wiggled. I laughed, then knelt to scratch her head. "She's adorable."

"Lyric!" Ember called. "Come back and say hello to Tessa." Lyric slunk back in and sat at my feet, then meowed.

"He says you can pick him up," Ember said.

"He says that?"

She shrugged. "Yeah."

I picked up Lyric and, with the back of my finger, rubbed his chin.

Aria, perhaps tired from wagging her tail so hard, lay on the bath rug and closed her eyes. Ember's eyes, however, were blue and narrowed as she leaned against the sink. Not unfriendly, just… guarded.

While Tristan and I were in the Underground, he told me that except for the physician and healers who'd examined me, and a handful of investigators and guards, no one knew the Kitteridge Killers were my parents. I hoped to keep it that way, but there was only one reason Ember would look at me like that. "You know, don't you," I said. "You know who I am. Who my parents are."

"My mom and dad just told me," she said.

"Does anyone else know?"

"Not yet. It's supposed to be confidential. But it's kind of hard to keep a secret in this town. Psychics *everywhere*."

"I'm sorry." The words pushed themselves from my mouth. "About my parents. For what they did to your dad. For attacking him. For giving him a heart attack."

She said nothing.

Because what *could* she say? "It's okay?" or, "No big deal?" It *wasn't* okay. It *was* a big deal. She almost lost her father because of my parents. An apology could never make up for that. *Nothing* I said or did could ever make up for that.

My blood burned with shame.

Finally, Ember spoke. "Your parents also tried to kill my brother. Twice."

My parents had tried to kill Tristan *twice*. Three weeks ago, before they knew I'd been kidnapped and was being held as bait, they planned for my mother to give Tristan a brain aneurysm via her psychokinesis. And just the other day, during my mother's Underground escape attempt, she tried to slice him open with a slash of her clawed hand through the air. The same way she'd sliced me open eight years ago.

Ember left without another word, taking Aria and Lyric with her. My burning shame kicked up to a boil.

Between Deirdre's nervous attempts at mothering me and Tristan's hypervigilance to keep me from losing control of the fog, I felt so smothered that I could barely breathe at the mall that day. I spent most of my time concentrating on balancing the fog, keeping away the visions of all the customers who'd shopped there in the past—nowhere close to the number of people who'd passed through Union Station, but enough to make me dizzy and weak. Through Herculean effort, I managed to keep the fog balanced, and Tristan didn't have a single warning premonition about me the entire day.

When we got back, there was a note on the kitchen table. A sheet of plain computer paper folded into thirds. My name was on it.

*Tessa*

I blinked, still not used to seeing my real name in print after using aliases for so many years.

"That's my mother's handwriting," I said.

"A guard dropped it off for you this afternoon," Dennis said as he grabbed a box of Cheez-Its from the pantry.

Tristan frowned. "She's allowed to contact Tessa? After everything she did to her?"

My hands fluttered to my belly.

"I think she's trying to redeem herself," Dennis said. He tossed an orange cracker in his mouth, exactly the way Tristan would.

There was no redemption for what my mother had done. I plucked the note from the table. A vision appeared of my mother crying as she wrote it, but I doused it with fog. When Dennis wasn't watching, I stuffed the note in the garbage can.

Upstairs, with Mac at his side, Tristan lounged on my bed, programming my new cell phone, while I sorted through my new jeans and sweaters. Deirdre had expressed that I should choose trendier clothes, brighter clothes, clothes like Ember would wear. But after so many years of needing to be invisible, I felt uncomfortable in anything that would draw attention to myself. The only clothes I truly liked were my new running outfits. January in northern Wisconsin was too cold for running outside, but as soon as spring came, I fully intended to start jogging again.

Would Jillian and Logan still be missing in the spring?

Too awful to consider, I tucked that question away in a cloud of fog.

Most of my new clothes I folded into the dresser or hung in the closet. The rest I tucked into my new getaway bag, which I would store in the trunk of Tristan's car. I had a blue denim getaway bag for the past eight years. This one was a polyester yellow, but it served a similar purpose: I needed to be ready to leave at any moment. Not to escape from Dennis Connelly, but to go get Jillian and Logan.

Deirdre had also insisted on buying me cosmetics and hair supplies, although I rarely wore makeup and I usually left my hair down and loose, or up in a ponytail for jogging. I left those items in the bag and stored them in a dresser drawer.

As I straightened Jillian's ballet shoe and Logan's sheet music on the dresser in front of the mirror, Tristan's cell phone dinged. "Finally," he said. "I've been texting my buddy Nathan all day, but he hasn't replied yet. I want you to meet him."

"You didn't tell him about my parents, did you?" After Ember's wary reception, I didn't want Tristan's friends to know who I was.

"Not yet. But he's my best friend, and you're my girlfriend. He won't care who your parents are. I mean, he'll be shocked at first, but he won't hold it against you. No one will." He checked his phone. "It's not Nathan, but this is even better."

"What is it?"

He grinned with pride, brightening from the inside out. "Something you need to see. Come on, it's easier on my computer." He led me down the hall to his bedroom. I looked around while he sat at his desk and opened his laptop. Tristan's bedroom in Twelve Lakes was temporary and therefore undecorated, but this one, his real room, had personality. Walls painted navy blue, displaying posters of classic rock bands and autographed sports memorabilia. A shelf cluttered with trophies from his tennis, cross-country, and skiing competitions. Yearbooks from elementary, middle, and high school. A sloppily made bed. Speakers on his desk. A globe. Paperbacks, mostly legal thrillers and crime procedurals. Battered ACT and SAT study guides. A model airplane. I lifted the fog to see a vision of him making it from a kit with his dad, when he was nine years old.

It smelled like him in here. Soap and strength and masculinity. I loved this room.

"So what do you want to show me?" I asked.

"One of the guys at the APR is a cyberpath. Craig Schultz. He can intuitively interface with computers," he said. "I called him this morning and asked him to hack into the Amtrak computers to see if Jillian and Logan went there when they got off the commuter train at Union Station."

"And?"

"And…watch." He gestured to his laptop. A black and white image appeared of a long ticket booth, stretching wall to wall, with multiple windows for making purchases. Ticket agents stood in three of the windows. A pair of teenagers, weary and disheveled, approached an agent.

"That's them!" I cried. "That's Jillian and Logan."

"It's the security footage," Tristan said. "You were right, Tessa. They went to Amtrak."

I couldn't breathe, couldn't take my eyes off the laptop. I wanted to hug it to my chest. I wanted to reach in and pull Jillian and Logan out of the computer.

"They bought tickets," I said, watching the grainy image of Logan slipping two tickets into his pocket. "Where to?"

"Craig said they bought tickets to New Orleans," Tristan said, reading the email on his phone. "Probably because it was the first train scheduled to leave."

"Maybe they're still there," I said. "Jillian's always liked the warmer states. At the very least we can pick up their trail." I raced to the guest room to finish packing my getaway bag. When I returned a minute later—I had eight years of fast-packing experience—Tristan was still at his computer. "Tristan, come on. We have to go."

He turned to me, his face no longer bright with pride, but grim and gray.

The hope that had blossomed in my chest withered. "What happened?"

"Watch." He rewound the video a minute back.

The view on the screen changed to the waiting area. Jillian and Logan huddled on two of the seats. Jillian was shivering, and crying again. Logan had one arm around the back of her seat. His other clutched the duffle bag of money on his lap.

My siblings talked to each other, heads close, without moving from their seats. I could see their lips moving, but their image was so small and grainy that I couldn't figure out what they were saying.

Occasionally they'd peer around the lobby, but stayed seated as if they were too scared to move. At one point Logan gazed directly at the security camera. He seemed to be looking right at me. I watched as his eyes widened, going from fear to outright terror.

He flew from his seat, pulling Jillian up too, and pointing at the camera. They flung their getaway bags over their shoulders, grabbed the duffle bag of money and dashed away.

The following images, spliced together by Craig, showed my siblings fleeing from the Amtrak lobby, back through the concourse and through the crowd in the Great Hall, then out of Union Station.

They were gone. Again.

"I wonder what spooked them?" Tristan murmured.

"Our parents taught us to avoid places with security cameras," I said. "They told us Dennis Connelly had the resources to track us that way."

Our parents had been correct.

"They probably didn't go to Louisiana," I added. "Not after they realized they were caught on camera buying tickets for New Orleans."

Tristan pulled me into his lap. "I'll ask Craig to check the Greyhound computers next."

"If there's security cameras, they wouldn't go to the bus station either," I said, my muscles heavy with disappointment. "They must have gotten a car and driven out of the city."

"This was just the first try, Tessa," he said, wrapping his arms around me. "I have lots of ideas. And there's still a chance they'll go to Nebraska to find Jillian's boyfriend."

I sat frozen, unable to take my gaze from the computer screen.

"Tessa." Tristan caressed my cheek. "Clockwise. Did you hear me?"

"Play the video again," I said. "From the beginning. I want to see them again."

He dragged the cursor back to the beginning of the video, and played it again.

And again.

And again.

# CHAPTER FIVE

INNER THAT NIGHT was an extra-large half-pepperoni-half-veggie, delivered from Argento's Pizzeria. Tristan and I set the table. It was one of the first times in my life I'd ever done it. When I was living with my real family, my mother would simply float the plates and utensils over and have them set themselves. The beverage would take itself out of the fridge and pour itself into our glasses.

I missed that. I missed things flying around by themselves. Here at the Connelly's, everything just stayed wherever we put it.

Their yellow kitchen was clean but cluttered, like the rest of the house. Report cards, flyers for community events, holiday and birthday cards were stuck to the fridge with magnets. There was not a single cooking gadget in sight. They kept a stack of delivery and carryout menus on the counter, and the fridge and pantry were crammed with leftovers and snacks. A wooden plaque hanging on the wall declared, *Please excuse the noise and mess, we are busy making happy memories.*

My mother would have been appalled at the clutter and the prepackaged food. I was too, but I kind of liked that plaque. Objects didn't fly around by themselves here, but the Connelly family was just as chaotic as mine had been, only in a different way. Happier. No undercurrent of fear and despair and hopelessness.

I picked the green peppers off my veggie pizza. "Any word about Jillian and Logan?" I asked Dennis.

"If there was, Kellan would have called, honey." He looked at Tristan and me over his glasses. "You two are still looking for them on your own, aren't you?"

"Yes." I told him the truth. I hated lying, and besides, it was useless to lie to a telepath.

Tristan chuckled and finished his pizza slice in one huge bite.

"I figured you would," Dennis said with a sigh. "Just be careful, and don't interfere with Kellan's search."

"Or your studies," Deirdre added. "School starts tomorrow for both of you."

I couldn't believe the Connellys were making us go to school when my brother and sister were missing. But like my own parents, Dennis and Deirdre wanted me to live as normal a life as possible. And Tristan had already postponed college for a semester in order to investigate my family's case. I couldn't ask him to make any more sacrifices for me.

After dinner, Dennis and Deirdre went to the family room to watch TV, while I found a broom and dustpan in the closet and swept the floor.

Tristan took the broom from my hand and led me to the living room. "Tessa, before you start school, there are a few things you should know."

Before he could tell me, though, his eyes grew wide and guilt crossed his face, seconds before the doorbell rang. "Too late," he muttered.

"Who's here?" I asked.

Ember, her purple hair sporting new blue streaks, dashed through the living room carrying a pink electric guitar. "My band's coming over," she said. "We have an extra practice tonight. We need to write an original song for Battle of the Bands."

That's right; Ember was in a band. Lyre. One of my very first visions, just a couple days ago, was of Ember playing that electric guitar. Maybe Logan, after we found him, could join her band. Even if they didn't need a sax player, Logan could learn to play any instrument with a wave of his hand, courtesy of his hypercognition.

Ember answered the door, revealing a petite girl in a heavy winter coat and a black knit beret, her black hair tumbling from under it. I'd seen that girl in a vision this morning. She was the girl who was crying in the guest room. Melanie Brunswick.

*Tessa, I wasn't expecting her to come tonight,* Tristan flashed to me. As she entered the house, he stood and tucked in his shirt. "Hey, Mel."

"Hi," she said. Timid, sweet. Hesitant. Just an inch or two taller than me, she kept her eyes on her Doc Martens as she took off her coat. "I, um, just came over for band practice."

"You doing okay?" he asked.

She gave a little shrug. "Yeah."

"Do you need anything? Your car's working now? I texted Nathan a few weeks ago and asked him to fix it."

"He did. Thanks."

Chewing her lip, Ember surveyed the three of us. "Come on, Melanie. Let's go to the basement."

As if it were painful to do so, Melanie dragged her gaze to me, her violet eyes wide and wounded. "You're Tessa?"

I'd been using my real name for three weeks now, but it still felt dangerous to hear it cross other people's lips. "Yeah. Hi."

"I thought you'd be…different. Taller, maybe."

"Oh! Hey!" Ember clapped her hands. "Tessa, Melanie's a seeker.

Maybe she can help find your brother and sister."

Tristan pushed his hands into his pockets. "I already thought of that," he mumbled. "But Melanie finds lost things, not lost people."

"I heard that your brother and sister are missing," Melanie said. "I'm so sorry."

Shocked at how much it hurt to hear those words said aloud—*your brother and sister are missing*—by someone I didn't even know, I nodded and took Tristan's arm. At that, a vision blasted into my mind, one that explained all the awkwardness in a single moment.

Or rather, in a single kiss.

Tristan kissing Melanie. Right here, in this room. Bending down and kissing her, putting his lips on hers. Melanie kissing him back.

I pulled my hand from Tristan's arm like it burned. *She's your girlfriend?*

*That's one of the things I was about to tell you. She* was *my girlfriend. Now you are.*

Of course Tristan had a girlfriend before me. He was kind, and respectful, and supportive, and dependable. He had strong shoulders and deep blue eyes and sandy brown hair that turned gold in the sun. Tristan probably had dozens of girlfriends before I came along.

Melanie said, "I wish I could help find your brother and sister, but all I can do is find things like lost jewelry or keys. My uncle's in charge of their case. He'll find them."

Tristan stiffened, and I blinked. "Your uncle is John Kellan?"

She nodded. "Uncle Johnny."

Did she know that *Uncle Johnny* had kidnapped me? That he had punched me in the face? Did she know that he held a gun to my head and made me witness my parents being shot? That he held a personal vendetta against my family because my parents had murdered his brother-in-law?

While I was in the Underground, a vengeful Kellan told me that his sister was struggling to raise her daughter all alone. Melanie must be that daughter.

Which meant…

Oh no. Oh God, no. Horror crept up my throat on tentacles, and I stared at Tristan. *My parents killed Melanie's father?*

Grimly, he confirmed it with a nod. *That's another thing I was going to tell you.*

That's why her last name was familiar. Timothy Brunswick was one of the recruiting agents who'd come to my house in Virginia eight years ago. His name was printed under his photograph in the evidence binder, along with all the other victims. His eyes appeared in the fog while I was passed out at Union Station, and in my nightmare last night, hurt and glowering and dark and accusatory.

The fog whooshed in and I stumbled into an armchair, heart beating double-time, pumping blood, my parents' killer blood, through my veins. "I'm sorry. I'm so sorry."

Tristan shouted for me to breathe. I pushed the fog away, but kept it close. "I'm so sorry," I said again. I would never stop saying it. I *should* never stop saying it.

The doorbell rang again, and more of Ember's bandmates piled into the house. Ember pulled Melanie, her face deathly white, into the basement after them.

"Does she know?" I asked Tristan, my voice trembling. "Does she know it was my parents who…"

Tristan kicked at the coffee table. "Kellan told her."

Another vision of Tristan kissing Melanie started to form, so I pushed myself up from the chair and stumbled into the kitchen. Melanie Brunswick. Tristan's ex. Beautiful: much prettier than me. Kind and sympathetic: she wished that she could help find my siblings. And forgiving: she wished she could help, even though she knew my parents had murdered her father.

"How long were you with her?" I asked Tristan, who had followed me into the kitchen.

*…A long time,* he admitted silently.

*How long?*

"We were kids at first," he said. "She's a couple years younger than me. Your age. After our fathers were attacked…" He sighed. "My dad survived and hers didn't. She was so sad. I kind of… I don't know. She needed me, so I took care of her. As friends."

"Then as you got older," I finished for him, "it turned into more than friends."

"Yeah."

"So you've basically been with her since you were ten. Eight years."

He took my hand. "Tessa, there's something else—"

I shook my head. No more confessions. Not yet. I slid my hands into the sleeves of the red hoodie I'd borrowed from him. "Did Melanie ever wear this hoodie?"

He chuckled. "No."

*Can you do* this *with her?* I asked. *Talk to her like this?*

*No.* He took my left hand from my sleeve and wiggled the thin band of pearls around my fourth finger. "I never gave her a promise ring, and I never had warning premonitions about her, either."

What I really wanted to know, I couldn't find the strength to say out loud. *Were you in love with her?*

"I thought it was love. But now I know what love really is." He nuzzled my neck with his lips. *It's us. You and me.* "She knew it was happening before I did. She said she could hear it in my voice when I called her from Twelve Lakes. I felt awful about it. I didn't want to hurt her. But it would've hurt her more if we stayed together when I was in love with someone else. So we broke up. I love *you,* Tessa. Only you. Always you."

I let Tristan kiss me. I believed him. He loved me. I could feel his love for me in every touch. See it in every glance. Hear it in every word.

I slid my arms around his neck and pressed close against him. So bold and strong, so daring and caring and brave. A true hero. He rescued me. Melanie had needed him, so he'd taken care of her. He rescued her, too.

He rescued Melanie, and then he fell in love with her.

Then he rescued me. Now he loved me.

On the counter, its handle half covered by a magazine, a steak knife glittered and glimmered, sparkled and glowed.

Was Tristan in love with me only because he rescued me?

I tried to extinguish the thought with fog, but it kept reigniting.

# CHAPTER SIX

HAD THE nightmare again last night. With another victim added to the mix.

The silver knife had glittered and glimmered, sparkled and glowed, as usual. But Melanie Brunswick's father had been killed by that knife, and last night she joined him in the group of my parents' victims. Her wide, wounded violet eyes blended with the others to become a single pair of vast, vengeful, venomous eyes, dark as a starless night and black as a cavern of coal. Demanding revenge. Demanding blood.

Tristan had stumbled in to the guest room to wake me, but now, hours later, the Nightmare Eyes still lingered, glowering at me from above.

I tried to shake them off. Today was my first day at Lilybrook High, and Tristan's first day at Heron University. Jillian and Logan still hadn't shown up at her boyfriend's house in Nebraska, and until we had a new lead, there was nothing we could do but go to school anyway. Besides, Tristan's career aspirations were to be an investigator at the APR, and then executive director, like his dad. He needed a college degree for that.

Car keys in hand, backpack slung over one shoulder, Tristan lingered in my doorway as I made my bed. "My buddy Nathan texted this morning," he said. "He's going to look out for you. He's a senior, so you probably won't have any classes with him, but he'll try to find you in the hallways between classes. Look for him. Tall guy. Dreadlocks. He's really excited to meet you. Remember that, okay?"

"Okay. Thanks." I was excited to meet Tristan's best friend, too.

"You sure you can keep the fog balanced?" he asked. "Lilybrook High is a small school, but it's almost a hundred years old. Lots of history. Which means lots of visions."

"I'll be fine. Please don't worry about me," I said, knowing he would anyway.

"You have your phone?"

"Yep. Fully charged." White, sleek, and shiny, my new phone looked almost exactly like the one Tristan had given me in Twelve Lakes, the one that was now locked away in the APR's evidence room. And this one didn't have a secret tracking app installed.

Deirdre rushed up behind him in a flowered robe and with her hair still wrapped in a towel. She ran a preschool at the APR for the little psionic kids who hadn't learned to control their abilities in public yet, and she was running very late. "Tristan, you should've left already. I don't want you speeding or getting in an accident."

"Mom, you know you don't have to worry about that." He tapped his temple. "Warning premonitions, remember? And I have plenty of time."

Heron University was a little less than an hour away. Tristan had originally planned to live in the dorms on campus, but now that I was here, he would drive back and forth each day. Thank goodness. I did not want to live here without him. When I agreed to live at the Connellys' house, it was to be with Tristan, not his parents. Dennis and

Deirdre were kind and generous—much too kind and generous to a girl whose parents had tried to kill both Dennis and Tristan—but they were still relative strangers.

Deirdre turned to me. "Give me fifteen minutes, Tessa. I'll drive you to school."

"But you're running late," I said. "Ember told me that she walks. I'll go with her."

Her hands flittered to her throat. "Are—are you sure?"

"Yes." She looked hurt, so to soften the blow, I added, "You bought me a whole bunch of school supplies and a brand new book bag. Everything I need. I'm all set. Thank you, Deirdre."

Brows knit, she nodded, then whisked back to her bedroom.

"I know she's trying too hard," Tristan said, "but she wants you to feel welcome here."

"I do," I said. But the Nightmare Eyes glowered down on me, reminding me that one day, Deirdre was going to wake up to the fact that my parents had tried to kill her husband and her son. And then she would regret taking me into her home and her heart.

Lips still tingling from Tristan's record-setting goodbye kiss, and stomach filled with orange juice and a slightly burned strawberry Pop-Tart prepared by Deirdre, I set off with Ember for Lilybrook High. I wore my new white coat and new mittens, a new pair of jeans, a new pair of sneakers, and Tristan's old tennis hoodie. Tucked at the bottom of my new book bag were Jillian's ballet shoe, protected in a baggie, and Logan's sheet music, folded carefully in an envelope. I couldn't seem to leave them behind.

Ember had gathered her purple-and-blue hair in a spiky ponytail high on her head and wore a raspberry-colored down jacket. This was the first time we'd been alone since our exchange in the bathroom the other day, and neither of us knew what to say. Piles of snow and massive, bare trees lined the streets as we walked the half-mile route to the high school. The Nightmare Eyes followed, tethered to me like a shadow. I looked behind me, certain I would see them hovering in the sky like a gray cloud.

Finally Ember spoke. "What are you looking at?"

I saw nothing but a blue sky, a bright sun, and white clouds. There were no hovering, hateful Nightmare Eyes. "Just looking around," I answered. "Getting to know the neighborhood."

"Are you nervous for your first day?"

"Kind of. But I'm used to being the new kid. We moved a lot."

"You must have a ton of friends all over the country."

Bitterly, I shook my head. "It was too hard to make friends and lie to them, and then leave them when my family ran again. I couldn't even tell them my real name."

"Well, you should be okay at Lilybrook High," she said. "You're a lab rat. We all hang out together." From one of the branches above, a little blackbird fluttered down to a pile of snow. Ember took off her mitten and wiggled her fingers at it.

"A lab rat?"

"A Lab *Brat*. Capital L, capital B." She pulled something from her pocket—a baggie of birdseed. "The Agency for Psionic Research is also known as the Lab. So we're Lab Brats. Get it?"

"Just being psionic makes me a Lab Brat?" I asked.

"Yeah."

"But do they know I'm..." I couldn't bring myself to say *the daughter of the Kitteridge Killers* out loud. "...who I am?"

"I'm sure some of them know by now," she said. "But you're Tristan's girlfriend. The Lab Brats will accept you."

Just a few days ago, I didn't even know I was psionic. And now, not only could I see the past with my retrocognition and communicate telepathically with my boyfriend, I had a group of instant friends.

Maybe, for the first time in eight years, school wouldn't be so bad.

"The Lab Brats have to follow some special rules, though." Ember crouched and poured some birdseed in her palm. "The neutrals think the APR is just a boring lab called the Northern Wisconsin Science Laboratory. We can't let them know it's specifically for psionic research. We also can't let them know about our abilities, and we can't use our powers against anyone or to cheat."

"That doesn't sound too bad." I'd still have to follow special rules and keep secrets like I had when I was living with my real family, but this time I'd be keeping those secrets along with a large group of friends. The Lab Brats. "It could even be fun."

"It is." Ember whistled, and the blackbird hopped over, confidently pecking a seed right from her hand.

"Is that someone's pet?" I asked.

"Nope." With her free hand, she gestured to the woods beyond the neighborhood. "He has a nest over there by Lilybrook Lake."

"Do you feed him every day?"

"I've never met him before."

An echoey, hollow bang came from the woods, muffled and far away, but loud enough to make Ember jump, and the bird flitter off. A gunshot.

"Stupid hunters," she shivered. "This time of year they hunt wolves, rabbits, foxes… " With the cuff of her jacket, she wiped her eyes.

"Poor defenseless animals," I said. I could have cried myself.

We continued down the sidewalk, Ember kicking at snowbanks. "My friend Kimber and I? Last summer we used to hike around the lake to the hunting cabins. We'd spy on the hunters, and Kimber would use her psychokinesis to jam their guns so they couldn't kill anything. One time, we did it to some hunters while they were eating by a campfire, and I told a couple of deer to go over and take the food right out of their hands." She laughed, sweet and high. "The hunters tried to shoot them, but their guns didn't work. They got *so* mad. It was hilarious."

I had to laugh too. "I'd love to see that. You'll have to take me with you next time."

"When our parents found out, they said it was too dangerous and won't let us do it anymore." She grinned at me anyway. "Tristan told me that you're a vegetarian."

"I am."

She nodded approvingly, like I'd passed a test. "I didn't know what to expect," she said. "About you living with us, you know, because of who you are. Who your parents are."

"I'm sorry," I said, because I was. I was so sorry, so ashamed, of who I was. My shame burned through me, boiling and blistering.

"And also because of Melanie," Ember added. "She wasn't just Tristan's girlfriend. She's a backup singer in my band, and she's one of my best friends. When they broke up, she was devastated. She still is. He didn't get warning premonitions about her, but she felt safe with him. And Tristan's got a huge hero complex. He liked protecting her. And now..." She shrugged, then pocketed the baggie of birdseed. "But Lyric, Aria, and Mac like you. And if they like you, I like you. You're nice. And you're living with us, so it's kind of like having a sister. I guess that's pretty cool."

We grinned at each other. And just like that, I had my first friend.

The fog trembled upon my first step into Lilybrook High School. The building had been updated several times over the years, so everything—the big windows, the tile floor, the blue lockers—looked shiny and new, but almost one hundred classes had graduated from this school. If I raised the fog too high, I would see every single person who'd ever walked these halls, and probably pass out. Same with bringing in the fog too low. If I was still neutral, I wouldn't have to worry about becoming overwhelmed by visions or fog. But my whole life I'd wanted a psionic ability to be like the rest of my family, and now I had one. My retrocognition was a strength, not a weakness. It made me special.

And at Lilybrook High, it also made me a Lab Brat.

Taking a deep breath, I lowered the fog an inch, then raised it half an inch. Balanced. Perfect. I forced myself onward.

I was used to being the new girl at school and the curious looks that came along with it. This was the first time, however, that I could use my real name. The Nightmare Eyes slunk behind me, reminding me that I was the daughter of killers. I also felt my classmates' eyes on me as the assistant principal led me on a quick tour.

"That's Tristan Connelly's new girlfriend," a girl whispered as we passed, and pride exploded in me like a starburst.

I was taking a heavy course load, but I was looking forward to the challenge. When my family was on the run, my mother and father insisted that we maintain a steady B-C average so we wouldn't attract attention. I'd struggled to earn those grades, but now that I knew my life wasn't in danger, I should be able to concentrate on my studies. I could earn A's, and I would welcome the attention. Maybe I would even get on the honor roll. When Jillian and Logan got here, they would soar to the top of the class. With his hypercognition, Logan would probably take all AP classes and graduate as valedictorian.

Quiet, stable, peaceful lives. Normal lives.

We were going to love this place.

I was a little disappointed that Ember and I had no classes together— she was a freshman and I was a junior. It was also too late for me to take Driver's Ed, so I'd have to wait until next year for that. But otherwise, I was happy with my classes. I was especially excited about my first-period Explorations in Art class. I used to love to paint when I was younger, but my family didn't have enough room in our getaway car to haul my paintings from hideout to hideout, and it was too painful to watch them burn. So I'd quit. But now, at Lilybrook High, I could finally take Art again. The potbellied, paint-splattered teacher, Mr. Vargas, even gave my pencil sketch of a leaf an impressed grunt.

I had to dash all the way across the building to my chemistry class, where I was assigned to partner with a skinny boy wearing a Maroon 5 concert T-shirt. Nice enough guy, but he barely spoke to me. I couldn't even try to start a conversation with him. The Nightmare Eyes burned into me, and the fog rumbled around me, and I was concentrating so hard on keeping everything balanced against the visions that I didn't hear a word the teacher said.

I tapped the phone in my back pocket to make sure it was still there. I missed Tristan—it felt like half of me was missing—but I was happy he hadn't called. That meant he wasn't having any warning premonitions about me. Good. The fog was looming, but I was in control.

In the foreign language hallway between second and third period, Ember and I almost bumped into each other. We giggled at our shared clumsiness before heading to our respective classrooms. But where were all the other Lab Brats? Ember said we all hung out together. If any of my classmates were Lab Brats, they didn't tell me, and I didn't want to risk lifting the fog too high to find out for myself. I kept my eye out for Tristan's friend Nathan. I saw lots of tall boys, but none with dreadlocks.

Just after the bell rang for fourth-period geometry, a girl with the most beautiful hair I'd ever seen, long and shiny and auburn, slid into the desk in front of mine. She wiggled her French-manicured fingers at one of her friends. When the teacher started scribbling formulas on the whiteboard, the girl swiveled in her seat to face me, her eyes the color of coffee and cream.

Was she a Lab Brat? "Hi," I said as cheerfully and as loudly as I dared.

Her gaze flitted down to my hoodie. Her lip curled up in distaste. And then she snarled, "Tristan broke up with Melanie for *you?*"

Before I could reply—not that I could get any words past the lump that had instantly appeared in my throat—she turned back around.

Why would that girl speak to me with such venom? Maybe she thought I'd manipulated Tristan into breaking up with Melanie. Maybe it was the way I was dressed. She wore shiny black boots and a pencil skirt with a ruffled white top. In Tristan's enormous hoodie, I looked like a slob compared to her.

Maybe she knew who my parents were.

*Please, please let her hate me because of the hoodie, and not because my parents are the Kitteridge Killers.*

The girl turned her head, glancing at me over her shoulder. "It's not the hoodie."

I sank back in my chair and slid my hands in my sleeves. Whoever this girl was, she was telepathic, which meant she was a Lab Brat. She knew who my parents were. Ember said the Lab Brats would accept me simply because I was psionic, and because I was Tristan's girlfriend.

But Ember was wrong.

# CHAPTER SEVEN

N THE CAFETERIA, I was jostled and propelled through the lunch line to buy my salad and milk, then scouted the tables for a seat. While my family was on the run, we had to sit near an exit in case we needed to make a speedy getaway. But now I could sit wherever I wanted. I spotted Melanie Brunswick sitting next to that telepathic girl with the auburn hair. Their table was half-empty, but although everyone at the table—the other Lab Brats, I assumed—looked straight at me, they didn't wave me over.

Whatever confidence I had left drained from me like water from a sieve.

The tables near the back window were empty. I could sit there.

Everyone at the Lab Brats' table watched as I walked by them. The telepathic girl put her arm around Melanie, like she was shielding her from me, and whispered something.

"Leave her alone, Winter," Melanie mumbled.

I collapsed into a seat at an empty table and brought the fog in a little, to numb myself from the sting of the Lab Brats' rejection. They were all looking at me, some emotionless, some curious, some judging. Except for Melanie. She just stared at her tray.

I pretended to ignore them. I concentrated on picking the green peppers from my salad, then acted like I was super-interested in reading a red flyer that was taped to the wall, promoting a blood drive. It said to contact Nathan Gallagher for more information. Maybe Nathan Gallagher was Tristan's buddy.

I took the napkin from my tray to spread it across my lap. Under the napkin was a piece of paper, torn from a spiral notebook and folded into quarters. A note. Someone must have slipped it onto my tray when I wasn't looking.

From my back pocket, my phone rang. 'Wildflowers,' by Tom Petty and the Heartbreakers: Tristan's ringtone.

He would only be calling to warn me about something. It had to be the paper on my tray. I reached to answer his call.

No.

I needed to know what that note said, and Tristan would only tell me not to open it.

Shadowy dread crushed me from all sides. Knowing I shouldn't, but unable to stop myself, I unfolded the paper.

Scrawled with ink thick and red, the letters were designed to look like dripping blood.


## KILLERS' SPAWN


Heart pounding in my ears, my body grew hot, then cold. My phone rang and rang and rang.

I shot a glance at the Lab Brats. Cheeks pale, violet eyes wide, Melanie shook her head. Next to her, the auburn-haired telepathic girl smirked.

I shoved the note into my pocket. At all of my old schools, no one knew who I was, and I was glad. I didn't want any friends back then.

But now it was different. I *wanted* friends now. At Lilybrook High, I was no longer hiding behind an alias. I could finally have friends who knew me as Tessa Carson.

But Tessa Carson was the daughter of the Kitteridge Killers. Tessa Carson was Killers' Spawn. Who would want to be friends with that?

My phone rang and rang, then finally fell silent.

My feet itched to get up and run, to get me out of this place and never come back. But no. I gripped my chair, digging my fingers into the seat, to keep myself from fleeing. I'd promised myself I wouldn't run anymore. I would stay here, and I would not let a mean girl and her cruel note bother me. I had Tristan, and I had Ember, and I even had Dennis and Deirdre. That was all I needed. And if they rejected me one day because of what my parents did, I would have Jillian and Logan. As soon as I found them.

I stayed in the lunchroom, but when the fog came rolling in to numb me, I didn't push it away.

Get through the day. That's all I needed to do. Just get through the day. Go to my locker, get my books, go to class. Go back to the Connellys' and hole up in their guest room.

Clouded in fog, I headed to my locker after lunch. Taping a red blood drive flyer onto each shiny blue locker was a boy with blond dreadlocks held back in an elastic.

Nathan. Finally. Tristan was his best friend. He would accept me, at least.

I approached him with a smile. "Hi, Nathan? I'm Tessa. Tristan's girlfriend."

He did not smile back. Instead, he looked down at me with eyes the color of tarnished steel. "You were there," he said.

"Where?"

A cell phone rang, but not with the 'Wildflowers' ringtone. It wasn't mine. The heavy metal ringtone was coming from Nathan's jeans.

Instead of answering his phone, he grabbed my arm and yanked me over to him. He dropped his blood drive flyers, and my book bag slipped off my shoulder and fell to the floor. Jillian's ballet shoe! Logan's sheet music! I tried to pull away to get my bag, but he jerked me close, his touch burning through Tristan's hoodie.

"When my father died," he said. "You were there."

"Your father? I wasn't—" My stomach plummeted and the world around me narrowed, darkened. Not another one. Not again. "Which one was your father?" I asked, defeated.

"Kip Gallagher. He was on the recruiting team that your parents attacked. Tristan's dad, Melanie's dad, and my dad."

Tristan, Melanie, and Nathan. My parents had attacked their fathers, leaving two dead and one critically wounded. In their grief, the three of them had bonded. One had become Tristan's girlfriend, and the other his best friend.

Until I came along.

"I was there that day," I appealed to Nathan, "but I was outside, locked in Dennis Connelly's car. I didn't know what was happening inside my house. I didn't know anything at all, until a few weeks ago."

He squeezed my arm tighter and shook it. "I was nine." He ground the words out through clenched teeth. "I was only nine years old when your scumbag parents killed my father. Do you know how they killed him?"

I did know. I'd seen it in a vision when I held my parents' wedding rings while I was in the Underground. I saw the murder weapon in my nightmares. It glittered and glimmered, sparkled and glowed.

"They stabbed him," he rumbled over his ringing phone. "Your mother threw a knife at him with her PK, and when he tried to crawl away, your father stabbed him again. Multiple times."

The air turned into a solid block of fog and I couldn't inhale. "I'm sorry," I squeaked. "I'm so sor—"

"It sickens me that you're here." In his pocket, his phone rang and rang. "Every time I look at you I have to be reminded that your parents killed my father. You shouldn't be allowed to go to this school. You shouldn't be allowed to live in this town."

His hand, squeezing my arm, also pushed a vision into me: a young version of him, blond hair cut short, wearing a too-big black suit. Crying in a cemetery, beside a coffin as it was lowered into the ground. Next to him was a tall, grim, teenage boy, and on his other side, sobbing into a tissue, was their mother.

Then instantly, the image vanished, although I hadn't lowered the fog. "Stop that." His fury lashed at me like a whip. "Don't you dare use your retrocognition on me."

"Did you do that?" I asked, breathless. "Did you cut off my vision?"

His phone rang again. He released my arm to yank the phone from his pocket. "What!" he shouted into it. "…How did you… You get premonitions about *her*? Oh, that's just great. …Go to hell, Connelly. Have fun with Killers' Spawn."

He thrust the phone back into his pocket and glared at me. "And you, Spawn, you stay away from my blood drive. No one wants your tainted blood. Not in that way, anyway." He stormed away, his feet scattering the red flyers like leaves in the wind.

I dove to grab my book bag. Fingers fumbling, I checked that Jillian's ballet shoe and Logan's sheet music were unharmed, then sank to the floor. Sunlight streamed through the high windows, bright and blinding, reflecting on the lockers. The bell rang and students began flooding the hallway, stepping around me, but I didn't move.

After a few seconds, when my hands stopped shaking and my heart resumed beating, I called Tristan.

"Tessa? Are you okay?" His voice was rough with worry.

"Yeah." I tried to laugh, but it came out sounding like a sob. "You didn't call to warn me about him."

"When you didn't answer last time, I called him instead," he said. "But this time my warning was, I don't know, faded. Weak. I didn't think it was a real premonition. Especially when I saw it was Nathan with you."

He sighed, and I could almost feel his anguish through the phone. "He texted this morning that he would look out for you. That he was excited to meet you."

"I guess you misinterpreted that text," I said. "You didn't tell me that his father was one of the agents who…" The end of that sentence was too awful to say out loud.

"I didn't want you to feel guilty around him, like you did with Melanie. He told me he would tell you himself. So you would see it doesn't matter."

"It does matter, Tristan. It matters a lot." The Nightmare Eyes glared down on me.

"What he did to you, what he said to you just now, it's not like him. I don't know why he would do that."

I knew why. The Nightmare Eyes knew why too.

"In the cafeteria," Tristan started, then paused. He drew a breath before continuing. "Did that note really say what I think it said? Killers' Spawn?"

Hot shame flooded my senses. Those words sounded especially heinous coming from him. "Yeah."

"Why didn't you answer my call? I would have told you not to open it."

"That's why I didn't answer. I wanted to see what it said. Telling me not to read the note wasn't going to erase the words on it."

"But I could have fixed things. I can't protect you if you don't answer my call," he said. "I knew I shouldn't have left you. I'm too far away. Maybe that's why my premonition was so weak. I'm coming home."

"Tristan, no. I won't let you quit school just so you can sit around and wait for warning premonitions about me."

"But—"

"I'm fine, Tristan. I'm over it already." He wanted me to say yes, please come home. He wanted me to say I needed him. But he already lost his job at the APR because of me, he gave up his girlfriend for me, and now he lost his best friend because of me. I couldn't let him give up college for me too.

"I have to get to my next class." I made my voice sound perky and hoped he didn't hear it crack. "So do you. See you tonight I love you bye." I hung up before he could protest.

# CHAPTER EIGHT

"STUPID LAB BRATS," Ember said as we entered the Connellys' house after school.

"It's not your fault," I muttered. "You didn't know." She seemed as hurt as I was.

Mac and Aria greeted us cheerfully, barking and yipping, but their tails stopped wagging and they started whimpering as they picked up on Ember's distress. She sank to her knees and buried her head in Mac's fur, then picked up Aria and gave her a kiss. Lyric slunk from behind the sofa and rubbed Ember's legs, mewling. She scratched behind his ears, the tightness in her shoulders loosening.

"Tessa needs to feel better too," she told the animals. They obediently turned to me, and I obediently petted them as Ember snapped leashes to the dogs' collars.

She was right: I did need to feel better, and petting the animals helped.

"Come with me," she said, handing me Mac's leash.

Before we even had a chance to warm up, we headed back outside to take the dogs for a walk. Mac pulled me along behind him, and Aria pranced on her little paws next to Ember. "Did they say things to you about your parents, right to your face?" Ember asked.

"Yeah."

"Me too. They said you shouldn't be allowed at our school, that you shouldn't be allowed to live in our town. I had no idea they were going to be like that, Tessa. I'm sorry."

"Thanks." Maybe it was a bad idea for me to go to Lilybrook High. Just like the scars on my stomach reminded me of my parents' crimes, my mere presence at that school reminded everyone else. Going to Lilybrook High was like throwing myself into a pit of vengeful lions.

"Winter Milbourne is the one who told everyone who your parents are," Ember said, her breath coming out in little clouds. "Did you meet her today?"

"Not officially." With my free hand I touched the Killers' Spawn note in my pocket and lifted the fog, just a tiny bit. There she was, the telepathic auburn-haired girl, writing the note in geometry class as she sat right in front of me, then having a Lab Brat named Lucy teleport the note onto my tray as I passed them in the cafeteria.

"Her dad is the head warden at the Underground," Ember said. "That's probably how she found out about your parents so fast."

Ah. My mother gave the warden a heart attack with her psychokinesis, during her failed escape attempt. Thanks to the quick action of Tristan and the guards, he survived, but it explained Winter's animosity toward me.

Was there anyone in Lilybrook whom my parents *hadn't* hurt in some way?

"Winter is also Nathan's girlfriend," Ember said. "When she started saying all those things about you, I thought he would help me stop her. But he was even worse than she was."

"Yeah." My arm still ached where he'd grabbed it. "Tristan's really upset about that."

We halted when Mac stopped to sniff a tree trunk. "What I don't get is, Nathan's a really good guy," Ember said. "He's like the most charitable person on the planet. When he was a kid, he started a blood drive in honor of his dad. He has a coat drive every fall, and he volunteers at a food pantry every week."

"You know what's ironic?" I sighed. "My mother depended on coat drives and food pantries to survive when she was a kid." She'd grown up impoverished, friendless, and abused by her stepfather. "Then as an adult, she murdered the father of someone who volunteers at places like that."

Ember shifted uncomfortably at the mention of my mother. Above me, the Nightmare Eyes glared and glowered, and my blood burned, burned, burned. I unzipped my coat and breathed in the cold January air, but I still burned.

Mac finished sniffing the tree and pulled us onward. "Nathan's a safeguard, like his dad was. He's also clairvoyant, like his mom." Ember said. "Tristan and Nathan always planned on being investigators together. Partners."

We walked a block before she spoke again. "Probably not anymore, though."

Like a shadow, the Nightmare Eyes hovered high in the guest room as I read my history textbook and waited for Tristan to get home from college. Ember had to leave for her volunteer job at the animal shelter, but she sent Mac, Aria, and Lyric to keep me company, and now they sprawled on my bed, leaving me only a small corner of it. Mac kept his head on my lap. I didn't mind. I liked having them there. The animals didn't care that I was Killers' Spawn.

I jumped when Dennis and Deirdre knocked on my door frame. "Ember called to tell us what happened today," Deirdre said. "Honey, I'm so sorry. Nathan's mother is one of my friends. I'll talk to her."

Dennis pushed his glasses up his nose. "The school has a zero-tolerance policy for bullying. I'm going to report him and Winter Milbourne. They'll be suspended."

"Please don't." Getting Nathan and Winter suspended would only give them another reason to hate me. "It was no big deal. Nathan is Tristan's best friend, so he can't be that bad. He'll come around." I forced my lips into a smile. "He needs to do that blood drive. Suspending him will do more harm than good."

Dennis and Deirdre reluctantly agreed not to report them, but made me promise to tell them if it happened again.

When they left, I raised the fog to numb myself and got lost in it. Until someone grabbed me, slid his hand behind my head, caressed my cheek with his thumb, and pressed his warm lips to mine.

Tristan.

I wrapped my arms around his neck. He shooed the animals away and I shooed the fog away, then he fell into the bed on top of me.

"This was the longest we've been apart in weeks," he said, nuzzling my neck. "And the farthest."

"I missed you."

"I'm sorry about Nathan," he said. "And about that note. I'll fix everything."

"Please don't talk about that while you're kissing me," I replied, then took his face between my palms and looked into his eyes. Big, blue, beautiful eyes, filled with love. The complete opposite of the Nightmare Eyes. I crushed my lips back onto his.

"Kids!" Deirdre called from downstairs. "Dinner! I picked up sweet and sour chicken!"

Was someone calling us? Deirdre, maybe? If she was, I couldn't hear her. Tristan was here with me again, and he loved me.

Later that evening, Tristan sat at his desk to write a paper for his criminal justice class while I curled up on his bed to read *The Scarlet Letter* for American Lit. His computer dinged—an email.

He gave a little triumphant fist pump. "It's from the APR," he announced. "The board accepted my request to work with Brinda Lakhani to find your brother and sister. We have a meeting with her tomorrow at five."

"Who's Brinda Lakhani?" I asked.

He gave me a grin, lighting up from the inside out—first his eyes, then his smile. "Brinda Lakhani is going to tell us where to find your brother and sister."

# CHAPTER NINE

*L*ATE THE NEXT afternoon, with Tristan on one side and Dennis on my other, I hurried down the white-pebbled path to the Agency for Psionic Research. The first time I'd entered this building, I'd been dragged in by John Kellan. Handcuffed, blindfolded, gagged. Terrified.

No one had to drag me this time, and terror had been replaced with hope. Brinda Lakhani. Whoever she was, she was here at the APR, she was going to help me find my siblings, and I loved her already. Tristan told me to bring along Jillian's ballet shoe and Logan's sheet music, something I would have done anyway. I carried them with me everywhere.

We rushed past the snow-dusted wooden sign that falsely identified the facility as the Northern Wisconsin Science Laboratory, and into the unassuming, industrial brick structure. In the lobby, the security guards greeted Dennis and Tristan warmly. "Thought you retired, Mr. Connelly," a hefty guard with rectangular glasses joked to Dennis. "But you still come in almost every day."

Tristan chuckled, and Dennis grinned. "Deirdre would prefer if I stayed home," he said, "but retirement doesn't agree with me." Dennis had retired as executive director last year because the stressful job was bad for his heart, which had been weak ever since my mother tried to kill him by giving him a heart attack.

Before shame could swell up inside me, Dennis placed a gentle hand on my shoulder. The guard looked at me with unease as he buzzed open the security door to let us through.

It was almost five o'clock, and most of the APR employees were leaving for the day. As we passed them in the hall, some raised their eyebrows in surprise, or maybe disapproval, at the sight of me.

Did they *all* know I was Killers' Spawn?

In response to one dark-haired woman's apprehensive glance, Tristan brought my hand to his lips and kissed it.

"While you're here," Dennis said, "do you want to visit your parents? The warden told me that your mother's been asking for you."

My heart squeezed into a tiny ball. "No."

"Absolutely not," Tristan said at the same time.

"She's been neutralized," Dennis said. "It's safe. It might do you some good to see her."

"I'm not ready." I would *never* be ready. The woman I remembered as my mother didn't really exist. The real woman was a liar. A thief. A killer. I wanted nothing to do with her.

Tristan stopped suddenly and gripped my hand. Everything grew silent. Coming from the boardroom was a woman with a wide jaw, dressed impeccably in pressed slacks and white shirt, and a gold badge that read Executive Director. Following her was a man with a red beard.

John Kellan.

My lungs wouldn't inflate. My heart wouldn't beat. Kellan had kidnapped me. He hit me, he chased me down and drove me far away, locked me up in a dark cell, and put a gun to my head.

The woman shook his hand and returned to the boardroom, but

Kellan stayed, turning to me with a bored blink. Hanging from a lanyard around his neck was a new red badge that boasted Lead Investigator.

Stiffly, Tristan pushed me behind him.

But I wasn't running away anymore. I wasn't hiding anymore. I stepped out from behind Tristan and forced myself to meet Kellan's grimy blue eyes. He was telepathic, so I smothered my fear with fog. "You sent a security guard to search my house in Twelve Lakes," I said, slowly, to keep my voice from shaking. "You didn't even care enough to go there yourself."

"I'm understaffed," Kellan said with a shrug. "Believe it or not, Miss Carson, I want to find the targets as much as you do. I don't like loose ends."

"Jillian and Logan aren't *targets*. They aren't *loose ends*." I no longer had to pretend that I wasn't afraid, because I wasn't. I was angry. "They're my brother and sister. And if you find them, you need to take me with you to get them."

One corner of his lip curled up in amusement. "Why would I do that?"

"Because you'll bring them here by force. If I'm there too, they'll know it's okay to come." Then I added, "And I need to make sure you don't hurt them."

I hoped my words would shame him, but he only snickered.

Dennis, however, rubbed his chin. "She makes a good point. They won't trust anyone but her. Take her with you once you know where they are."

At that moment, Nathan Gallagher came out of the boardroom, his dreadlocks long and loose. I stiffened, instantly on guard. Kellan clapped him on the back like a proud parent. "I just brought Nathan on as a junior investigator," he said.

"Thanks again, sir. It's a huge honor." Nathan smiled, but when he turned to us, that smile turned into a sneer. "Kellan used to have a different junior investigator," he said, "but that traitor fell in love with his target and almost ruined the mission."

Tristan cringed, clearly hurt. "I don't regret a thing," he said, pulling me into his arms. "And I know you don't mean what you said to Tessa at school. And that note? Come on, buddy. You're better than that."

A vision pushed into me, a vision of a young Tristan and Nathan, right here in this hallway, both wearing yellow Lilybrook Middle School T-shirts as they taped blood drive flyers to the wall. Tristan nodding in earnest agreement as Nathan said through clenched teeth, "Yeah, but even if the Kitteridge Killers are captured, they'll just be sent to the Underground. They get to live, but my dad will still be dead. How is that fair?"

I shoved the vision into the fog, but the guilt remained.

A man in a black APR jacket and red scarf came rushing around the corner, glancing at his watch. He was in a hurry, but stopped when he saw us. In his early twenties, he had the same blond hair as Nathan, but cut conservatively. Same straight nose, too, but eyes of tawny brown instead of hard steel.

He frowned at Nathan. "Did you apologize like I told you to?" he said.

"You can't tell me what to do, Cole," Nathan said. "You're my brother, not my father." He cut a glance to me. "We don't have a father."

Dennis stepped between us. "Cole, hello," he said, his cheery tone an attempt to thaw the icy tension. "How are things in the Lab?"

"Good," Cole said. "We tried to test a potential recruit today. A pyrokinetic. But the guy was so nervous that he couldn't set a single fire. It took me all afternoon to calm him down enough to make a few sparks on his fingertips." As Dennis chuckled, Cole turned to me. "You're Tessa Carson."

On guard, I nodded. He seemed nice, and Dennis liked him, but he was Nathan's brother. My parents had murdered his father.

"My brother has some…issues with you," he said, placing his hand on my shoulder, "and he feels very angry and hostile right now. But he won't bother you again. Got it, Nathan?" He glanced at his watch again. "It's late. Mom's waiting for us. Go wait for me in the car."

Muttering something under his breath, Nathan stormed away. Dennis shook his head at him, then pulled Kellan aside. The two telepathic men began a silent conversation—an angry one, judging by their tense postures and jabbing fingers.

Tristan watched Nathan leave. "I don't get it," he said. "I thought he'd understand."

Cole mirrored Tristan's bewildered and disappointed expression, and sighed.

My heart broke for Tristan. I destroyed his lifelong friendship with his best friend. And now, I was also the source of disagreement between two brothers. My siblings and I had our squabbles, but we never had such bitter animosity for each other. My presence in Lilybrook had caused the rift between Nathan and Cole.

"Don't feel guilty, Tessa," Cole said.

How did he know I was feeling guilty?

He smiled. "And now you're surprised. And confused."

"Um, yeah," I said. "Are you telepathic?" Telepathy seemed to be the most common psionic ability around here.

"No mind reading for me," Cole said. "I'm an empathic clairvoyant. I can feel the emotions of others. I'll do my best to keep Nathan away until his feelings toward you are more compassionate."

Maybe that was why Cole didn't hate me—he was feeling *my*

emotions, not his own. If he wasn't an empath, he'd probably hate me as much as Nathan and Kellan did.

Cole zipped up his jacket and rushed off. Dennis, still deep in his argument with Kellan, waved us away, so Tristan and I went to see Brinda Lakhani without him.

Tristan took my hand as we climbed the back stairwell to the second floor. "Brinda's precognitive," he said. "She's the one who predicted where we would find your family. Remember that drawing of twelve lakes in the evidence binder?"

I did. While trying to prove my parents were innocent, I had Tristan help me swipe the binder of evidence the APR had collected against them. That binder also contained notes from the APR's psychics who'd predicted where my family would go. One note was a crayon drawing of twelve misshapen circles in blue, with wave symbols. Twelve Lakes.

We stopped at a closed door covered with crayon scribbles and heart and butterfly stickers. A wooden plaque with the name BRINDA painted in pink block letters hung in the middle. "Brinda's a little girl?" I asked.

Tristan raised his finger to his lips. "Shh. In a way she is. No talking, though. She doesn't like noise." He brushed his hand on the door rather than knocking on it.

The door opened a tiny crack, and from up high, an olive-brown eye peered out. Tristan grinned and wiggled his fingers.

The door swung open wider, and a tall Indian woman with shiny black hair jumped up and down at the sight of him, clapping her hands but stopping just before they touched. Tristan held his arms open and she threw herself into them.

An older gentleman, black hair peppered with gray, sat at a short table inside the room. Smiling, he raised his hand in greeting to us. His other hand held a red plastic beach pail filled with Crayolas.

Brinda hugged me next, towering over me as she wrapped me in her arms. *She is a child,* I sensed as I timidly hugged her back. A child in a woman's body. Eyes young and innocent, like she'd never been sad or scared in her life, and all she'd ever known was love and adoration and peace.

How different from my life. How wonderful. I hugged her tighter.

*She's forty years old,* Tristan told me telepathically, *but she never developed mentally past the age of four. She's never spoken a word.*

*Does she live in here?* The silent room was set up like a playhouse. It even had a wooden play kitchen. Every surface—walls, table, floor—was covered with stickers and crayon marks.

*This is just her playroom. She has no idea she's making predictions for the APR.*

*Who's that?* I gestured to the man at the table.

*That's her dad. He's neutral. One of the few neutrals who knows about this place. They lived in New York until an APR sensor discovered her when she was five. Then they moved to Lilybrook.*

Brinda stared at me for a moment, head tilted, then she curled her fingers into a claw and swiped across her stomach. She pointed at me with her eyebrows raised.

My hands fluttered to my belly. Yes, that's me, I confirmed with a nod.

Her eyes wide and sympathetic, she gestured for Tristan and me to sit at the table, and offered each of us a plastic teacup. We held them up so she could pour invisible tea from a pink plastic kettle. I pretended to take a sip.

*Put the ballet shoe and sheet music on the table,* Tristan instructed. I did, and Brinda put her teacup down and grabbed the shoe.

I cringed at her rough treatment of the shoe, and had to force myself not to speak as she bent it back and forth. Mr. Lakhani wagged his finger, and Brinda stopped, placing it on the table. She touched it gently, then looked at her dad for approval. He nodded.

Brinda held out her palm, and he obediently reached into his pocket and presented her with a sticker. A red heart. She handed it to Tristan and pointed to the ceiling. With a silent chuckle, Tristan stood, and stuck it where she directed.

Brinda turned back to the items on the table. The air in the silent room became still and heavy as her eyes dulled, her expression flat, emotionless. A mannequin.

Mr. Lakhani slowly raised the pail of crayons. Brinda pulled out a red crayon, then, on a sheet of drawing paper from the stack on the table, drew an oblong rectangle and a square. With a black crayon, she drew four circles underneath it.

*Is that a truck?* I asked Tristan. *Like a red pickup truck?*

*Looks like it,* he replied. *Maybe that's what Jillian and Logan are driving. Or what they will drive in the future. We should check car dealerships.*

*Yeah. There's probably thousands of them, but someone's bound to remember two teenagers buying a red pickup truck with cash.*

Brinda slid the drawing aside, then took another sheet. With a black crayon she scribbled a shapeless loop, then stabbed it with black dots.

*That kind of looks like the shape of the United States,* Tristan said.

I didn't see it until he said it, but he was right. It did look like the U.S. *What do the black dots mean?*

*Maybe all the places they're going to go?*

I hoped not. There were dozens of them.

Brinda made a few more drawings, most of them shapes that could be cars or buildings. One page had two black curves that at first I thought were smiles, but when she added black lines sticking down from them, made them look like closed eyelids with eyelashes. Another was a circle on what could be a short pedestal.

*I know what that is.* Tristan squeezed my hand excitedly. *That's a crystal ball. Maybe they're going to visit a psychic.*

*That makes sense,* I said. *We tried to ask that college professor for help.* In Twelve Lakes, Jillian, Logan, and I had sought help by emailing a professor who taught parapsychology, hoping he was psychic, or at least knew others who were. That endeavor ended tragically when he died of a brain aneurysm—one that our mother had planted in him. But Jillian and Logan didn't know that part of the story. It was entirely possible that they'd ask another psychic for help.

*The APR has a huge database of psychics around the country,* Tristan said. *I'll get that list. We can ask them to be on the lookout for Jillian and Logan.*

Brinda's next drawing was not as easy to interpret. It featured two brown rectangles, one vertical and one horizontal, with four lines sticking from the bottom of the horizontal one—legs? She added a small black circle inside the vertical rectangle. *That could be a deer,* I said, *with one eye.*

*Or a horse.*

*A horse with one eye. What does that mean?*

Brinda dug deep in the pail, finally withdrawing a silver crayon. She drew a large square, then filled it in. The silver reflected the florescent light from the ceiling, so bright I had to blink against it. Her eyes on me, Brinda took the red crayon again, and slashed it across the silver square. She slashed it, again and again, angry red slashes, hard enough to tear through the paper.

Tristan gripped my hand. *What does* that *mean?*

I shook my head as Mr. Lakhani forcibly took the crayon from Brinda. She pouted for a moment, then slid the ripped-up paper across the table to me, and nodded.

That drawing was a prediction about me.

Through the slashes of red, the silver glittered and glimmered, sparkled and glowed.

Silently, Tristan stacked the papers. *We'll take these home to interpret them,* he said. He took the drawing of the silver square and angry red slashes, but he hesitated first, like he didn't want to touch it.

# CHAPTER TEN

OW, SOFT THUDS on my ceiling woke me up early Saturday morning. A rustling. Mac whined from my floor. Then, from across the room, a low chuckle that could only belong to Tristan.

"Tristan?" I asked, rubbing my eyes. "What's going on?"

"Shh," he whispered. "It's still early. Go back to sleep if you can."

No problem there. My school days were spent keeping the fog balanced, avoiding Melanie's hurt, betrayed gaze, and pretending Nathan's glares and Winter's smirks didn't bother me. My evenings were spent half-doing homework, trying to interpret Brinda's crayon drawings, and retreating from Deirdre's nervous mothering. My darkest hours were spent biting back screams against the glowering, glaring, glimmering Nightmare Eyes. And every minute of every hour of every day was spent wondering where Jillian and Logan were.

Tristan caressed my cheek and I drifted off again.

Soon, though, he woke me up again with a murmur. "Happy birthday, Clockwise." His lips brushed over my neck, my collarbone. "The girl with wildflower eyes. *My* girl with wildflower eyes."

Wildflower eyes still closed, I ran my hand over his scruffy jaw. My birthday. Seventeen. The first birthday in eight years that I didn't think would be my last.

The first birthday in my life that I wasn't spending with my family.

Did they even know it was my birthday? My mother knew, I was certain. She might even be hoping I'd come visit her in the Underground today, but I wasn't ready to see her. My unconscious father definitely did not know it was my birthday. Jillian and Logan, wherever they were, would know. But they thought I was dead, murdered by Dennis Connelly, so they would be especially sad today.

Today was my birthday. I was seventeen. And I did not have a family.

God, I wanted my mom. I wanted my dad. The mom and dad I grew up with. The mom who braided my hair and taught me how to cook and called me Babydoll. The dad who helped me with my homework and called me Tessa Blessa.

No. *No.* The mom and dad I grew up with were liars. Thieves. Killers. They destroyed lives. The atrocious things they did burned through my blood like a disease. Tainting me, marking me, scarring me. Branding me Killers' Spawn. I hated them, and I never wanted to see them again.

Tristan smoothed the hair from my forehead. "Okay, birthday girl, open your eyes."

The soft thuds against my ceiling *were* making me curious, so I shoved my ugly thoughts into the fog and pried open an eyelid. Silver balloons danced around the lavender streamers that hung all over my room. I smiled sleepily at Tristan. "You did this?"

"Yeah, but it wasn't easy," he said. "You were so restless, and I didn't want you to wake up and see me."

"It's beautiful."

"Lavender was the closest I could find to periwinkle."

"It's perfect. I love it. Thank you." One balloon had my name on it. TESSA. Each letter a different color: red, yellow, blue, green, purple. I was still not used to seeing my real name written on paper. To see it emblazoned on a balloon was something I'd never even imagined.

The balloons swayed back and forth, up and down, around and around. Hypnotizing. The silver Mylar reflected in the mirror, making little prisms that danced on the walls.

Silver, like the square on Brinda's drawing.

Silver, like the angry flashes of the Nightmare Eyes.

Silver, like the ribbon from my Winterball dress that Kellan used to capture and blindfold me.

Silver, like the knives my parents used to murder Timothy Brunswick and Kip Gallagher.

I shoved those thoughts into the fog too. Today was my birthday, and my beautiful, blue-eyed, broad-shouldered boyfriend had woken me up with seventeen balloons and streamers almost in my favorite color and kisses.

It was still early, and the house was quiet. Dennis and Deirdre were still asleep. I lifted my covers, inviting Tristan to crawl into bed with me. With a wicked grin, he slipped under the blanket. I grabbed him, kissed him hard, then kissed him again, harder. I couldn't kiss him hard enough, or passionately enough. My love for him was a tangible thing, mountainous, colossal, and a kiss could not contain it.

He slid his hand behind my head, but didn't kiss me back. For a long moment he gazed at me and caressed my cheek with his thumb. "How is it possible," he breathed, "for one person to be so beautiful?"

Then he dove at me. My mouth, my neck. "Every part of you." He peppered kisses along my collarbone, then below it. "Every inch. Beautiful."

The professional Borderline that he'd dictated when he was an agent and I was his target existed no more. His lips traveled lower and lower, down to my breasts, then even lower. He lifted my flannel pajama top and ran kisses across my stomach as if it hadn't been defaced by five hideous scars, then his kisses traveled back, a centimeter at a time, all the way up to my lips.

He suddenly flew from the bed, moments before there was a sharp rap on the door. "That's enough, you two," Deirdre's stern voice called from the other side.

Mortification spread through my cheeks, making them impossibly hot. The door swung open and Deirdre came in. She looked from me to Tristan, who was sprawled casually on the overstuffed chair and giving her an innocent shrug. She didn't believe it for one moment. She gave me a final glance, and maybe there was terror on my face—my own mother would have gone ballistic and slammed things into walls, maybe even me—because in a slightly softer tone she said, "Happy birthday, Tessa. Come downstairs. We have presents for you."

When she left, Tristan grinned devilishly and tossed the tousled hair from his eyes, but I wanted to hide under the covers and never come out. "Your mother is going to kick me out of your house."

"She will not." He grabbed my hand and pulled me from the bed. "Come on, Clockwise. Time for presents."

Downstairs, more streamers in lavender, pink, and green twisted around the banisters and hung from the chandelier. A store-bought cake with white frosting, sprinkles, and *Happy Birthday Tessa 17!* in pink icing sat on the dining room table. "Breakfast birthday cake is our family tradition," Tristan said.

"Open your presents first," Ember said, clapping. At her feet, Aria yipped and wagged her tail. Dennis and Deirdre piled presents around me. The only things I really wanted were Jillian and Logan, but the Connellys were trying so hard, I couldn't help smiling.

I kept waiting for one of them, or all of them, to remember that I was Killers' Spawn.

"The big one is from Dennis and me," Deirdre said.

The box was huge, actually. Dennis and Deirdre looked so pleased, so proud. I untied the green bow, tore the Snoopy and Woodstock wrapping. Lifted the flaps and peered inside.

Silver flashed.

No, not silver. Stainless steel pots and pans. Cookie sheets and mixing bowls. A whisk, a spatula, a timer, a food thermometer. Little jars of spices. Aluminum foil and parchment paper. Cookbooks. Flour, sugar, extra-virgin olive oil, a variety of specialty vinegars. And a cutlery set: Six knives with black handles and long silver blades.

This time, the silver blinded me. The knives looked identical to the set in my family's kitchen in Kitteridge, Virginia, the ones my parents used to stab Kip Gallagher and Timothy Brunswick.

I blinked, and when I could see again, I saw that Deirdre's smile had faded. "You don't like it?" she asked. "Tristan said you like to cook."

"I, um…" I *did* like to cook. I used to cook dinner every night with my mother. But my mother was a killer. All those evenings we'd spent cooking together were a lie.

"We can return everything and get something you like," Deirdre said, her hands flittering to her throat. She looked like she was holding back tears.

I didn't want to make her cry, and it truly was a thoughtful gift, so I put a smile on my face. "The cooking stuff is great, Deirdre. Really.

Thank you."

That seemed to make her feel better, because she smiled back.

"Mine next," Tristan said. He handed me a shoebox shape, semi-heavy, in periwinkle paper.

I unwrapped it: Tubes of oil paint.

He handed me more boxes, and I unwrapped them one by one: Brushes, from tiny to large. Then palettes, and paint cleaners, a drop cloth, and a dozen canvases in all sizes.

"I set up an easel in the sunroom for you," Tristan said.

My parents had taken painting away from me. But I could do it now. I could paint. I could paint, and then I could hang my canvases on the wall, on every wall, for everyone to see. My parents couldn't take painting away from me, ever again.

Tristan understood that.

"Thank you, Tristan." My heart was so full of love for him I thought it would explode out of my rib cage. *Thank you so much.*

He tucked me under his arm and held me tight.

"My turn!" Ember sprang up. She darted from the room and returned, holding a small wicker basket. Lining the basket was a fluffy cream-colored blanket.

And curled up on the blanket was a tiny orange kitten.

"She's the runt of the litter," Ember said. "Her mother rejected her."

She placed the basket on my lap. I couldn't stop staring at the kitten. The runt of the litter. My brother and sister used to taunt me with that name because I was so small and didn't have a psychic power.

"Ember," Dennis said, "I told you to stop bringing animals home from the shelter."

"You also keep telling me that Tessa's a member of this family now and I need to make her feel welcome," she said. "I have Lyric and Aria, and Tristan has Mac. So I'm giving Tessa a cat. She needs a pet of her own, too."

I *wasn't* a member of this family. But I wanted this orange kitten. The runt of the litter. Tiny, parent-less, and taken in by the Connellys. We belonged together.

The kitten yawned and rolled onto her side, her paws pink and curled. What was it like to sleep that soundly, to feel that safe and content? No dreams of silver knives and Nightmare Eyes for this little kitten.

Ember continued to pout. "You know she'll behave, Dad. I'll make her the best-behaved kitten in the world. Please? You won't be sorry. One day this kitten will save Tessa's life. You'll see."

Tristan laughed. "Dad, come on," he said. "Look at Tessa. She loves that kitten already."

"Dennis," Deirdre said, one eyebrow raised.

"Please?" I begged.

Dennis gave a sigh that was half exasperation and half laugh. "Fine."

Ember and I exchanged grins. The kitten was mine. "Thank you, Ember." I rubbed the kitten's chin, softly, so I wouldn't wake her. She purred.

"What are you going to name her?" Ember asked.

She was light orange, and sweet and warm all curled up in her basket. Like orange marmalade on toast—Jillian's favorite breakfast. "Marmalade," I said. "She's my little Marma lady."

While we were eating my birthday breakfast cake, the doorbell rang. Dennis went to answer the door and came back with an envelope in hand. "For you, Tessa."

Tristan, Deirdre, and Ember looked confused, but I didn't have to open it, or even lift the fog, to know who had sent it. My hand fluttered to my belly.

Dennis handed it to me. "One of the guards dropped it off."

Because everyone was watching, I opened it. Another plain sheet of computer paper from my mother, this time folded into quarters to look like a greeting card.

*Happy birthday, Babydoll*

…was as far as I got before the words became blurry, and my lungs shriveled up, and my blood burned through my veins.

I tucked it under my paper plate, telling everyone I would read it later. But when I cleared the table, I swept it into the trash can with the rest of the garbage.

After breakfast, Tristan and I played with my sweet, adorable new kitty for a while, then I put my new cooking supplies away. I vowed to cook something soon, if only to please Dennis and Deirdre. I found places for everything in the cluttered kitchen, straightening the disorderly cabinets and drawers as I went along. But I couldn't put the knives away. I *wanted* them put away, but every time I looked at them, the blades glittered and glimmered, sparkled and glowed. I couldn't bring myself to touch them.

I didn't want to cook, but I did want to paint. Specifically, I wanted to paint something for my boyfriend, who had given me the best birthday I'd had in eight years. I sent him upstairs to study, telling him that he would never become a lead investigator for the APR, and then executive director, if his grades were less than excellent. Then Marmalade padded along beside me as I took my new painting supplies into the sunroom, which was separated from the kitchen by sliding glass doors.

Sunlight streamed through the glass walls, making the room warm and cozy despite the snowy outside view. Marmalade stretched out in a patch of sun while I set up. Deirdre used this room for crafts, and she had stacks of unopened supplies in a low cabinet and half-finished projects on a table. I placed a small canvas onto the easel, sat on the stool, and squeezed some paint onto a palette. Swirling my brush over the colors, I stared at the plain white canvas.

I had no idea what to paint.

A few feet away in the kitchen, Deirdre dug through a pile of papers while listening to an audiobook, while Mac sat at her feet and whipped his tail. Dennis came in to grab another piece of cake. Aria yipped while Ember whined into her cell phone. "But Kimber quit last week. You can't quit the band too. We need you." Her gaze landed on me, and when she saw me looking, she yanked the glass door shut.

Her argument and Aria's yipping continued, along with Deirdre's audiobook and Mac's panting, but the noise was muffled enough now that I could tune it out. I stared at the canvas again.

Hmm. A painting. For Tristan.

A patch of wildflowers on bright green grass. That's what he saw when he looked in my eyes. That's what I would paint for him.

I put the brush to the canvas, sweeping shades of green across it, then dotted bright yellows and blues and purples over that.

I turned seventeen today. The first birthday I had without my family. Was my mother sitting in her cell, watching the door, expecting a guard to come any second and escort her to the visiting room to see me? Did my comatose father have even the tiniest inkling that his middle child, his Tessa Blessa, had turned another year older? Had Jillian and Logan done anything to commemorate my birthday?

I pictured my mind opening up, and I sent a message to them: *You're safe! I'm safe! I'm alive and I'm safe and I'm trying to find you!*

The only thing I felt in return was the Nightmare Eyes as they glowered and gleamed, dark as a starless night and black as a cavern of coal, weighing down on me from above. Burning into my soul. Accusing me. How dare I eat cake and paint and play with my new kitten, when Jillian and Logan were alone and lost and scared? How dare I enjoy myself, when my parents had murdered dozens of people, including two people from this town? Melanie, Nathan, and Cole were fatherless because of my parents. Winter's father had a heart attack because of my mother. *Dennis* had a heart attack because of my mother. My parents had planned to kill Tristan.

How dare I enjoy myself today, when I was Killers' Spawn?

"Tessa."

Tristan's voice echoed in the fog. "Tessa, you okay?"

I raised the fog a little to clear my head. "I'm fine," I said.

"Are you crying?" He caressed my cheek with his thumb.

"No," I said. But when I wiped my cheeks, they were warm and damp. "How's studying going?" I asked, to change the subject. "Getting a lot done?"

"I spent most of the time making contact lists of psychics and car dealerships," he said. "I want to follow up on Brinda's drawings. But then I had a warning premonition about you. Something about eyes." He glanced down at the canvas, brows furrowed. "What are you painting?"

"A patch of—" The twin disks of black smeared on the canvas were nothing like the wildflowers I'd intended to paint. "Oh. I guess I need more practice."

"Those are the eyes in my premonition," he said, frowning.

Eyes? Yes, the black circles on the canvas could be eyes. But they looked more like my Nightmare Eyes than my wildflower eyes.

I lifted the canvas from the easel and leaned it against the wall, facing away from us, then replaced it with a fresh, clean one. Tristan stayed with me, and as he nuzzled my neck, I painted the patch of wildflowers I'd originally intended. I darkened some areas and highlighted others, adding shades and tones to give the flowers dimension and depth.

"There," I said when I finished. Not bad. Obviously painted by an amateur, not good enough to display in a gallery or anything, but it was much better than my first attempt.

"Wildflowers," Tristan said. "For your wildflower eyes."

"I made it for you. To thank you. For getting me the perfect gift. And for helping me look for Jillian and Logan."

"It's good, Clockwise. *Really* good."

"It'd be a lot better if you weren't tickling me with your kisses the whole time," I said, and swiped a dab of green paint on his nose.

He kissed me, getting the green paint on my nose too. "Sign your painting so I can hang it in my room."

I dipped a thin brush into some paint on the palette, then signed my name in the corner. *Tessa.* My name glittered and glimmered, sparkled and glowed, reflecting in the sun.

I'd painted my name in silver.

I didn't remember putting silver paint on my palette. I must have done it while I was painting the Nightmare Eyes.

# CHAPTER ELEVEN

ROM THE PAGES of the binder, my parents' victims glare and glower, and meld together to become a single pair of eyes, dark as a starless night and black as a cavern of coal. The knife pivots on its point as it glitters and glimmers, sparkles and glows. Slowly, blood drips down the blade, drop by drop, drip by drip, then faster and faster, until it forms a river, a river of blood, a flood of blood. Blood from me, my tarnished blood, my tainted blood, my contaminated blood.

In a low rumble the victims chant *Killers' Spawn, Killers' Spawn, Killers' Spawn.* And the Nightmare Eyes watch it all from high above, as they glower and gleam, and flash silver with grief and shame, despair and rage.

The effort of holding back a scream woke me up. From my bedside, Tristan was shaking me. "You're safe, Tessa."

Safe. I was *safe.* Safe with Tristan. Safe with the Connellys. Safe in Lilybrook. I even had my new kitten sleeping at the foot of my bed, purring contentedly. There was no reason to have these bad dreams. No reason to feel the Nightmare Eyes hovering over me, even while I was awake.

Except.

My parents were killers.

Except.

My blood was tainted.

Except.

Nathan Gallagher hated me. Winter Milbourne hated me. Kellan hated me.

Except. Except. Except.

Tristan sat on my bed. "I came in here because I had another warning premonition," he said. "It was those eyes again. The ones you painted earlier."

Should I tell him? About my dream, about the Nightmare Eyes?

Above me, the Nightmare Eyes simmered. They didn't want me to say anything. They wanted me to keep them a secret. A secret of shame and guilt.

But Tristan already knew about that. He just didn't know how deep it went. "Those eyes are from all the people my parents killed," I confessed. "And Kellan, and Nathan. Winter. Melanie, too. They glare at me. Their eyes become one giant pair of Nightmare Eyes."

"That's what you've been dreaming about? Every night?"

"Every night." Since I started, I may as well tell him the rest. "And a knife. The one my parents used to kill your dad's team."

Shaking his head, he slipped into the bed, under the covers.

"Tristan," I gasped. "We'll get in trouble."

"Shh." He pulled me to him, my back against his chest, and reached under my pajama top. He rested his open palm on my stomach, covering all of my scars. "I wish I could make these disappear," he whispered, his breath warm on my neck. "Maybe then you could stop feeling so guilty about your parents and the nightmares would stop." His hand on my belly was warm, too. The good kind of warm, the loving kind of warm, and it soaked into me, into every cell.

"No more nightmares tonight," he whispered. "I'll keep them away."

One by one, my muscles relaxed, and I snuggled against him.

"Us," he murmured.

"You and me," I replied, and closed my eyes. Together, our breath grew slower and deeper. No more nightmares. Not with Tristan holding me like this.

Instead of a nightmare, I had a vision: Tristan, lounging on the sofa downstairs, his arm around Melanie. Nathan and Winter sitting next to them. All of the Lab Brats, laughing and joking around, wearing green and yellow and watching the Green Bay Packers on TV. Melanie staring up at Tristan like a rescued damsel worshiping her heroic knight. Tristan goofing off, booming with laughter.

So carefree. So content. Tristan was *never* like that around me. Around me, he was always stressed and worried and concerned. In Twelve Lakes, he'd tried to keep me safe—safe from my killer parents, safe from a vengeful Kellan. Here in Lilybrook, he was trying to find Jillian and Logan. Whatever dragons he had slain for Melanie were nothing compared to the dragons he was trying to slay for me.

With the exception of Melanie, none of the Lab Brats had come over since I'd gotten here. No football parties. No booming laughter.

My parents had stolen money and stolen lives. I had stolen Tristan's happiness. How long until he realized that? What would he do when he discovered he couldn't slay my dragons?

In my vision, Tristan's laughter echoed, then faded into the fog.

# CHAPTER TWELVE

HE ART STUDIO was the one place at school where I could forget about the Nightmare Eyes. Art was first period, but I wished it was my last class so I could have something to look forward to all day. I understood now why Logan loved composing music, and why Jillian loved dancing. Being creative felt like freedom.

Our unit on mosaics had ended last week. I'd decorated a vase using glass tiles in different shades of purple. Mr. Vargas had given me an A. My first A in eight years; my first since my family fled from our big red brick house in Virginia. Deirdre, upon seeing my vase that evening, had promptly placed it on the mantle over the fireplace among Tristan and Ember's school projects and trophies.

This morning, a royal blue bowl filled with carefully arranged fruit sat on the center table of the art studio. Mr. Vargas wasn't there, but he'd left a note next to the bowl that read simply,

*Paint me.*

Gladly.

My classmates and I settled onto our stools and squeezed paint onto our palettes. As usual, no one spoke directly to me, but I overheard enough to understand that Mr. Vargas often left his students alone in the classroom so his direction would not inhibit our creativity. I took a brush in hand and studied the fruit arrangement for a few moments, then divided the canvas into six equal boxes. After mixing some yellow and green together, I painted the fat curve of the pear, in the bottom left square. The curve of the giant strawberry, complete with seeds and leaves, filled the next box, and the curve of the orange in the box next to that. The curved parts of the purple grape, the shiny red apple, and the yellow pineapple completed the top row. Any part of the canvas that remained white, I painted royal blue to represent the bowl.

The bell rang, and I appraised my project with a nod, not so much proud of my artwork as I was that I'd kept the fog balanced while I'd painted it. No angry black smears across the canvas. Just colorful fruit. I left my painting on the easel to dry, certain my success in art class would carry me through the day.

I was proven wrong less than an hour later, when my Spanish teacher passed out a test.

We had a test today? I didn't remember hearing about a test. The words on the paper didn't even look familiar.

I struggled through the test, guessing at most of the answers. My classmates turned theirs in before I was halfway done. "Señorita Tessa," the teacher said from her desk in Spanish, "we can't wait all—"

The door flew open, and Tristan, *my* Tristan, strode into the classroom and over to me. Coatless in a Heron University hoodie, hair tousled, breathing hard, as if he'd dropped whatever he'd been doing at his school and rushed to mine at full speed.

"Tessa," he said, "We have to go. Now."

Prickly dread crawled up my stomach and into my throat. Something was wrong. Tristan was supposed to be in class, an hour away. He wouldn't be here if something wasn't wrong. I swept my things into my book bag and rushed to the door, the movement instinctual after eight years on the run.

"She's in the middle of a test, Tristan," the teacher called after us. "You're not even a student here anymore. You can't just come in—"

"Sorry, Señora Diaz, but this is important," Tristan replied in perfect Spanish, and whisked me out the door.

"Tristan, what's wrong?" I pleaded as we rushed down the hall, my dread turning into nausea.

He stopped, rubbed my arms because I was shivering, and his lips slowly spread into a broad grin. "I did it, Clockwise. I found Jillian and Logan. I know where they are. Let's go get them."

# CHAPTER THIRTEEN

ILLIAN AND LOGAN. Tristan found Jillian and Logan. That's all I could think as Tristan drove at top speed through town. I wished I was psychokinetic so I could make the car go even faster. Better yet, I wished I could teleport. "Where are they?" I said, barely able to speak through my elation. "How did you find them?"

"I used Google Images to find places that matched Brinda's drawings." He shrugged, like it was no big deal.

We flew past a long line of cars that were crawling along at the speed limit on Main Street. "I searched for buildings that were similar to the ones she drew, and things like a one-eyed deer," he said. "Names of towns that could possibly match any of her drawings. I found a few matches, but none of them panned out. But one drawing, that one with the two black curves and the lines sticking down from them? Got a direct hit."

"The one that looks like closed eyelids?"

"There's an old motel in Braddock, Tennessee called Forty Winks," he said. "That closed eyelids symbol is its logo. I checked, and they don't have a security camera, so I figured Jillian and Logan might feel safe if they stayed there. I emailed their photos to the manager and asked him to contact me if they show up. It took a few days, but he called me this morning just as I walked into my first class."

He grinned at me, lighting up from the inside out: first his eyes, then his smile. "Jillian and Logan came in early this morning and booked a room."

I could not breathe. Jillian and Logan were in Braddock, Tennessee, at the Forty Winks motel, right now. This very moment. "Go, Tristan! Hurry!"

Tristan pressed hard on the gas. He turned off Main Street, but instead of turning onto the highway, he turned onto a small road lined by trees.

"Where are we going?" I asked. "Isn't this the way to the lake?"

"The Lilybrook airfield's on the other side of the lake," he said. "Driving to Tennessee would take too long, even if I go at top speed. I got us a charter flight."

"A charter? Can you afford that?"

He shrugged again. "Being an agent for your case in Twelve Lakes was a full time job. I may have lost that job, but I still have the money I made. Most of it's in the bank, but I keep a bunch of cash in my desk at home."

"But still, a charter. It must be so expensive."

"I'm not going to let a little money get in the way of finding Jillian and Logan for you."

We reached the little airfield in less than ten minutes. There were three small planes outside the low, wide hangar. The fancy one had a big *NWSL* painted in navy along the side—Northern Wisconsin Science Laboratory, the APR's plane. The others were smaller, but just as shiny and clean. A pilot was waiting to escort us on board the smallest plane. I grabbed the yellow getaway bag I kept stashed in the trunk of

Tristan's car, and we rushed on board.

Tristan and I sat next to each other in two black leather seats, me bouncing up and down like a little kid. I couldn't stop shivering as we took off, but I wasn't cold. No, I was excited. Anxious. Impatient. And so happy that I wanted to do cartwheels.

Instead, once the plane reached cruising altitude, I unbuckled my seatbelt and slid over to Tristan, straddling his legs with mine. We were the only two passengers on this little plane, and the pilot was up front, behind a partition. "You did it," I said. "You found my brother and sister."

"I promised you I would, Clockwise."

I cupped his face in my hands, unable to stop looking into his big blue eyes, eyes that were filled with love as he looked back at me. "Tristan, you're amazing."

He slid his hands over my hips and pulled me in closer. "*You're* amazing. And you're beautiful. You're everything."

I lowered my lips onto his, and we didn't stop kissing until the plane landed in Braddock, Tennessee.

Jillian and Logan. Jillian and Logan! I was finally going to see them again. How would they react when they saw me, the sister they believed was dead? My heart broke into a thousand pieces at the thought of telling them the truth about our parents. But once they accepted it, it would be such a relief not to be alone anymore. They would understand my grief and shame, and share it with me. The three of us sharing it would make it easier for all of us to bear.

We landed at a small airfield near Braddock, then Tristan rented a car, bribing the agent with charm and a few extra bucks because he was underage. He drove us a few miles through the snow-frosted mountainous region to the Forty Winks Motel. "Look at the eyes," I exclaimed as we neared the motel. On a hand-painted wooden sign, high over the road, were two enormous closed eyelids, smaller than my Nightmare Eyes but much more amicable. Almost identical to the shapes that Brinda had drawn. "You were right, Tristan. You did it."

As we pulled into the parking lot, I wrinkled my nose as I observed the motel. Run-down and dirty, rotting wood with peeling paint. A smaller sign boasted *Weekly and Munthly R tes!* Typical of the motels my family stayed in while we were on the run.

No matter. This was the last dingy motel my siblings would ever have to stay in. Jillian and Logan were coming home with me, today. They were just a few feet away, behind one of those scuffed white doors.

We dashed to the lobby to get their room number, and I gasped. "They were here. I can see them!" Through the fog, standing right there at the registration desk. Right *there.*

"Balance, Clockwise," Tristan said. He didn't sound worried, though. Just a gentle reminder from my constant protector. "Keep the fog balanced."

I brought in the fog a little. Jillian and Logan had been standing in this spot just a few hours ago. Jillian looked tired; shadows under her eyes, hair stringy and dyed dark brown. Sunken cheeks. Was she not eating enough? Logan looked thin and tired, too. Both wore plain baseball caps pulled down low.

It was so good to see them again, even if they were just intangible images. I'd be seeing them for real in just a few minutes.

A plump woman in a green sweater-vest and a silver name tag— *Valerie Simmons, Clerk*—appeared behind the desk. "Can I help you?"

Oh. She was real, not a vision. I shook the fog back into place.

"We're here to see the manager," Tristan said. "He's expecting us."

Valerie looked over her shoulder. "He must have gone on his coffee break," she said in the cutest Southern accent I'd ever heard. "I'll go get him." She disappeared into the back office.

I couldn't wait for the manager. I could find Jillian and Logan's room on my own. I lifted the fog and filtered through the visions until the one I needed came to me. I saw Jillian slide some cash to the stocky middle-aged man behind the desk—Lyle Berri, my visions told me—and he handed her a key dangling from a diamond-shaped tag. Printed on that tag was the closed-eyelid symbol. And underneath that: a number.

"Room 160," I said.

Then I started running.

I ran from the lobby, back outside and down the corridor of white doors, vaguely aware of Tristan rushing after me. Room 101, 118, 124. Why did this motel have to be so big? 132, 146…160. There it was. At the end.

I raised my hand to knock on it at the same time Tristan skidded to a halt a few feet behind me. "Tessa."

The door was open. Just an inch.

That wasn't right. My family had always kept the doors locked, double-locked, when we were on the run.

I felt it then, through the fog. Fear. Jillian and Logan were scared. Something had frightened them. I could feel their fear, feel their panic, bleeding through the fog, seeping into me.

A vision showed them rushing out the door and down the corridor, then disappearing completely.

We had been so close. *So* close. My heart hurt, like someone had taken it in their fist and squeezed it dry.

"They're gone, Tristan," I said. "We were too late."

# CHAPTER FOURTEEN

"ET'S LOOK INSIDE their room," Tristan said as he held me against his chest. "Maybe you'll see what made them run away again."

Inhaling disappointment instead of oxygen, my muscles replaced by rocks, I pushed open the door to room 160 and went inside.

The television screen was shattered. The drawers in the cheap dresser were half-open. Something had scared them, startled them enough to shatter that TV and leave in a rush. But although they'd fled in a hurry, they made sure to leave nothing personal behind. The drawers: empty. The mattresses: sheetless. Except for a lamp that lay in pieces on the worn carpet, whatever they had touched—a menu, a map, perhaps a newspaper—they had taken with them to burn. "They're doing everything our parents taught us," I said. Our parents had taught us too well.

A groan came from the bathroom.

Jillian? Logan?

It couldn't be them. But please, *please...*

Tristan and I darted to the bathroom. The door wouldn't budge, so he shoulder-charged it. It splintered, and when he pushed it open, I was blinded by silver.

No. Just a plastic silver-plated name tag, reflecting the light hanging over the sink. Not a knife pivoting on its point. A name tag. But that name tag was attached to the green sweater-vest of a stocky man crumpled on the grimy floor. The man groaned again, blood trickling from a deep gash on his forehead, and reached for us with stubby fingers.

Tristan dropped to the man's side. "Tessa," he said, "call an ambulance."

The silver name tag flashed again, catching the light, reflecting on the walls. It glittered and glimmered, sparkled and glowed.

"Tessa!" Tristan's sharp voice made the silver light shatter and disappear. "Call 911." He was applying pressure to the man's cut with a washcloth. I shook my head to clear it, and with shaky fingers, used my phone to call for help.

The man stirred, his name tag falling off as he struggled to sit up. *Lyle Berri, General Manager,* it read, and as I watched, it glimmered, just once, like a wink.

"Those two kids," the man moaned. "The lamp flew off the table and hit me on the head. All by itself. Did they do that? Did they make that happen?"

"No, sir," Tristan said soothingly. "You don't remember that right. You tripped and hit your head."

*Jillian and Logan attacked this man*, he said to me silently.

"No," I said aloud. "They would never—"

Then the fog lifted, and showed me that they did.

She asks Logan to go back to the lobby of this shabby Tennessee motel–it's Tennessee, right? They're in Tennessee?–to get some food from the vending machines. As soon as he leaves, she breaks down again. She's been crying all week, ever since they went to Nebraska and Gavin's mother told them he'd died of a brain aneurysm over two years ago, the night her family left that town.

That college professor they contacted from Twelve Lakes had died of a brain aneurysm, too. There was no way that was a coincidence. Dennis Connelly had killed them both. It was obvious.

Gavin. Smart, shy, beautiful Gavin. No one else thought he was beautiful, but she did. Dennis Connelly had killed Gavin, sweet Gavin who wrote her poetry and quoted Shakespeare and Wordsworth, simply because her family had escaped. Did he kill him out of vengeance? Or had he questioned him first, torturing him, hoping to get information about her family?

And then Gavin's mom told them that someone had stopped by just a couple weeks ago, a very polite man in a black jacket, looking for them.

So now they knew: Dennis Connelly was still hunting them. Even though he'd already killed Mom and Dad and Tessa, he was still after them.

When Gavin's mom told them that she was going to call the man in the black jacket to tell them they were there, as the man had instructed, they fled. They destroyed the rusty red pickup, bought a different car, and zigzagged around the country for days, stopping only for gas and food, until Logan saw the giant sign with closed eyelids on this motel in Tennessee. After ensuring the old motel had no security cameras, he'd insisted they get a room and sleep for a few hours before hitting the road again.

How can she sleep, when Gavin is dead, and Mom and Dad and Tessa are dead, and Dennis Connelly is still after them?

He rushes back to the room after making a run to the vending machine in the lobby, gripping a sheet of paper, slamming the door behind him. "Jillian—"

"Don't start," she says with a sniffle. She's on one of the beds, rotating the heart charm around the gold bracelet that Gavin had given her, and going through Tessa's getaway bag again. "I told you, I'm not getting rid of these things. It's all we have left of them."

"We have to go. Now. Dennis Connelly knows we're here."

Her eyes grow large. At her silent command, the chain on the door slides itself into the lock. "How do you know?"

He peeks out the window from behind the curtain. "The guy in the green vest at the registration desk. He was watching us."

"But why do you think—"

He shoots the paper over to her. "I saw this on the counter."

She plucks it from the air and gasps. Two black and white photos, side by side: one of Jillian. One of Logan.

"Connelly must've known we would come here," he says, "so he sent that Lyle guy to act as manager and wait for us. The same way he sent Tristan Walker to wait for us in Twelve Lakes. The same way he sent someone to Gavin's house in Nebraska. Connelly's probably on his way here right now."

With a wave of his fingers, the washcloths fly out of the bathroom. They hadn't been here long; they hadn't touched much so there wasn't much to burn. Just a map of the city and a few washcloths. He decides to take the bed linens and pillowcases as well. Can't be too safe. They'll burn everything later.

Jillian hoists both her and Tessa's bags over her shoulder. He gives the room a quick glance. No sign that they'd ever been there. They open the door, and that man with the green sweater-vest is leaning against the wall outside their room, obviously watching it.

Every muscle in his body goes rigid. "Get out of the way," he says. He clenches his fists. He will fight this guy if he has to.

Jillian whimpers. The dresser drawers start trembling, the lamp vibrates, the television screen shatters. "Hey!" the man shouts, and when he charges inside, she squeals. The lamp flies off the table, slamming with full force into his head. The man groans and falls to his knees, then, clutching his head, collapses to the floor.

Jillian stares at the man in horror, hands clamped over her mouth. "I didn't mean—"

He puts his hands to his knees. Think. *Think.* The guy's not dead, he's still alive, struggling to get up. They need to stop him from following them. He drags the man into the bathroom and slams the door shut, using his PK to jam the doorknob so it won't turn.

Then he and Jillian grab all the getaway bags and flee.


I chased the vision of Jillian and Logan as they ran from the motel room, down the aisle, and into the parking lot. Their images were fading, but I tore after them anyway, raising the fog higher and higher. What kind of car were they driving? Which direction did they go?

I raised the fog again. So many cars had driven through this lot; minivans and sedans and rumbly old delivery trucks. If I could just see the car my siblings hopped into. *Please.* Just a glimpse.

Something grabbed me, yanked me, and a siren blared, sending the fog back in with a whoosh.

I was standing in the middle of the parking lot of the Forty Winks motel, Tristan was gripping the hood of my sweatshirt, and the only moving vehicle was a red and white ambulance. It pulled to a stop in front of room 160.

"You ran right in front of that ambulance," Tristan shouted, frantic. "I was yelling for you to stop. Didn't you hear me?"

"Logan saw their photos on the registration desk," I blurted, the words tumbling over each other. "They panicked. That's why they attacked the manager and ran. And they know Gavin's dead. They already went to Nebraska. Gavin's mom told them someone's looking for them."

Tristan stood shocked for a moment, then pulled me into his arms. "Can you lift the fog, very slowly, very carefully, and see what kind of car they were driving? I'll have the APR put out an all-points-bulletin. But you have to be careful. Don't lift the fog too high."

I lifted the fog as high as I dared, but there were no more visions. Just the glowering, gleeful Nightmare Eyes above, and the weedy, crumbling parking lot at my feet. Beyond the parking lot was the street, and beyond that were businesses and houses and roads, and then more roads. North, south, east, west—it didn't matter which way they went. All the streets in Tennessee, all the roads in the country, went in one direction: away from me.

# CHAPTER FIFTEEN

RISTAN AND I returned from our failed trip to Tennessee, stumbling into the Connellys' house after nightfall. Tristan had called his parents from the plane to tell them what happened, and the moment I stepped inside, Deirdre pulled me into a too-tight hug. "You ran in front of a speeding ambulance? Honey, what were you thinking?"

"I wasn't thinking," I mumbled into her chest. "I was looking for Jillian and Logan." I stayed in her arms for a few moments before pulling away. It felt good to be hugged like that.

I missed having a mother.

Deirdre gave Tristan a hug too, then scolded him. "This is exactly why I told you to let the APR handle the case. Leaving class and taking Tessa out of school was bad enough, but she could have been killed, Tristan."

He hung his head. "I know. You're right. If anything happened to her, it would've been my fault."

"Tristan, I lifted the fog too high," I said. "I didn't hear you shouting for me to stop. It *wasn't* your fault."

He shook his head anyway. "I promised I would keep you safe, and instead I almost got you killed."

Dennis came in, phone in hand. "I just hung up with Kellan. I asked him why he didn't know Jillian and Logan went to Nebraska."

"And?" I asked.

"He did know about it." He rubbed the back of his neck. "Gavin's mother called him right after they ran off. Kellan never reported it. It happened almost a week ago, but he said he's been too busy to file the report."

I felt like I'd been punched in the chest. "Who cares about filing a report? He should have called us the second he heard from Gavin's mom."

Tristan cursed under his breath. "He just didn't want anyone to know he screwed up."

"The good thing is," Dennis said, "I convinced him to take on an additional investigator, someone who'll be dedicated full-time to your case."

"Me?" Tristan asked, hope in his voice for the first time in hours.

"I suggested it," Dennis said, "but Kellan won't work with you. Sorry, Tristan."

That wasn't fair. Tristan already had the dedication and the desire. If he also had the resources of the APR, we'd find Jillian and Logan in no time.

"Who is it, then?" I asked Dennis.

"Kellan's selecting the new agent tomorrow," he said. "He said to meet him at the APR at four o'clock."

I couldn't pay much attention in school the next day. Not because I was busy keeping the fog balanced against the visions, or pretending that Nathan and Winter's scornful glares weren't bothering me. Well, I was busy doing that, but I also couldn't pay attention because after school, I was going to the APR to meet the new investigator assigned to my case. I couldn't concentrate on anything else.

When I got home, I gave Marmalade a quick cuddle before Dennis drove me to the APR. Tristan was waiting for us, having left class early for the occasion.

"Tessa, do you want to visit your parents first?" Dennis asked as we walked to the elevator that would take us down to the investigation offices. "I'm sure your mother would like to see you. The warden told me she asked if you received her birthday card."

Tristan shook his head, and I shook mine. "I just want to meet the new investigator." I had the ballet shoe and sheet music with me. Same with Brinda's drawings. I didn't want to give them up, but the investigator would need them.

John Kellan marched toward us as we waited for the elevator, his red Lead Investigator badge swinging from a lanyard around his neck.

"How could you not have told us that Jillian and Logan went to Nebraska?" I demanded, arms crossed. "We might have found them by now."

"I was getting to it," Kellan said. "I have over a dozen cases and I'm understaffed. Filing reports is not my main priority."

Dennis frowned at him. "John, introduce Tessa to the new investigator. Then you can get back to your eleven other cases."

"With pleasure." Instead of turning to the elevator, Kellan pivoted on his heel. "This way. He's in the Lab."

"The Lab?" Tristan said through tight lips. "Those guys aren't trained in investigations."

Kellan snorted without turning around. He led us to the end of the hallway and into the bright, glass-walled Lab, which looked more like a lounge than an industrial science laboratory.

I'd been here once before, while Tristan and I were staying in the Underground. The round tables, comfortable chairs, and plate glass windows gave the place a sense of receptive openness, but beyond the windows were tall trees, and surrounding the trees was an electrified fence.

One-way mirrors lined one interior wall, and they caught the light from the windows and reflected into the Lab, making everything luminous. Several APR employees wearing green Lab badges sat at the tables, interviewing potential psionic subjects. Cole Gallagher was interviewing a boisterous, brown-haired woman as she gazed into a wide bowl of water and described the visions she saw in it. Mirroring her confident expression, he gave us a nod as we passed him.

"This way," Kellan said, and we followed him into one of the offices lining the perimeter of the Lab. The sign on the door read *Technokinetics*. I'd been in this office before too, when Tristan asked an elderly large-nosed man to recharge my cell phone.

"I already tried with the Techno guys, Kellan," Tristan said. "I had Craig Schultz hack into the Amtrak computers."

"I know," Kellan said, opening the door. "That's what gave me the idea. Craig can hack, but I found you someone even better. Miss Carson, meet your new, dedicated, full-time investigator. Aaron Jacobs."

Surrounded by piles of circuit boards, cords, and various electronics, a scrawny guy sat at the back of the room. He faced three computer monitors, the images on them flashing as his fingers clickety-clacked over a keyboard. Without stopping, he stole a glance at us over his shoulder. Young, no more than three years older than me, wide mouth and chapped lips, black hair parted down the middle and sorely in need of a trim, and dark brown eyes behind glasses that were much too big for his face. He turned bright red at our scrutiny and returned to the monitors.

"Hey, Aaron," Tristan greeted him, then flashed to me, *Super-smart guy. Graduated from Lilybrook High when he was twelve and from Heron University when he was fifteen. But he knows nothing about investigations. I can do better on my own than he can here.*

*Then why would Kellan pick him?*

*Aaron's mom is the executive director. I bet Kellan's doing this to suck up to her after messing up so badly in Nebraska.*

Dennis rubbed his chin. "Why Aaron?" he asked Kellan. "He doesn't have the necessary training to be an investigator."

"He doesn't need it," Kellan said. "Aaron is a cyber-mind. He's basically a computer in human form. He'll scan webcams and security cameras to find the targets. Like facial-recognition software, but a thousand times faster and more accurate."

Dennis nodded approvingly, but Tristan crossed his arms. "Jillian and Logan are purposely avoiding places with cameras. Aaron will never find them that way."

Aaron's fingers hesitated on the keyboard, then stopped, his shoulders sagging.

"They can't avoid all cameras," Kellan said. "And Aaron's all we got. Unless you want me to assign Nathan Gallagher to the case." He smirked at me, knowing full well that I wouldn't want that.

Kellan handed Aaron a file. "That's everything you need to know about your targets. We took pictures of them a few weeks ago, so the photos are recent. Just do your computer magic to look for their faces. They're on the road, so start with traffic cams, gas stations, drive-throughs."

Keeping his head ducked so low his glasses almost slipped off, Aaron opened the file. I went to stand next to him so I could look over his shoulder.

A photo of Logan was the top picture. Carrying his sax on the driveway of our house in Twelve Lakes. His face was serious, his brown eyes looking cautiously down the street, making sure it was safe.

Jillian's photo was next. Also taken in Twelve Lakes, this photo was a close-up of her looking out our upstairs window, one hand holding back the curtain, her gray eyes staring into the distance, blond hair falling over her shoulders.

"She's dyed her hair brown since then," I told Aaron, remembering my vision of her brown hair in Tennessee. "And they both might be wearing baseball caps." He didn't respond, just looked at Jillian's photo. I held out the ballet shoe and sheet music. "Do you need these?"

He shook his head.

I tried giving him Brinda's drawings next. "Would these help at all?"

Another shake.

Tucking the items back in my bag, I gave him more direction. "Try truck stops," I said. "We used to eat in truck stops a lot. And twenty-four-hour diners. Try convenience stores, too."

The number of truck stops, drive-throughs, convenience stores, and gas stations in this country had to number in the millions. No wonder Aaron was shocked into frozen muteness. Kellan had assigned him an impossible task.

"Jillian likes warm places," I said. "Maybe you should start with the Southern states. And don't bother looking in the states we've already lived. They won't return. Tennessee is out too, and probably Louisiana. That narrows it down for you a little, right?"

Aaron still said nothing.

I found a piece of paper and a pen. "This is my phone number," I said, jotting it down. "Call me the second you find something. Any time, day or night. I'll answer on the first ring." I slid a sideways glance to Kellan. "Don't bring Kellan with you to get them. He'll just hurt them. I'll go with you instead."

Kellan snorted. Tristan fisted his hands. Dennis frowned at both of them.

But Aaron didn't respond.

Finally I gave up. I went to Tristan, seeking comfort under his arm. We didn't have to say anything, telepathically or out loud. We both knew it would be almost impossible for Aaron to find them.

Even Dennis failed to suppress a disappointed sigh. He mouthed to me, *I'll talk to the board of directors.*

"Thanks, Aaron," I said. "Good luck." Disheartened, we turned to leave.

"She's beautiful."

The choked words came from Aaron.

I paused in my steps and looked back.

"Your sister," he said. "She's beautiful."

"Yes," I said. "She is."

He traced his finger down Jillian's photo.

I glanced up at Tristan, and smiling, I broadcast my next thought loudly, so he would hear it, and Dennis would hear it, and Kellan would hear it too.

*Aaron Jacobs is going to find my brother and sister.*

# CHAPTER SIXTEEN

"**M**AKE SURE YOUR getaway bag is packed," I said to Tristan as we entered the kitchen the next morning, hand in hand. I held Marmalade in my other arm, and Mac plodded along at our feet. Tristan nodded with a huge yawn. Poor thing was exhausted. I had actually fallen asleep a little early last night, convinced that with Aaron's additional help on the case, I would soon find my brother and sister. But Tristan was up most of the night writing a report for his criminal justice class and doubling his efforts to contact the psychics in his database. "As soon as we get a lead, we need to leave."

"Oh no, you won't." The protest came from Deirdre, who was leaning against the kitchen table, still in her flowered robe. Her skin seemed extra pale against her messy copper hair, making her freckles stand out even more. Dennis stood next to her, one arm around her shoulders, his expression grim.

"I'm sorry, Tessa," he said. "But you can't leave Lilybrook."

"Why, because Tristan and I skipped school to go to Tennessee?" I asked. "We'll make up the work we missed."

"It's not about school," Deirdre said.

Tristan tightened his hold on my hand. "You had a dream, didn't you, Mom?"

She bit her lips and gripped the back of the chair, then gave a quick nod. "Last night."

"A precognitive dream? About me?" I'd been hoping Deirdre would have another dream about me—specifically, a dream about me finding Jillian and Logan. But she was so tight, so tense, so *terrified.*

"Tell me exactly what you dreamed," Tristan said, "so I can stop it from happening."

She kept her grip on the chair. "In the dream, Tessa, you left Lilybrook for your brother and sister. But you ended up inside a little house. The walls were silver. Silver walls. So bright it was blinding."

"Silver?" On the counter near the sink, a steak knife glimmered.

"Silver, and then..." She let out a huge exhale. "Red. The entire room filled with blood. A flood of blood."

The knife glimmered and glowed, and my pulse quickened, sending my tainted blood through my veins with every beat of my heart.

*Brinda Lakhani drew the same exact thing,* Tristan flashed to me, then aloud he asked his mother, "When is this supposed to happen?"

"I don't know when, I don't know where, I don't know how." Shaking, Deirdre stumbled over and clutched my shoulders. And when she looked down at me, the agony in her eyes made my heart stop beating. "The only thing I know, Tessa, is that if you leave Lilybrook," she said, "you are going to die."

# CHAPTER SEVENTEEN

 WAS GOING to die.

Inside a little house with silver walls, I was going to bleed to death.

Because Deirdre had a dream.

"How will it happen?" An anxious dread settled in my stomach like a rock. From the counter, the knife flashed again.

"I don't know," she said. "I just know that it will."

"What kind of house has silver walls?" I asked.

"It doesn't matter," Dennis said solemnly, "because you'll never be in a house like that. Deirdre's dreams always happen, Tessa. The only way to keep them from happening is to change the course of events. She dreamed that you left Lilybrook because of your brother and sister. So, to change the course of events, you won't leave. You'll stay in Lilybrook."

"Tristan changes the course of events with his warning premonitions all the time," I said. "So if he has one about me while we're away, I'll listen. I won't ignore him anymore. I'll do what he says. Immediately. I promise."

"That's not good enough," Tristan said. He put his hands on either side of my face and caressed my cheeks with his thumbs. "You almost got hit by that ambulance in Tennessee because you had lifted the fog so high that you were lost in the visions. You walked right in front of it, even though I was yelling for you to stop. It wasn't that you ignored me—you didn't hear me. Or what if…" He grimaced, guilt shadowing his face. "What if something like Twelve Lakes happens again?"

My shame was my parents; Tristan's shame was his failure to keep me safe from Kellan in Twelve Lakes.

"But what about Jillian and Logan?" I asked. "I can't let a dream stop me from finding them."

"Aaron Jacobs is looking for them," Dennis said.

"I'm looking for them too," said Tristan. "I may not be a human computer like Aaron is, but I'm still searching for matches for Brinda's drawings, and I'm still contacting psychics around the country. I'll find them for you, like I promised I would. I'll bring them to you, here, in Lilybrook."

"No. No!" How could they not understand? "They won't trust anyone but me. I have to go to them. It *has* to be me. I *have* to be able to leave town."

The tightness in Deirdre's face turned from worry to anger. "Dennis spent eight years looking for you," she said. "Tristan moved away his senior year and delayed college for you. They *risked their lives* to bring you to safety. That you would even *consider* ignoring my dream—"

Dennis took her hand. "You can't be with your brother and sister if you're dead, Tessa."

From atop the fridge, Marmalade mewed.

I stared at the Connellys, and they stared back at me. Deirdre: hurt and resentful. Dennis: decisive and stern. Tristan: distressed and determined.

Tristan and Dennis were almost killed because of me. I owed it to them to stay alive.

And despite the shame that crawled around inside me like a disease, despite my tainted blood, despite being Killers' Spawn… I didn't want to die. I wanted to live to see my brother and sister again. I wanted to give them happy, stable, peaceful lives.

I couldn't give Jillian and Logan happy, stable, peaceful lives if I bled to death inside a little house with silver walls. I needed to live.

For the past eight years, I'd fled from town to town to stay alive. And now, to stay alive, I needed to stay put. I could not change my past, but I could change my future.

"Fine," I mumbled. "I'll stay in Lilybrook."

As I stood at the mirror in the guest bedroom and brushed my hair for school, Tristan came up behind me. He put his hands on my hips and drew me back against him. "I have to leave for class, but I want to let you know that you don't have to worry about a thing," he said. "Nothing's changed except you can't leave Lilybrook. You'll still get Jillian and Logan back."

"What do you think it means, though?" I asked. "A silver room?"

"My mom's dreams can be symbolic. She dreamed that you had wildflower eyes, remember? You *do* have wildflower eyes, but not literally. The silver room can be anything. I think the silver is your fog. Maybe it means that instead of lifting it too high, you bring it down too low and pass out again, like you did in the Underground."

"Hmm. That could be. But the red? The blood?" I asked.

"I don't know. You'll hit your head on something when you pass out? You'll get hit by a car?" He shuddered.

"What if it means someone's going to kill me?"

"Don't even talk that way. Who would want to kill you?"

I met his gaze in the mirror. "Nathan."

A muscle pulsed angrily in his jaw. "I told him to leave you alone. Has he threatened you?"

"No. He hasn't even spoken to me. But he still hates me. He's in my nightmares. His eyes become part of the Nightmare Eyes."

Tristan considered it, then shook his head. "I don't know what's going on with Nathan, but he wouldn't hurt you. He's a safeguard, Tessa. He protects people. I'll call him on my way to class this morning and talk to him again. Besides, my mom's dream will only happen if you *leave* Lilybrook. And you're not going to do that. You are going to stay here, where it's safe. I will bring Jillian and Logan to you."

Before I could protest, he added, "I'll find a way to show them that they can trust me. I promise, Tessa."

I studied Tristan's face in the mirror. He looked tired, but his jaw was set. He failed to keep me safe in Twelve Lakes, and he was determined to make up for that in Lilybrook.

His phone dinged and he swiped the screen. "It's another psychic responding to my email," he said. "He owns a metaphysical shop in New Mexico. He even has a crystal ball, just like in Brinda's drawing. He said he'll keep an eye out for Jillian and Logan and call me right away if they show up."

He wrapped his arms around me. "See, Clockwise? I'm getting lots of responses like this. Everything will be fine."

I turned so I faced him and brought him in close, inhaling his scent of soap and strength and masculinity. The tighter he held me, the more my lungs opened up. Even the Nightmare Eyes dimmed a bit. I needed to stay here, in Lilybrook, in Tristan's arms.

I couldn't leave Lilybrook to look for my siblings, so Lilybrook would have to be my headquarters. Command Central. The mission: Find Jillian and Logan. Tristan and Aaron were my soldiers. From my post as Commander-in-Chief, I would oversee their investigations and help in every way I could.

# CHAPTER EIGHTEEN

ISS BENNETT, THE enthusiastic geometry teacher, jabbered away while scribbling angles and formulas on the whiteboard. The dry-erase markers squeaked, their acerbic scent permeating the room and making me slightly nauseated. The colorful triangles, squares, and circles reminded me of Brinda's crayon drawings. Chin propped in hand, I pretended to be copying the shapes and formulas into my notebook, but actually, I was writing a message.

*Jillian, this is Tessa. I'm alive. I'm safe.*

The Connellys believed that I was contentedly going about my life while imprisoned in Lilybrook because Deirdre dreamed of a little silver-walled house that filled up with my blood, and had left the responsibility of finding my siblings to Tristan and Aaron. But I wasn't contentedly going about my life. For the past three days, I'd been trying to contact my sister. Psionically.

I knew I couldn't contact her telepathically—I could only do that with Tristan, and only when we were close. But when my family lived in Twelve Lakes, Jillian had been trying to develop remote vision, the same psionic ability our father had. Or at least, the psionic ability our dad used to have, before the APR neutralized him. Jillian made some progress before her terrible headaches and bloody noses had driven her to quit—headaches and bloody noses that were manufactured by our mother so Jillian wouldn't discover our parents' murderous secrets.

Maybe now that our imprisoned, neutralized mother could no longer give her those headaches, Jillian could develop her remote vision again.

Jillian thought I was dead, so she wouldn't purposely send out her mobile eye to find me. But maybe if she thought of me, she would see me in Lilybrook. Alive. Safe.

Chances were slim. Almost zero. But I had to try.

As Miss Bennett scrawled formulas on the whiteboard, I continued my letter to Jillian.

*I'm in Lilybrook, Wisconsin. Come to Lilybrook. It's safe here. You don't have to run anymore. I have so much to tell you and Logan....*

I'd filled almost a page, willing Jillian to see it through my eyes, when the sound of my name brought me back to the classroom. I looked up from the notebook to see Miss Bennett, marker in hand, looking at me expectantly.

"Oh. Um… could you repeat the question, please?" I stammered.

"What is the formula for the surface area of a pyramid?" she repeated, not patiently.

I turned to my notebook to find the page with that formula, and saw that I hadn't written a long letter to Jillian after all. After a few lines I'd stopped writing words, and instead had drawn a pair of circles, filled in solid black.

My Nightmare Eyes.

"You should know that formula by now, Tessa," Miss Bennett said.

"I…" I sputtered, staring at the Nightmare Eyes on my paper. "I don't. I'm sorry."

Miss Bennett shook her head. "Can anyone help her out?"

In the seat in front of mine, Winter shot her hand up and quite cheerfully provided the formula.

"Very good, Winter." With a disappointed look at me, Miss Bennett continued her lesson.

Cheeks burning, I gave my head a little shake to break the hold the Nightmare Eyes had on me. I flipped to a blank page and obediently copied the information from the whiteboard onto my paper. But once Miss Bennett turned her attention to someone else, I started a new letter to Jillian. This time, I kept it short and simple:

*Jillian, it's me, Tessa. I'm alive. I'm safe.*
*Come to Lilybrook, Wisconsin. It's safe here.*

I stared at it, hard, until my eyes dried out and the words turned blurry. Then I blinked, and stared at the words again.

Was Jillian seeing this? What if the fog was blocking her ability to see through me? I'd been writing notes to her for three days; maybe the fog was the reason she wasn't seeing them.

I should lift the fog a little…. A little more…

I stared at the note again.

*Jillian, it's me, Tessa. I'm alive. I'm safe.*
*Come to Lilybrook, Wisconsin. It's safe here.*

Something shifted in my peripheral vision—Winter, turning to smirk at me over her shoulder. She was listening to me, telepathically. Her amused snarl burned into me, along with the Nightmare Eyes, reminding me that I was Killers' Spawn.

Ignoring both Winter and the Nightmare Eyes, I lifted the fog higher, and focused on my note.

I couldn't tell if Jillian was seeing through me or not. The only thing I could sense was the multitude of students who'd sat in this chair before me. Trenton Abrams, last period. He thought Miss Bennett was hot. Amber Fakhoury, two years ago, wishing Tristan Connelly would dump Melanie Brunswick and ask her out instead. Kiarra Davis, ten years ago, doodling hearts and stars in her notebook.

The bell rang, and fog still raised, vaguely aware of Miss Bennett telling me to pay more attention next time, I shoved everything into my book bag and walked out of the classroom. If Jillian had connected to me via mobile eye, she would be seeing everything I was seeing and hearing everything I was hearing right now.

"Jillian," I murmured, holding a textbook in front of my mouth so no one would think I was talking to myself, "can you hear me? It's me, Tessa. I'm alive. I'm trying to find you."

The halls were so *crowded*. Was everyone heading to an assembly or something? If Jillian was watching through me right now, she'd see that I was in a high school, not locked away in a gray cell somewhere. As I pushed through the students, I saw a blue flyer taped to the wall:

LILYBROOK HIGH PEP RALLY TODAY!
GO LIGHTNING!

I let my gaze linger on it. "See that, Jillian? I'm in Lilybrook, Wisconsin," I murmured behind my textbook. "Come to Lilybrook. It's safe here."

It was becoming hard to concentrate. Everyone was on their way to that pep rally, all walking and talking. So *loud*. The mass grew bigger and denser by the second, everyone chattering. Brian Edes plodded along. Susie Berkowitz and Tamara Yonkers rushed past him. Girls in acid-washed jeans, boys in brown leather jackets. Junie Lyons. Ben Guntherson.

The bell rang but the hall wasn't emptying. Girls in poodle skirts and saddle shoes passed by, intermingling with scruffy boys in fringed vests.

Poodle skirts.

That wasn't right.

The students in the hall weren't really there. They *used* to be there, but they weren't now. Now they were visions.

The pep rally flyer wasn't there either.

The fog. I'd lifted it too high.

Dizzy, woozy, I stumbled to the row of shiny lockers, leaning against them for support. Big mistake—the lockers forced more visions into me.

Rochelle Mellon in bell-bottoms and sporting big, feathered hair.

Darren Szostak wearing a royal blue T-shirt that boasted LILYBROOK HIGH CLASS OF '88.

Tristan Connelly, in a hockey sweater, walking down the hall with a worshipful Melanie Brunswick to his left and a short-haired, laughing Nathan Gallagher to his right, just two years ago.

The visions of Tristan and Melanie continued walking, but Nathan's stopped. Stayed. Stared.

"N-Nathan?" Was he real?

No—just a vision. He disappeared, swallowed up by other visions, more and more visions, crowding the hallways, shoving and clamoring.

I tottered away from the lockers. But the visions were still there, multiplying, growing denser and louder.

I had to bring in the fog. I had to bring it in *now*, before I lost control and the visions became solid, and I started spiraling into nothingness.

I pulled it in, but it wasn't enough.

I pulled it in lower. Thicker. Lower and thicker again.

More, I needed more fog. One big yank, and the visions disappeared. But I could see nothing *but* fog. I breathed in fog. My muscles turned into fog.

So much fog. Too much fog. I'd gone too far. Everything was fog, no sight, no air, no strength, why didn't Tristan call, he didn't call to warn me—

Then everything disappeared.

Blackness. Absolute and all-encompassing.

But even in the blackness, there was something. Something gleeful and threatening.

My Nightmare Eyes, darker than even the black fog surrounding me. Watching me. Dark as a starless night and black as a cavern of coal.

I could not move. The eyes kept me paralyzed. Their rage burned through me. They wanted to keep me in the black fog forever.

Something twinkled. Something silver.

*~killers' spawn~*

I heard the words, booming through my subconscious, low and rumbling, as if they were spoken aloud, or perhaps whispered in my ear. I struggled to escape from the hateful words, from the eyes' hateful glare.

A knife. Long and sharp and silver. Its blade glittered and glimmered, sparkled and glowed.

I had to get away. I had to get away from the ominous eyes, from the glimmering silver.

I had nowhere else to go except deeper into the fog. With a desperate heave, I pulled the fog in closer, darker, thicker. It came, quick and solid, and it consumed the glimmering, glittering silver, it consumed the Nightmare Eyes, and it consumed me.

I found out, after I woke up in the APR's clinic with Tristan holding my hand and begging me to come back to him, that a security guard had found me. Unconscious, alone, and crumpled on the floor of the school's hallway. The school nurse had called Dennis, who'd rushed me to the APR.

I also found out that Tristan never called because he hadn't gotten a warning premonition about it. He didn't get a warning premonition of the visions overwhelming me. He didn't get a premonition of the fog overpowering me.

I also found out that it was the next day. While the Nightmare Eyes had me pinned under their hateful gaze, the sun had set, and risen again.

Dr. Sheldon, the kind, warm physician who had taken care of me in the Underground, placed one hand behind my neck and her other on my forehead as I sat on the curtained-off cot in the clinic. "Don't move," she said. Closing her eyes, she bowed her head.

She'd kept me here overnight while I was lost in the fog. Deirdre and Dennis had stayed until about midnight, and Tristan had stayed the entire night with me, holding my hand. Now he hovered close as Dr. Sheldon determined if I was ready to go back to the Connellys' house.

"So much fog," she muttered as she looked into my mind. "But there's something else… something dark. A starless night. A cavern of coal." She shuddered, then opened her eyes. "Any idea what that means?"

"That's just my nightmare," I said.

Tristan took my hand back. "She gets them every night." His hair was messy and his button-down shirt was wrinkled from sleeping in it overnight, curled up in a chair next to my cot.

"I can certainly understand why you have nightmares," Dr. Sheldon said, "but that darkness is terrifying. It felt… hateful."

Terrifying. Hateful. Shameful. It all burned through my blood. "It's just a nightmare," I muttered.

Dr. Sheldon made a note on her chart. "Well, you're back in control of that fog of yours, and nightmares are no reason to keep you here."

"So she can go home?" Tristan asked.

"Yes, she can." Dr. Sheldon slipped her pen into her white doctor's coat. Before she left, she put a warm hand on my shoulder. "Be careful with the fog, sweetheart. I understand why you want to practice using it, but we don't want that to happen again. The second you feel it slipping out of control, you need to stop."

"I will." Relieved I could get out of here, I slipped from the cot. Tristan held out a hand for me to hold in case I was shaky, but I wasn't. I changed from the blue cotton hospital gown and into the clothes Tristan brought for me—my usual jeans and one of his hoodies.

"I don't understand why I didn't get a premonition about you fainting," Tristan said as we left the facility. A thin layer of snow had fallen while I was unconscious, and it crunched under our feet as we walked to Tristan's car. Though I didn't need him to, he held my elbow so I wouldn't stumble. "I could have called you. I could have warned you and stopped it from happening."

"It's not your fault, Tristan," I said. "*I* raised the fog. *I* lost control of the visions. *I* pulled the fog in too low."

"Why, though? Why were you playing with the fog in the middle of class?"

"I wasn't playing with it." I confessed my plan, that I'd been trying to contact Jillian psionically in the hopes that she was trying to develop remote vision again. "I thought maybe the fog was blocking her ability to see through me. So I raised it. Then I lost control." I sighed. "But I know now that was a stupid idea. Jillian could only piggyback on our dad's mobile eye. She was never able to move beyond that. Besides, I can't spend twenty-four hours a day staring at a sign that says Lilybrook, Wisconsin."

Tristan had stopped, and now he was staring at me, incredulous. "How could you put yourself in danger that way? My mom's dream—"

"Your mom's dream will only happen if I leave town to look for my brother and sister. There was nothing in that dream that said I can't look for them from within Lilybrook."

"That's not—" He scrubbed his hand in his hair. "You raised the fog that high, then pulled it in that low, on *purpose*. That's exactly why my mom's dream will happen if you leave Lilybrook."

"I was trying to connect with my sister, who is missing, and scared, and heartbroken. You can't be mad at me for that. And you didn't have a premonition about me fainting, so you couldn't have stopped it from happening anyway."

He exhaled, his whole body deflating. "You're right. I promised you that I would keep you safe. I failed you in Twelve Lakes, I'm failing you by not finding Jillian and Logan, and I failed you again yesterday."

It was usually me who shivered, but this time it was Tristan.

I took his hand and gave it a kiss. "You're not failing me. I don't blame you for any of that."

"Well, you should. I blame myself."

We reached his car, and he opened the door for me and helped me inside.

We drove back to his house in silence.

# CHAPTER NINETEEN

ENNIS AND DEIRDRE wanted to keep me home from school the next day, but I convinced them to let me go after I'd promised not to play with the fog anymore. I had to triple-promise Tristan. "Please be careful with the fog," he said. "Please. What if I don't get a premonition again? Even if I do, I'll be too far away to stop it from happening." He raked his hands through his hair. So worried. So anxious.

I took both his hands in mine. "Tristan. I know you want to keep me safe, but you also need to trust me. I *will* be careful." I stood on my tiptoes and kissed his lips. "Please don't worry about me."

Not at all comforted by my promise or by my kiss, he cupped my face in his hands and brushed his lips on my forehead, then reluctantly left for school.

Twenty minutes later, bundled up in coats and mittens, Ember and I shuffled through a layer of snow on our way to Lilybrook High. Determined to prove to Tristan that he didn't need to protect me as much as he thought he did, I concentrated on keeping the fog balanced. But as always, Jillian and Logan were in the forefront of my mind.

A blackbird descended from the trees, and while Ember stopped to feed it, I gave Aaron Jacobs a call. "Any progress?" I asked, keeping my tone chipper and optimistic. One negative word from me would discourage him.

"Their 1-last known location was in Braddock, Tennessee," he mumbled, tripping over his words. "S-so I started there, and I'm moving outward in all directions."

"That's a good plan, Aaron," I said. "Tristan said you were super-smart, and wow, you are."

"But I haven't found anything."

"You just have to keep looking," I said. "Don't let Kellan intimidate you. You can do it."

He was quiet for a moment, then said, "D-does your sister… I mean, I know I'm not… but do you think she'd like…"

"She likes guys like you, Aaron," I said. Jillian had had lots of boyfriends—silly, pretty, empty-headed boyfriends. But the only boy she ever loved was Gavin, and she loved him because he was sensitive, sweet, and super-smart. Just like Aaron.

He said nothing for another long moment. Then: "I'll find them."

"I know you will. Bye, Aaron."

Ember finished feeding the bird, and we continued to school. She'd been quiet around me lately, and I thought I knew why. I'd been so preoccupied with finding my siblings that I'd neglected our friendship. And Ember was the only friend I had.

"How's your song coming along?" I asked. "I'd love to hear it."

"My song?"

"You said your band had to write an original song for Battle of the Bands."

"Oh." She looked off into the trees. "I don't know if we're doing Battle of the Bands anymore. The keyboardist and the drummer quit. I can't find anyone to replace them."

"Did they quit because of me?" I asked as my blood started to burn. "Because I live in your house?"

"No," she said, but she wouldn't meet my eyes.

The warning bell rang as Ember and I climbed the front steps to the school. She rushed inside, but I stalled before entering the building. I filled my lungs with the cold February air and balanced the fog. The last time I was here, I'd lost control of the visions, then the fog, and passed out. I had to be extra careful to keep the fog balanced from now on. I had to show Tristan that he didn't need to protect me so much. I took another deep breath, nudging the fog a little higher, then a little lower.

"Are you okay?" a sweet voice said beside me: Melanie, her black hair tumbling from under her black beret.

"Yeah," I said, a bit surprised that she'd asked. "Thanks."

"I heard you fainted in the hall the other day," she said with genuine concern in her voice. "I just wanted to make sure it wasn't happening again."

"I'm fine," I said, now really surprised. "Thanks, Melanie."

Melanie Brunswick truly was kind. And sweet. I could understand why Tristan had loved her.

She would make a good friend. I gave her a smile, a real smile.

She started to smile back, but then she cleared her throat and looked down at her Doc Martens. "I feel bad for everything you're going through, Tessa. I really do," she said. "But... my dad... and Tristan..." Her gaze flitted to my hand—to my promise ring. "I've lost so much. I'm sorry, but I can never be friends with you."

She rushed into the building without looking back.

In art class that morning, Mr. Vargas returned everyone's fruit bowl paintings we'd made last week. Except for mine. All I got was a slip of paper that read, *See me after school.*

I shoved the note into my pocket. What had I done wrong? I liked my painting, how I'd divided the canvas into six squares and painted just a part of each fruit. But maybe he wanted us to paint the fruit as he'd presented it. Realistic, not abstract.

After last period I went to the art studio. Mr. Vargas was bent over the counter, cleaning paintbrushes in the sink and wearing a ratty cardigan splattered, as all of his clothes were, with dried paint. "No one realizes how expensive these brushes are," he mumbled to me. "You have to take care of your brushes."

That was why he called me in after school? I was always concentrating so hard on keeping the fog balanced that it was entirely possible that I'd neglected to clean my brushes. "I'm sorry, Mr. Vargas," I said. "I forgot. I won't do it again."

"Oh, it wasn't you, Tessa." He wiped his hands on his sweater to dry them, then went to his desk. He picked up my abstract fruit painting and tucked it under his arm. "Come with me," he said, and sauntered from the room.

I followed him to the cafeteria. He stopped at the back wall and held his arms out wide, facing it, my canvas still in one hand. I had to step out of the way so he wouldn't hit me with it.

"Tell me what you see," he said.

Was I supposed to see something? If I didn't have the fog balanced, I'd see dozens of visions, but Mr. Vargas wasn't asking about visions. He was neutral. "Um, a wall?" I said.

"I know you can do better than that. Try again. What do you see?"

"Um…" Oh! "A giant canvas?"

"Yes!" he said. "Excellent. Now what do you see on this giant canvas?"

I stared up at the wall for a minute. We were in the cafeteria, so that meant food. He couldn't mean… "My painting? My bowl of fruit?"

"Yes. Your bowl of fruit." He held my painting in both hands, arms straight out. "I want you to recreate this same piece, on a much larger scale, big enough to fill this entire wall."

"But everyone will see it," I said.

"Everyone *should* see it."

He couldn't be serious. "It's just fruit."

With one eye closed, he tilted his head, then tilted the canvas the opposite way. "I've been teaching for twenty-seven years, and every year, I present that same bowl of fruit and tell my students to paint it. Do you know what I get? I get paintings of the same bowl of fruit, from every student, every year. Some are truly awful, most are decent, and a few are excellent. Yours is one of the excellent. You took it in a new direction."

"I thought you were going to fail me for not following instructions," I said. This was incredible. I had to raise the fog a little to make sure I was hearing him correctly.

"I didn't give any instructions to follow," Mr. Vargas said. "You've only been here a few weeks, and you're unpracticed. Undeveloped. However, you have a raw talent, Tessa. You are a very gifted artist."

Gifted.

Jillian was a gifted dancer. Logan was a gifted musician. All the talent in the family had gone to them, I'd always assumed.

I'd painted before, sure. As a hobby. I was decent. Maybe good. Never excellent. Never *gifted*. But I was psionic now, when I'd never been psionic before. Maybe my retrocognition wasn't the only thing the fog had suppressed all those years.

I could envision my painting, super-sized, on the wall. The curve of the yellow-green pear, stretching from the floor halfway up the wall. The shiny crimson apple. The plump purple blueberry. Greedily, I eyed the white cinder blocks. The strawberry would go right *there,* in the upper corner. The wall's bumpy texture would be perfect for the orange.

I was stuck in Lilybrook because of Deirdre's dream. But when Tristan brought my brother and sister to me, I would bring them to this school and lead them to the cafeteria. Then I would stand them in front of the mural, spread my arms, and announce *I painted this.* They would be so proud.

Breathless, I appraised the blank white wall, a wall that wouldn't be blank or white much longer. "When can I start?"

# CHAPTER TWENTY

STARTED ON my mural the very next day.

With a pencil in my left hand, I lightly sketched the arc for the meaty part of the pear. To steady myself, I pressed against the wall with my right hand and a few visions appeared through the fog. A girl wearing her hair in two braids with a headband made from daisies. A boy with hair short in the front and long in the back.

I stepped away from the wall and adjusted the fog, bringing it closer until the visions disappeared. It left me a bit dazed, but still aware. The perfect state for painting. I put my pencil to the wall and completed the curve of the pear, then sketched until it was time to go home.

Although Tristan continued to contact psychics and search for matches of Brinda's drawings, and Aaron worked nonstop on his webcam search, there had been no new leads in their investigations over the next week. So every day after school, I would meet Mr. Vargas in the art room and gather my supplies. He'd help me carry everything down to the cafeteria, bring me a ladder if I was painting up high, then leave me to my work. I'd have to spend a few minutes getting the fog adjusted to just the right level, then I'd dip the brush into the paint, and get started.

The students in the clubs that met in the cafeteria left me alone, but I could feel them watching. On occasion I felt Nathan Gallagher's eyes on me as well, watching my every move, as if he peeked into the cafeteria to see what I was doing. A few times I'd turn around, but he would disappear before I saw him. Once I felt John Kellan watching me, but that was impossible. I was keeping the fog thick and close to keep the visions away; I must have been lost in memories of the night he had forcibly taken me from Twelve Lakes.

The Nightmare Eyes were always there. They always watched.

When it was time to go home, Mr. Vargas would come to help me clean up, but I would never notice him. He would have to clear his throat or tap me on the shoulder to bring me out of my daze. My muscles would be sore from crouching and bending and reaching and climbing the ladder. My left hand would be stiff from holding the brushes. And though I never remembered crying, my cheeks would always be damp with tears.

# CHAPTER TWENTY-ONE

ONE SUNNY MORNING a couple weeks later, as I was hanging up my coat in my locker at school, Tristan texted me. *Just got an email from another psychic. She had a vision of J & L with an animal that looked like a horse. It had one eye.*

I had a drawing of that one-eyed horse in my book bag this very moment. Heart leaping to my throat, I texted back: *Brinda's drawing!*

*Yep. Told you my method would work. Now we just have to find that horse.*

Finding a one-eyed horse would be difficult, and of course, that vision could be symbolic, like Deirdre's dream. But this was the first development we'd had since Tennessee. We were getting closer. We'd find Jillian and Logan any day now. I was sure of it.

The second I sat down in chemistry, the intercom buzzed. "Sorry for the interruption," the secretary said in a bored voice. "Please send Tessa Carson to the office."

I jumped up, and without even checking with the teacher, bolted from the classroom. This had to be about Jillian and Logan. Finally. Finally! Was it Tristan waiting for me in the office, or Aaron? Tristan had gotten that lead about the one eyed-horse, but it had to be Aaron waiting for me—Tristan would have come straight to the classroom to get me.

In the front office, I skidded to a stop. Aaron wasn't there, and neither was Tristan. But Cole Gallagher was there, wearing a regulation black jacket from the APR, his tawny eyes dour, his lips in a straight line. "Dennis needs you at the Lab, Tessa."

"Why? What happened?" I asked. "You look like it's bad."

Cole slid a glance to the secretary, who was watching with sharp green eyes, clearly curious about why the new girl was needed at the top secret science lab down the road. "You know I can't discuss that here."

"Did Aaron find my brother and sister?" I asked.

"Tessa. Please." He took my arm. "Dennis says it's urgent."

Insides prickling with anxiety, I left with Cole. In his Jeep, I asked him again. "Just tell me if they're okay." I slid my hands into my sleeves.

"I feel how anxious and scared you are," he said, "but I don't know anything about your brother and sister. I'm sure they're okay. They probably went deeper into hiding after what happened at that motel in Tennessee."

It took less than five minutes to get to the APR. I shivered as we hustled down the pebbled path into the building—cold because I'd left without grabbing my coat, and also, yes, because I was scared about why I'd been pulled out of school and brought to the Lab. Cole put a timid arm around me, to offer warmth or comfort or both.

Dennis waited for me in the lobby, somber and pensive. "Dennis, what's going on?" I asked. "Did Aaron find Jillian and Logan? Did something happen to them?"

Dennis thanked Cole for fetching me, then guided me through security. But instead of heading down the main hallway, he turned to the right, into the elevator that led to the Underground.

That's when it hit me: "You're taking me to see my parents, aren't you?"

He pressed the Down button, and the doors closed. "I am."

"But I told you I'm not ready." I covered my belly with my hands. I would never be ready. They were liars. Thieves. Murderers. They made me Killers' Spawn.

"You don't have to see your mother," Dennis said as the elevator brought us down. "But your father needs you. As you know, he's been unconscious the whole time he's been here. But lately he's been stirring and mumbling. More and more every day."

"He's finally waking up. That's good." I didn't want anything to do with my father, but I was relieved he was waking up.

"He's still incoherent. He keeps reliving the night Kellan abducted you," Dennis said. "Today, he became frantic. They can't calm him down. I was here to check on Aaron, but when I heard what was happening with your father, I suggested that you come see him. He's not aware of his surroundings, but maybe he'll sense that you're safe, and calm down on his own. Are you willing to see him?"

"Of course. Yes." My father must be in agony, reliving what was probably the worst night of his life. I didn't want him to suffer like that.

A gum-chomping, muscle-bound man met Dennis and me at the elevator—Mr. Milbourne, the head warden. Winter's father. Nathan and the rest of the Lab Brats would know all about my Underground visit by the end of the day. I could just picture the gleeful, vengeful gleam in Nathan's eyes. He would probably be happy my father was in such a tormented state.

Mr. Milbourne grunted a greeting and led us through the prison. Dim and dank, smelling of mildew and hopelessness. He led us past the cell where I'd stayed for three weeks, the cell Kellan had thrown me in after he kidnapped me. The cell I'd refused to leave until I could free my innocent parents.

The cell where Tristan had proven that he truly loved me.

An armed guard unlocked the gate of the high security wing, the hall silent except for our footsteps. As a condition of their incarceration, all inmates had been neutralized. But as I passed each cell, I couldn't help but wonder who was inside, what their powers had been, and what crimes they had committed. I was grateful they were all locked behind windowless, steel doors.

We rounded a corner, and an echoed howl came from behind the door at the far end.

My father's cell.

As Mr. Milbourne swiped his badge through the security pad, I held my breath, gaining the courage to see my father for the first time since I'd left the Underground.

If he'd been lying peacefully in his hospital-type bed, it may not have been so bad. It was his hysteria that set me trembling, that made my legs refuse to move and a small whimper escape my throat.

My father was even thinner than when I'd last seen him. Pale. Cheeks sunken, hair gray. Unshaven and bedraggled. His eyes, however, were open, and alive with panic. They darted, wild, back and forth. He howled, struggling with ferocious effort against the padded cuffs connected to the bed rails.

"We don't know where he's finding the strength," Dennis said. "They had to restrain him so he wouldn't hurt himself."

Mr. Milbourne stood in the doorway, stiff-legged, massive arms crossed over his massive chest. Coming up behind him was the woman

I'd seen talking to Kellan outside of the boardroom a few weeks ago.

"Tessa, this is Beverly Jacobs, the agency's executive director," Dennis said over my dad's howls. "She's Aaron's mother."

Her gold badge shone brightly, and her face was smooth and hard as ice as she acknowledged me with a quick nod, then turned to Dennis before I could greet her. "I hope this works, Dennis," she said.

"Me too," he replied grimly, and nudged me further inside my father's cell.

Various pieces of medical equipment lined the perimeter of the antiseptic-smelling cell, some of them attached to my father by tubes. The screen to his heart monitor shone brilliantly, casting an eerie white glow over the tiny room, and beeped frenetically, though the sound was barely audible over Dad's frantic wails.

"Mr. Carson," Dennis announced. "Look who came to see you. Your daughter, Tessa."

My father whipped his head in our direction. "Oh thank God thank God thank God, you have to *do* something!" he crowed. "You have to help her! Help her! Help her!"

I whimpered, bringing my hand to my mouth in shock. He was talking about Kellan, the night he kidnapped me and held me as bait, to force my parents to surrender.

"He's going to kill her. He's going to make her pay for what we did. Make her pay. Make her pay. Make her pay!" He threw his head back and wailed.

I rushed to his side. "Dad, that man, he didn't kill me. See? I'm right here. I'm safe."

"Tessa Tessa Tessa!" he croaked.

"That's right. It's me, Tessa."

His eyes, feverish and wild, opened wide. He sat up as much as the restraints would allow, the tendons in his neck straining with the effort.

"He's going to kill her!"

He didn't know it was me. His terror was almost tangible. It came off him, forcing its way through the fog, rolling like waves, one after another. "He took my baby girl, my Tessa Blessa. He's going to kill her."

"Daddy, no." I put my hand on his arm, hoping my touch would comfort him. "That night happened a long time ago. It's over. I'm safe now."

But he continued to writhe. "He took her and he's going to kill her," he howled, bucking against the restraints. "Someone has to save her. Please save her. Please save my Tessa Blessa!"

"It's not working," I cried to Dennis over my dad's howls.

"No. It's not," Dennis sighed. "I thought you'd be able to get through to him, but he's looking right at you, and he doesn't recognize you."

"Wait," I said. "I know what to do." Slowly, I pulled up Tristan's hoodie and revealed the five jagged scars on my stomach: the only thing my dad ever truly saw when he looked at me. "Dad. Look."

His gaze shifted down, coming to a rest on the scars. "T—Tessa?"

"Yes." I exhaled with relief. He knew me now. I let the hoodie drop back down.

"Tessa," he whimpered. "He's going to kill you, Tessa, Tessa, Tessa."

I took his hand and gave it a light squeeze. "No, he's not. John Kellan just needed you to think he was going to kill me so you'd surrender. But it's over. I survived. I'm safe."

Dad stared at me—at my stomach—and began crying.

"Oh, Daddy. Please don't. Please don't cry." I didn't know which was worse—seeing my father in the throes of abject terror, or seeing him so weak and broken. "I can stay for a while. Would you like that?"

He nodded with a whimper. Then a cry. Then he howled, wailed, screamed, his eyes growing wide again with terror. "He's going to kill her!"

"Dad, no, it's me," I cried. "I'm safe. Look at me. Look!"

As I let go of his hand to lift my hoodie again, he grabbed my wrist. "Someone has to help her! Save her! Save her! Save my Tessa!" His body stiffened, back arching off the bed, and he squeezed my wrist with unyielding strength.

It hurt. It *hurt* but I couldn't pull away. "Dad," I cried. "Let go. You're hurting me." His grip became tighter still. He was going to crush my bones if he didn't let go.

Dennis tried to uncurl his fingers, but he couldn't budge them. Mr. Milbourne stepped over and tried to help, but the two men together could not loosen my father's fingers.

Dad howled, and the heart-wrenching terror in his eyes cut off and changed into something different. It took me a moment to identify it. I saw it every day in other people's eyes, in John Kellan's and Nathan Gallagher's and Winter Milbourne's. But I never expected to see it in my own father's eyes.

Rage. Fury. Hatred.

And they were black. Dark as a starless night and black as a cavern of coal.

My father blamed me for putting him here. Blamed me for destroying our family. Blamed me for betraying our family by telling Tristan our secrets. My blood burned through my veins.

A smile slithered across his lips, and slowly, purposely, he squeezed my wrist tighter. And tighter. And tighter.

I heard the snap before I felt the pain. I clamped my mouth shut against a scream—never ever *ever* scream—and it came out as a strangled shriek.

Still, he kept his grip on me, squeezing my wrist tighter, tighter, impossibly tight, grinding the bones together. He was crushing them to dust.

The fog rushed in, numbing me, making me dizzy, making everything far away.

"Shoot him," Mrs. Jacobs said from behind me.

"No," I tried to shout it, but it came out as a moan. "Please don't shoot my dad."

"It's just a tranquilizer," Dennis said. "It's the only way we can weaken him."

Mr. Milbourne pulled a gun from his holster. Pressed the barrel to my father's neck.

"Don't," I whimpered, my head light and swimming. "Please. He may never wake up from it."

I didn't hear the whistle as the tranquilizer shot from the gun into my father. But I did hear his violent gurgle as his body slowly sank back onto the bed. "Tessa Tessa Tessa," he whimpered as the sedative took him away. "He's going to kill her. He's going to make her pay for what we did. Someone save her. Save her. Save my Tessa. Save my Tesssss… ahhhhh…."

Silence. Screaming silence.

My father's grip on my wrist loosened, and Dennis gently, so gently, uncurled his fingers. "How the hell was he able to do this?" he spat at the warden. "How did he get so strong?"

Mr. Milbourne shook his head. "I've never seen anything like it."

"Adrenaline," Mrs. Jacobs said. She hadn't moved from the doorway the entire time. She'd just watched. "Adrenaline, fueled by hysteria."

I flinched when Dennis touched my wrist. Groaning, I cradled it against me. I couldn't move my hand.

More painful than my wrist, though, was the rage in my father's eyes. It still coursed through me, burning through my bloodstream, my tainted, tarnished blood.

"Let's go to the clinic," Dennis said. "We need a healer to look at your wrist."

"It's broken," I said, my voice sounding far away.

"I don't see how that's possible, honey. He was strong, but he couldn't have been *that* strong. It's just a bad bruise."

I didn't have the strength to correct him. I'd heard the snap. I felt the pain.

Keeping my swollen and twisted wrist tucked into my body, I looked at my father one more time before leaving. He seemed peaceful now, sleeping so deeply like that.

"He didn't mean to hurt you, Tessa," Dennis said as we made our way through the Underground's hallway. "He didn't know what he was doing."

Dennis was right. He had to be. Despite the focused glee in my father's eyes, he couldn't have known what he was doing. He couldn't hate me. He couldn't.

Besides, my father's eyes were hazel. Not black. Hazel.

I must have imagined the whole thing.

# CHAPTER TWENTY-TWO

"Oh, yeah. It's definitely broken," Amy Van Der Sande said as I sat on a low table in the APR's clinic. Amy was the healer who masqueraded as Tristan's aunt while they were on assignment in Twelve Lakes. I liked her, but her cute pixie haircut and the bright polka dots on her scrubs didn't do a thing to make this drab clinic any cheerier. The fog was so thick I was shocked that Dennis and Amy couldn't see it.

"It's bad, Dennis." She hissed, as if it hurt to just look at my wrist. She'd had to cut the sleeve off of Tristan's hoodie; I was in too much pain to pull my arm through. "If this was a hospital for neutrals, she'd have to have surgery."

Dennis held his phone to his ear. "Yes, Tristan, Amy says it's broken." I could hear Tristan shouting through the phone.

"Is he coming?" I asked.

"Of course he is," Dennis said, ending the call. "He's already on his way."

"He didn't have a warning premonition," I said. "He's going to blame himself."

"I know," he sighed.

"So what happened, Tessa?" Amy asked. "Did you crush your wrist in something?"

"Just fix it, Amy," Dennis said. "Please."

*Thank you*, I mouthed to him. He knew I wouldn't want anyone else to know that my own father did this to me. If Amy was truly curious, she could probably read it in the inevitable report. My family's file was probably the thickest in the APR's history.

"I can't heal a bad break like this one completely, but I can get it started," Amy said. "Hold still." She held her open palm a half inch over my wrist, heat emanating from her hand.

We'd been in a similar position a few months ago, in Twelve Lakes. I'd had no idea she was healing my broken collarbone.

The swelling in my wrist lessened a bit, and then the pain. "This may take a few minutes," Amy said. "It's a really bad break. It's like your bones were crushed, and then… ground against each other."

My skin became very hot. "It's burning," I gasped, resisting the urge to move.

"That's good. You're healing." She slowly waved her palm over the break.

"I don't remember it burning when you fixed my collarbone," I said through gritted teeth.

"That was just a tiny fracture. It didn't require much effort. I basically looked at it and it healed."

"Hey, can you heal scars?" I asked. Maybe she could heal the scars on my stomach. My permanent reminder of my parents' crimes may not be so permanent after all.

"I can only heal injuries," Amy said. "Scars are the *result* of injuries."

"Oh." The disfiguring marks on my stomach were there to stay. "How's Heath?" I asked to distract myself from the pain. Heath was Amy's husband, and he served as Tristan's safeguard while they were in

Twelve Lakes. The quiet, shy man had punched Kellan in the jaw in retaliation for hitting me during the kidnapping, and for that, I would love him forever.

"He's good," Amy said. "Kellan won't let him safeguard any more investigators, but he doesn't care. He's safeguarding one of the board members now."

"Tell him I say hi. And thanks."

"I will, sweetheart," she said. "There. I've done as much as I can do." She lifted her hand away, and my skin cooled immediately.

My wrist still hurt, but it was no longer twisted or swollen. Still, I was surprised when Amy started wrapping it in strips of plaster. "A cast? I thought you healed it." I moved my wrist up and down, but a jolt of pain shot up my arm. I bit my lips to keep from screaming.

"And that," she said, "is why you need a cast. I'm a healer, not a miracle worker. You'll heal much faster than if you were treated at a neutral hospital, but the bones are still weak, and you could break them again if you're not protected. Go home and rest. No more school today."

Before Dennis and I left, Amy gave me a pill for the pain. Being pulled out of school this morning by an APR employee, then returning with a cast tomorrow, would definitely be fodder for both Lab Brat and neutral gossip. It was my left wrist, too. I wouldn't be able to paint my mural, and Tristan would have to help me do my homework.

And what would Jillian and Logan think, if Tristan or Aaron found them in the next few days? What would I tell them—that our father had broken my wrist?

Well, our mother had given me the five scars down my stomach. I could tell them that news at the same time, right after I told them that our parents had killed dozens of people.

Outside, Tristan was rushing up the pebbled path, carrying an enormous teddy bear, just as Dennis and I were walking down it. I gave him a weary wave with my casted arm. The pill Amy had given me was taking effect, eliminating the pain but making me woozy. All I wanted to do was crawl into bed, use Tristan's chest as a pillow, and sleep. Dreamlessly.

He greeted me with an anxious kiss. "Tessa, I am so sorry."

"It's not your fault, Tristan." My eyelids were so heavy. "My father broke my wrist, not you."

"It is my fault," he said fiercely. "I didn't have a premonition. Again. I don't understand what's wrong with me." He took me under his arm. "I'll take her home, Dad."

I waved a wobbly goodbye to Dennis, then leaned on Tristan as he walked me to his car.

He placed me in the passenger seat and buckled me in. I held the teddy bear on my lap and laid my head on it. So soft. My left arm was tucked safely between myself and the bear. I couldn't stay awake any longer. "My dad had Nightmare Eyes," I slurred to Tristan.

If he replied, either telepathically or aloud, I was asleep before his words reached me.

# CHAPTER TWENTY-THREE

EEMING ME HEALTHY except for my broken wrist, Dennis and Deirdre let me go to school the next day. Ember told everyone that I'd gotten it caught in the elevator doors, but of course the Lab Brats already knew the truth: that my own father, one of the Kitteridge Killers, had broken it.

Unable to paint my mural, after school I went back to the Connellys' house. Ember had gone to volunteer at the animal shelter, Deirdre had a meeting with the parents of one of her preschool students, and Tristan was still in class at Heron University. I called Aaron to ask if he needed anything, but he said no. He didn't have any new leads, either.

So I cleaned. As best I could with one hand, anyway. I moved all of the items that were cluttering the bathroom counter back to the cabinet, I cleaned the mirrors, I sprayed and wiped the kitchen counters. I went to the living room to dust the knickknacks and picture frames. Dennis was there, glasses low on his nose as he read through a pile of green binders on his desk: evidence binders from the Investigation unit of the APR. My parents' names were printed on one of them: *Andrew Carson - Gwendolyn Carson - Case #CARS5020*. That binder was the thickest in the stack. "What are you doing with that?" I asked.

"Oh, you know me," he said. "I've never been able to fully settle into retirement, so sometimes I consult on the open cases. Jillian and Logan's case is at a standstill, and I thought I'd take a look at your family's file. Would you like to see it? The others are confidential, but you can look at yours."

"No thank you," I said as Marmalade tapped me with her paw. I picked her up awkwardly with my one good arm. "I've already seen my file." Tristan and I had pored through every word in that file, multiple times, back in our Underground cell. I did not want to see the photos of my parents' victims again. I already saw them every night in my dreams.

Dennis returned to the file he'd been studying. "So how is our Tessa adjusting to life as a Connelly?"

I was a Carson, not a Connelly. I could only shrug in response.

He chuckled. "You still don't think of this house as home yet, do you?"

"Not really," I said honestly.

"I know how you feel," he said. "I was shuffled between my mother and various foster homes for years. Even after I was permanently placed somewhere, it took me a long time to think of it as home."

At that, a vision appeared in the fog. A young woman, just a teenager. Scrawny and dirty, hair stringy and eyes sunken from drug use. Pamela Connelly. A small boy with dark hair and wise, sad, blue eyes. Dennis. Even at that age, he wore wire-rimmed glasses.

"My mother loved me, but she was relieved when the state finally terminated her parental rights," he said. "She didn't admit it out loud, but I knew." He tapped his head—he was able to read her mind. "I was ten years old, resentful and rebellious. She was twenty-five, overwhelmed, a high school dropout and addicted to crack. We had a very tumultuous relationship."

Oh, poor Dennis. "I am so sorry."

"The first thing I did once I was hired by the APR was try to find her," he said.

"Did you?"

"Yes. She died two years after losing custody of me. She was under the influence and got in a fatal car accident."

"How awful," I said.

He looked at me over his glasses. "She used to tell me she could hear animals think."

"Like Ember?"

"Ember inherited her ability to communicate with animals from her. But my mother never knew she had a psionic gift. She thought she was insane. That's why she turned to drugs. They impeded her ability to hear them think."

My heart ached for Dennis. And for his mother. What a sad, lonely life she'd had.

My mother had a sad, lonely childhood too.

"What about your father?" I asked.

"My mother never knew who my father was, but with the help of the APR, I was able to identify him, eventually. He was her dealer. A neutral. He never knew about me. He died in prison, a few years after my mother died." He turned back to the binder.

"Ember looks like your mom," I said. "If Ember left her hair blond."

Dennis perked up, his blue eyes suddenly bright. "You think so?"

"Kind of, yeah. Ember looks healthier than she did. Happier, too."

"It's nice that you know what my mother looks like," Dennis said. "I don't have any pictures of her. No one else in the family has ever seen her."

*In the family.* Dennis said it so casually, like he truly considered me to be part of his family.

"Did you love her? Your mom?" I asked. "Even though she was a bad mother?"

"I loved her very much," he said. "I was also angry at her for a long time. But now I just feel sorry for her. If she'd grown up in Lilybrook, her life would have been completely different. That's why, when the APR found Deirdre and me, I chose to be on the recruiting team. I wanted to bring psionic families to Lilybrook, so no child would grow up feeling lonely or scared because of their abilities."

How different my mother's life would have been if she'd grown up in Lilybrook. She could have used her psychokinesis to help people, not to kill people. Instead, she'd grown up in a rickety old trailer with an overburdened mother and an abusive stepfather. When she finally came to Lilybrook as an adult, it was only to spend the rest of her life in a gray Underground cell.

My mother had brought tragedy to so many people, but her life was tragic as well.

Sleepy-eyed, Tristan leaned on the bathroom door frame as I tried to brush my teeth with my right hand. "Why are you up so early on a Saturday?" he asked through a yawn. "Another nightmare?"

Of course I'd had another nightmare. But that wasn't why I was awake. "I'm going to the APR to visit my mother."

He jolted upright. "What?"

"I'm going right after breakfast." Marmalade purred from the counter. I put down the toothbrush and scratched under her chin.

Tristan rubbed the heel of his hands in his eyes, like he was trying to wake up from a dream. "She almost killed you, Tessa. She tried to kill me. Twice. She tried to kill my dad. She's killed dozens of people. How can you want to see that woman?"

The venom in his tone hit me in the core. He hated my mother as much as Nathan did.

Understandable. I hated her too. I did. My hatred for her crawled around inside me like insects. But I needed to see her. Today. Right now. "She's my mother," I said. "What other reason do I need? Besides, maybe she has an idea where Jillian and Logan are. Maybe she can give us a lead."

He shook his head. "You can send her a note, then. Or have the warden ask her, or one of the investigators. You don't have to go see her yourself."

"Tristan, I can visit my mother if I want to," I said.

"She's going to hurt you."

"Are you getting a warning premonition?"

"I don't need a premonition," he said. "It's not a psionic thing. She's going to hurt you. I know it."

"She can't hurt me," I said. "She's been neutralized."

"Your father's neutralized, and he hurt you," he said. "From his hospital bed. While he was restrained."

"This is different." Why was he being so difficult? "My dad's not lucid. Mom is."

"I'm just trying to keep you safe," he said, lightly running his fingers over my cast. "It's my job to keep you safe."

A detonator went off inside me and I exploded. "Your *job*? I'm your girlfriend, not your assignment." I flung my casted arm away from him, and Marmalade bolted. "In case you haven't noticed, Tristan, even with your premonitions, you can't fix everything bad in my life."

He flinched like I'd punched him. "I need to do this, Tessa. Please. I need to keep you safe."

"And *I* need to see my mother," I said, and stormed past him out of the bathroom, almost bowling him over.

I marched downstairs, only to see Deirdre on the sofa, sorting through a storage container of Valentine's Day decorations. Half the room was already covered in red and pink hearts. She gestured for me to come sit with her, but I stayed where I was. "So," she said, "I hear you want to visit your mother."

"Are you going to tell me I can't go too?" I asked crossly. "It's a prison cell, not a silver room."

"I'm not going to stop you," she said. "I think it would be good for you to see your mom. But don't be angry at Tristan. He can't help wanting to protect you."

I snorted. "He didn't even have a warning premonition, but he thinks my mom is going to hurt me."

"It doesn't matter," she said. "Tristan has always taken care of the people he loves. Even if he wasn't precognitive, he'd be that way. But precogs like Tristan and me, when we see something bad in the future, we feel it's our responsibility to prevent it from happening. Tristan defines himself by his warning premonitions. When he fails to prevent something bad from happening to you, whether it's because you ignored his warning or he didn't have the premonition at all, he blames himself. He feels worthless."

Tristan wanted to be a hero. He *needed* to be a hero. His entire self-worth was tied up in being a hero.

If Tristan needed to be a hero, then he should go back to slaying dragons for Melanie Brunswick. Because *my* dragons were indestructible.

# CHAPTER TWENTY-FOUR

 OU'RE SURE?" TRISTAN had his arm around me as the elevator took us down to the Underground. "You're absolutely sure you want to do this?"

"You don't have to come with me if it bothers you this much," I said.

His only response was tightening his arm around me.

The elevator doors opened to reveal Mr. Milbourne waiting to escort us, arms crossed, chomping on gum. "Let's go," he said. "I don't have a lot of time today."

We followed him into the labyrinth of the prison. He didn't look back as I thanked him for allowing this unscheduled visit with my mother. As we neared the cell that served as my father's hospital room, I stopped. "Can I see my dad first?"

"No change in his status," he grunted. "Still unconscious."

"I still want to see him."

He slid a glance at my cast. "Fine, but for the record, you're doing this against my recommendation." He slid his badge through the keypad at the door.

*Mine too*, Tristan said silently.

I lingered in the doorway, leaning against Tristan. My father looked exactly as he had when I left him earlier this week. Sleeping, apparently at peace. Wrists in restraints. An IV needle piercing his arm. The only noise was the occasional beeping of his breathing and heart monitors, their screens reflecting the fluorescent light from above.

*Are you going in?* Tristan asked.

*Not yet.*

I watched my father from the doorway for a long, slow minute. He didn't move. Neither did I. I willed him to open his eyes.

"If you're not going in, then you need to leave," Mr. Milbourne said.

His words spurred me to my father's bedside. Tristan held my right hand. *You're too close*, he warned me silently. I stepped back, suddenly fearful my father would spring to life and attack me again.

"Dad," I whispered.

As if on cue, my father moaned. The monitors beeped faster.

"Dad," I said again, louder.

His head turned to the side, facing me. His eyes were still closed, but his breathing started coming in short, shallow gasps.

The beeping was faster now, almost frantic. A white-clad nurse rushed in and checked the monitors. "You should leave," she said to me. "You're disturbing him."

"Is he waking up?"

"No. Just go, please."

Gingerly, I stepped closer and reached out to him, but Tristan pulled me back. "Tristan, please. I need to see his eyes."

The monitors beeped faster, louder.

"Please leave," the nurse said again, insistently. Mr. Milbourne marched in, ready to take me out by force.

At that, Tristan stepped between us. "She wants to see his eyes. That's all. Then we'll leave."

The warden sighed and nodded to the nurse. "Do it."

The nurse, lips in a tight line, put her fingertips lightly on my father's eyelids and pulled them open. "Quickly," she said.

I held my breath and leaned forward. Despite his racing heart and shallow breathing, he stared vacantly back at me. Blank. Empty. Dull, lifeless. No panic, no fear, no grief or despair. No hatred or rage. No love, either. Just…nothing.

Before the nurse closed his lids, I double, then triple-checked.

Hazel. My father's eyes were definitely hazel. Vacant, but hazel. Not lucid and black.

It had just been my imagination.

Mr. Milbourne swept Tristan and me back out to the hall. As my father's door swung shut, the monitors beeped slower again.

Tristan insisted on accompanying me inside the visiting room to see my mother. I blocked his entrance, arms crossed awkwardly with my cast. "You'll just upset her." And me.

"But—"

"You need to keep me safe. I get it," I said. "But I will be safe. There's no way she can hurt me."

Mr. Milbourne flipped through some papers on a clipboard. "Doesn't matter anyway, Connelly. You're on her do-not-allow list."

"I can't go in there?" Tristan glowered. "What right does *she* have to keep a list like that?"

The warden chomped away on his gum. "I hear ya, but even inmates have rights. That list helps keep the peace around here. And I don't want to rile her up. She's a hard one to calm down."

"Don't talk about her that way," I said. They may be right, but I was feeling very defensive about my mother today. She had grown up alone and abused. She deserved a little compassion, even if I was the only one who was willing to give it. "Who else is on her list?"

"Everyone. The only visitors she'll consent to are Andrew Carson, Jillian Carson, Tessa Carson, and Logan Carson."

Of the four people on my mother's list of approved visitors, one was in a coma and two were missing. The only person left was me, and I had refused to see her until today.

I tried not to feel guilty about that, but I did.

"It's fine," I told Mr. Milbourne. "I'll go in alone."

"With a guard," Tristan said. "Two guards. And I want them armed with tranq guns."

"Tristan, that's a little extreme," I said.

"Do it, Milbourne," Tristan said. "Two armed guards. Her own father broke her wrist on your watch. You think the board will let you keep your job if she gets attacked again?"

The warden shrugged. "Not a problem. I'll go in there myself," he said, then called for *three* more guards.

*Ridiculous,* I flashed to Tristan. He stared straight ahead and did not move.

"Keep your eyes on the inmate at all times," Mr. Milbourne growled to the guards. "Stay alert. Do not hesitate to shoot if she does anything out of line."

Tristan had his own orders for me. "Do not touch her," he said. "I will be right here, outside this door. If you get a warning from me, *listen.* I mean it, Tessa. Do what I say, as soon as I say it."

Without acknowledging him, I stepped into the visitor's room with the guards. I glanced behind me to see Tristan pulling his hands through his hair, watching me until the door shut.

The four armed guards took their place, one in each corner of the small gray room. The air was thicker in here. I sat on a hard metal chair at the stainless steel table, placed squarely in the center of the room, and waited. No one spoke.

The door leading to the prison opened, and the guards stiffened. I mimicked them as a shot of nerves and fear ricocheted through me, then forced myself to relax. My mother, a crumpled form of gray, was brought in by another guard, who forced her to sit in the chair across the table, chained her to it, and joined the posse along the wall.

All these guards, all these precautions, for such a shattered, broken woman.

Shackled at wrist and ankles, as she had been on my last visit when I confronted her about her crimes. Hair short, as if it was cut without a mirror and with dull scissors. Pasty. Thin. Vulnerable and defeated, like she had been when she was a little girl. I made a point to study her eyes. They were anxious. Miserable. Grateful. Gray.

Her lips trembled, and two fat tears rolled down her cheeks. "Babydoll," she quivered. "I'm so glad you came. They told me you had finally come, but I can't believe anything they tell me. But you're here. You're here."

I could barely speak. "Hi, Mom."

I waited for her to ask why I hadn't come sooner, but she didn't. Perhaps she already knew.

"How are you?" I asked.

"I miss everyone. I miss my PK. They…they lie to me." She shrugged as much as she could in her restraints. "But I'm seeing a therapist. I've got a job in the kitchen, cooking for the other inmates. I like that. I do a lot of crossword puzzles."

"That's good." The therapist was probably the best thing for her, and I was glad they allowed her to cook and do her puzzles. "I'll bring you some crossword puzzle magazines. I can bring you some cookbooks too. Would that be okay?"

"Thank you, Babydoll. That's so nice of you," she said, eyes downcast. "How are you?"

I wanted to tell her, "The kids at school hate me."

I wanted to tell her, "I have bad dreams every night. My Nightmare Eyes follow me around and I can't get rid of them."

I wanted to tell her, "You made me Killers' Spawn."

I opened my mouth to tell her everything, about my shame and grief and burning blood, about how I couldn't find Jillian and Logan, about how I couldn't leave Lilybrook because of a dream about a little house with silver walls.

But she spoke first. "Have you grown?" she asked, lips trembling. "You look taller."

So. She wanted to stick to neutral topics. Maybe she wasn't ready to hear about the hard stuff. She looked too fragile to hear it, anyway.

"I'm still four foot ten, Mom," I said.

"Oh," she said, and tried again. "Your hair's gotten longer."

That observation was correct; my hair had grown an inch or two, because I hadn't thought about trimming it. I raised my arm to smooth it.

The movement pulled the sleeve of Tristan's hoodie back and exposed my cast. She gestured to it with her chin. "What happened?"

Quickly, I lowered my arm under the table. "A stupid accident. I'm fine."

"Have you seen Daddy?" she asked.

"A few minutes ago."

"Is he…still resting?"

That's what I'd told her last time. But she knew what *resting* really meant. "Yes."

She sighed heavily.

"I'm getting better at using my retrocognition," I blurted, to change the subject. "Sometimes, anyway. And I'm painting now, too. I'm painting a mural. It's in the cafeteria at school."

"Painting!" she exclaimed. "I remember you used to be a talented little artist. Do you have pictures of your mural?"

That would have been a good idea. "No, sorry."

"You'll bring them next time, then."

She was a killer, yes, but at this moment, I didn't see it. She was so frail and meek. She was resigned to her incarceration, to going to therapy, to healing. It was so easy to see her as she used to be, as my *mother*, and not as a crazed murderer. The mother who sat at the kitchen table, contentedly doing a crossword puzzle while batter mixed itself in a bowl and the vacuum cleaner moved itself around the living room. The mother who called me Babydoll.

Mom.

I would never forgive her for the things she'd done, but I didn't want to hate her anymore. I wanted her back in my life.

"And Jillian and Logan?" she asked. "Are they still mad at me? Or are they so busy with their music and dancing that they couldn't come with you today?"

She didn't know? "Mom, they're still missing."

Her smile faded. "What?"

"We can't find them. They're still running."

"Wh—wh—" she huffed as her eyes filled with tears. "But I thought you were all together. I assumed..."

"We'll find them," I said. "Soon. Any day now."

Mom put her chin to her chest and cried. She couldn't even wipe her own tears. I leaned over the table to wipe her cheek.

Mr. Milbourne, hand firmly on my shoulder, pressed me back into my chair. "Hands off."

"Wherever they are, they're together. They're safe," I assured her. "They were in Tennessee recently. We missed them by minutes. Do you have any idea where they could have gone? Any clue where we could look next?"

She sniffled. "The only place I can think of is Nebraska," she said, her lip quivering. "To see Jillian's boyfriend. But when they get there, they'll find out…" Her face contorted with grief.

"They were already there," I said. "They know Gavin's dead."

She broke out in fresh tears.

"Mom," I said, "how come you didn't know that they're still missing? Don't you ever ask about us?" I glanced at Mr. Milbourne, who shook his head.

My mother shook hers as well. "I did at first," she admitted, "but not anymore."

How could she not ask about us, her own children, every single day? "Why not?"

She leaned to me and whispered, "I told you. They lie to me, Tessa. I can't believe anything they say. They told me the most awful—" Her eyes slid to Mr. Milbourne and she sat back. "It doesn't matter. You're here now."

What horrible lies could he have told her? I looked at him with suspicion. He looked back with innocence.

"If you're not living with Jillian and Logan, then where are you living?" she asked.

"I'm living with Tristan and his family."

"You're what?" Her voice rose, just a little, but enough to make the guards tense and reach for their guns. My mother, cowed, sank into her chair. She turned her head to Mr. Milbourne. "It's all true?" she whimpered. "You weren't lying to me?"

"We have never lied to you, Mrs. Carson," he said solemnly.

She inhaled, steeling herself. "So it's true that Tristan is really Dennis Connelly's son?" she asked me.

"Yes."

"You're living with Dennis Connelly," she said. "In his house."

"Yes."

"Like you're part of his family."

"Mom, yes."

She flinched, and the guards tightened their grip on their guns.

I gripped the table, bracing myself for my mother's uncontrolled screams of fury, for the table to vibrate, for the guards to crumple to the floor. Braced myself to be flown across the room and into the cinder-block wall. Braced myself for my stomach to be sliced open again.

But the table did not vibrate. I remained in the chair. My mother wasn't capable of doing those things anymore.

"All those years," Mom whispered. "All the running and hiding. Leaving our home, leaving our lives behind. And now you're living with the man who started it all." Her eyes were closed, her body stiff, her hands in fists at her side.

I'd rather she scream and lose control. She was doing this so the guards wouldn't take her away, I knew that, but anything was better than this forced calm.

"Are you happy there?" she asked, forcing the words out in a little squeak. "Are you happy living with Dennis Connelly and his son Tristan?"

"Yes," I said, realizing it for the first time. "Dennis and Deirdre are doing everything they can to make me feel welcome. I'm friends with his sister. I even have a kitten. And Tristan is helping me find Jillian and Logan. He's doing great, Mom. He's working so hard."

My mother closed her eyes, deep lines forming around her lips as she pressed them tight. She drew a breath, held it, and let it out. "Get out."

"W-what?"

She rocked back and forth, her fists so tight that her knuckles were white. "I said get out."

"Mom, no. Please."

She finally opened her eyes. I half expected to see her eyes had turned Nightmare black. They were filled with anguish and anger and grief and pain, but they were still gray. She looked up at Mr. Milbourne. "Sir, please take this girl out of here. Put her on my do-not-allow list."

"Mom," I cried. "You can't mean that."

"Get out, Tessa!" she screamed, then whispered, "And don't ever come back."

She watched from her chair as Mr. Milbourne pulled me from the room.

I stumbled into Tristan's arms, but I barely realized where we were. Tristan was frantic, furious, asking why I was so upset. But I could hear nothing but my mother telling me to go away and never come back. My own mother never wanted to see me again.

My *mother*.

# CHAPTER TWENTY-FIVE

NSTEAD OF HEADING back home after visiting my mother, Tristan and I cut through the forest surrounding the APR to take a walk down Lilybrook's quaint Main Street. Next to a wrought-iron bench was a wooden sign: *Welcome to Lilybrook - A Friendly Place to Live*. The February day was warmer than average and the sun shone, but I was frozen all the way to my core as we strolled under the leafless trees and past the bus stop and pharmacy. "All these weeks, I couldn't bring myself to see my parents." I took his arm and put it around my shoulders, the way I felt safest. "And once I did, my father broke my wrist and my mother told me to go away and never come back."

"Your dad didn't know what he was doing," he replied, "and your mother didn't mean what she said." He kissed the top of my head.

"Yes, she did." My father may not have been in his right mind when he broke my wrist, but my mother had been aware of every word she said. She blamed me for everything. She would never forgive me for telling our secrets to Tristan, or for living with the Connellys. My father had crushed my wrist in a fit of crazed panic. My mother had crushed my heart in a fit of whispered anguish.

"I'll talk to Mr. Milbourne," Tristan said. "He won't put you on her do-not-allow list if I tell him not to. I'll talk to the board of directors if I have to."

"Don't," I said. "I'm not going to force her to see me if she doesn't want to."

I wasn't sure about visiting my father again, either. The nurse said I was "disturbing" him. What did that mean? Was my mere presence in his cell this afternoon enough to disturb his peaceful sleep?

The whole time I lived here in Lilybrook, I'd avoided seeing my parents, telling myself I wasn't ready. But now that I *couldn't* see them, it hurt. My mother rejected me, and it *hurt*.

We passed the police station and post office and dance studio, then came to Hawthorne's, the local diner popular for its blueberry pie. "You're cold," Tristan said. "Let's get some hot chocolate for the walk home."

Tristan was right this morning. I never should have gone to visit my mother. He warned me not to see her, he warned that she would hurt me. He knew it would happen, this morning at his house, and he didn't even need a premonition. He just knew.

At the counter, he ordered two hot chocolates to go, looking back over his shoulder to make sure I was okay.

Taking care of me. Being the hero. Being *my* hero.

His winter coat stretched across his broad shoulders as he handed me one of the hot chocolates.

Even his hands were big and strong.

Outside, we left Main Street and headed back through the forest. The heat from my hot chocolate seeped through the foam cup. Tristan's arm was around me. I was toasty now, warm to the core.

The snow-frosted trees reached to the sky, hiding the APR, hiding Lilybrook, and the world became just Tristan and me, a few chirping birds, a few snowbanks, and a wooden bridge over a frozen brook. My steps slowed as we crossed the bridge.

Tristan stopped too, looking past the bridge's railing. "In the summertime," he murmured, "this brook is covered with hundreds of pink water lilies. That's how the town got its name. Lilybrook."

His eyes seemed extra blue, out here in the sun.

His tousled brown hair sparkled with gold.

I licked my lips. "Tristan," I whispered.

He shifted his gaze to meet mine. Our breath came out in little clouds.

"Tristan, I need you."

One at a time, not taking my eyes from his, I placed our drinks on the bridge's railing, out of the way. Then I stepped closer, one step, two steps, until I was only an inch from him. I pressed into him, wishing I could disappear inside of him, where I would always be warm and safe and loved.

His chest moved up and down as he breathed. His heart beat through his jacket, and the stubble on his jaw glistened like gold in the sun. I inhaled his fresh, clean, masculine scent.

God, I loved him. I loved every ounce of him. All of him. Inside and out.

I was hungry now, ravenous. Ravenous for him. I stood on tiptoe and snaked my arms around his neck, my left arm heavy with the cast, and pulled him down so I could kiss his lips. He kissed me back, tenderly. But I did not return his gentle kisses, oh, no. I was too hungry for him to be tender. I ravished him with passionate and greedy kisses. He responded; his kisses became less comforting and more urgent and gluttonous. We stumbled off the bridge and sank down behind the trees, against a snowbank.

My hands roamed his body, unzipped his jacket, then slipped under his shirt. I needed to touch him. My cast, my stupid cast, prevented me from feeling him fully, making me clumsy and awkward, but he understood. With shallow breath, he shed his jacket and spread it on the ground, then rolled us over on top of it. I was finally able to run one hand over his chest, his stomach, his waist, and then his chest again.

He kissed me, then stopped and pulled back a little, just far enough to slide his hand behind my head and stroke my cheek with his thumb. "Beautiful," he whispered.

No, *he* was the one who was beautiful. He wanted to keep me safe. He wanted me to be happy. He wanted to be my hero.

I slid off my coat, then pulled my hoodie—*his* hoodie, I loved wearing his hoodies but now I needed it *off*, I needed to have as much of me touching as much of him as possible—over my head, and the air must have been cold but I was desert-hot as he kissed my stomach, ignoring my five twisted, ugly scars. He worked his way up, kissing every inch of me, my belly, my breasts, my collarbone, my neck, until he was back up at my lips.

Our kisses tamed as our heart rates slowed and our breathing returned to normal. Reluctantly, we slipped back into our tops and jackets. He lounged against the snowbank and I put my head against his chest. As I snuggled into him, I rested my casted arm on his stomach and watched it rise and sink as he breathed in and out.

*I need you, Tristan. I do.*

# CHAPTER TWENTY-SIX

*A*MY CUT OFF my cast a few days later. I'd only had to wear it for a short while, a much shorter time than a neutral without access to a psionic healer, but I was relieved, just the same. Every time I saw it, or felt its weight when I moved my arm, I was reminded how my own father had broken my wrist. I still felt the burn of the rage in his eyes. But now the cast was gone, and I could paint my mural again. And best of all, I could run both palms all over Tristan's chest, and cup his face in both my hands, and bring him to me for a kiss.

The very next day after school, I went to paint my mural. Mr. Vargas was almost as delighted by my return as I was. He helped set up my supplies in the cafeteria, then went back to the art room, leaving me to my work. The mural was about seventy percent finished; I had only the strawberry and the grapes left to do. The apple and the blueberry needed some touching up, I decided. More highlights and shadows. I would do those first, and then I could probably finish most of the strawberry before it was time to stop for the day.

I squeezed some paint on my palette, adjusted the fog to keep the visions away, then sank into the mural, the fresh smell of the paint, the strokes of the brush. A group of students passed through the cafeteria, their footsteps and chatter echoing through the fog. I lowered it to block them out.

A grunt shot through the fog like a bullet. *Spawn*, it sounded like. I glanced behind me only to see wisps of auburn hair and blond dreadlocks disappear around the corner. Winter and Nathan. Had they been standing there watching me, or had they just been walking by?

Didn't matter. They were gone now. I lowered the fog as far as I dared and resumed painting the shadow on the underside of the apple, and tried to ignore the way my blood burned through my veins, tried to ignore the Nightmare Eyes that glowered at me from above.

"Tessa, what are you doing?" Mr. Vargas asked a few minutes later, startling me.

"Painting my mural," I said. I glanced out the window. The sun was low in the sky. I'd been painting longer than I'd thought.

"Yes, but why are you painting *that*?" He pointed at the wall.

Two big black circles.

Oh, no.

"You know I love what you've done so far," Mr. Vargas said, brows knit, "and I would like to give you free rein, but I can't let you paint these eyes on this mural."

I climbed down the ladder. Took a few steps back. Looked up at the wall.

Black, bottomless. Angry and accusing. Unlike the rest of my mural, which was playful and whimsical, the eyes were so detailed they looked real. Lifelike. Pupils solid, sinister, eternal black, surrounded by sparkling silver irises. They stared at me, glowering with shame and grief and fury, dark as a starless night and black as a cavern of coal.

My Nightmare Eyes.

Their gaze locked onto mine. Held me prisoner. I couldn't turn away.

"You painted them over some of your completed work," Mr. Vargas said from far away. "I don't understand."

"I…" I stammered. "I don't…" My breath started coming in quick gasps. I tried to force my shaking hands up to my face, to cover my eyes, to sever the connection, to break the spell the giant black eyes had cast over me. But I was frozen.

He brought a finger to one of the black eyes and touched it, fascinated. "What compelled you to paint these?"

"Cover them," I said. "Please."

"Yes, I'm afraid we'll have to," he said with a sigh.

"I can't do it. I can't touch them." If I touched the Nightmare Eyes, I would lose myself. I knew it. The fog would disappear, it would be sucked up in a vacuum, and the visions would overpower me. I would never recover.

"Oh, don't be upset," Mr. Vargas said. "The eyes are…well, beautiful isn't the right word, although you did a beautiful job painting them. They're haunting. They make me feel …shame. Loss. Anger. Betrayal. Pain."

He shuddered. "Art *should* give people strong reactions. But I doubt anyone could eat with those hateful things staring at them. I'd love for you to paint them again, just not on a cafeteria wall."

"Cover them," I said again. I backed up, still unable to tear my gaze away. I stumbled over a chair and caught myself before I fell. That seemed to break the hold the eyes had over me, and I was able to look away.

Mr. Vargas frowned. "Are you okay?"

I turned and fled. I ran to the girls' bathroom and stood, shaking, over the sink. My hands were covered in black paint, and when I looked in the mirror, I saw that I had smeared some of that paint on my face. I looked ghoulish. Haunted. I ran water over a fistful of paper towels, and scrubbed, scrubbed, scrubbed.

The next afternoon after school, Mr. Vargas helped me carry my painting supplies into the cafeteria. The giant eyes were gone. In their place was a fresh coat of bright white paint. Mr. Vargas must have painted over the eyes after I left yesterday.

Half of my mural was gone, but that was okay. As long as the eyes were gone too.

Instead of going back to the art room as he had always done before, this time he sat at one of the tables, sketching with colored pencils.

I approached the spot on the wall where I had painted the eyes yesterday. I lifted the fog and tentatively touched the spot.

A slight jolt—*shame-guilt-despair-tarnished-blood-tainted-blood*—but it was a remnant of my own fog-laden thoughts from yesterday. It was stupid to let those painted eyes affect me so much.

Over the next few days I repainted the portion of the mural that I'd ruined by painting the eyes over it, then completed the strawberry and grapes. It took a lot longer than it used to; I had a harder time keeping the fog balanced because I was afraid to sink too deeply into it. I battled visions, and I was much slower now, but I was still able to paint.

A week later, Mr. Vargas told me to invite all of my friends to the cafeteria after school so they could watch as I put the finishing touches on the mural. He brought in a sheet cake, big enough to feed at least twenty people.

Four. That's how many people came. Tristan, Dennis, Deirdre, and Ember.

Four wasn't much, but it was enough.

Dennis and Deirdre wouldn't stop exclaiming over how wonderful the mural was, or how proud they were of me. I didn't try to stop their compliments. My mural was *good*. Bright and whimsical. The colors and shapes were perfectly balanced. My cheeks hurt from smiling.

"Stand in front of it," Deirdre said, pulling a camera from her purse. I posed and preened as she snapped a dozen pictures.

The only thing missing was my brother and sister. Their absence was like a hole in my heart.

Tristan picked me up and whirled me around, not caring that I was all paint-y and would ruin his clothes. "Now you need to sign it," he said.

I dipped a thin brush into silver paint and scrawled *Tessa,* very small, in the bottom right corner.

"You forgot your last name," Mr. Vargas said.

"No," I said, "I didn't forget."

I hadn't signed my last name on purpose. The Lab Brats wouldn't want the name *Carson* forever painted on the cafeteria wall.

# CHAPTER TWENTY-SEVEN

M R. VARGAS ASKED a week later if I wanted to paint another mural, this one in the field house. I told him not today; I loved painting, but there was something else I needed to do. Tristan and Aaron, though working ceaselessly to find Jillian and Logan, had made no headway in weeks. It was time to do something about it. So after school, instead of painting a mural, instead of going back to the Connellys' house, I went to visit Brinda Lakhani.

I brushed my hand on her sticker-covered door. She peeked out and I wiggled my fingers at her, then she flung open the door, gave me a hug, and even kissed my cheek. Her father waved me in. Smiling, in silence, the three of us drank our invisible tea.

When I thought Brinda was ready, I placed Jillian's ballet shoe and Logan's sheet music on the table. I had nothing else to show her. I just had to hope that she would see something new.

We continued drinking our tea. Brinda's gaze flitted to the shoe and paper occasionally, but never landed on them. Finally, her olive-brown eyes turned unfocused, and Mr. Lakhani held up her bucket of crayons. She reached inside, shuffled around, and pulled out a brown crayon.

On a plain sheet of paper, she drew a large triangle. Next, she took a gold crayon and drew a small circle in the middle of the triangle.

Then, she slid the paper to me, her eyes clear.

That was it. No more predictions. This one drawing would have to be enough.

To thank her, I gave her a rainbow sticker, which she promptly stuck to the window frame. After gathering everything—the drawing, Jillian's ballet shoe, and Logan's sheet music—into my bag, I waved goodbye to Brinda and her father and went back downstairs. A gold circle in a brown triangle wasn't much to go on, but at least Tristan and I had another drawing to find a match for.

On the way out, I passed the Lab. From the entrance, I could see the Technokinetics office.

Hmm. Maybe Aaron would like to see the drawing too.

Aaron jumped when I knocked on the door frame, but his fingers didn't slow as they flew between two keyboards, and his eyes didn't stop as they scanned six monitors stacked on his desk, all of them flashing random faces so quickly that my brain couldn't decipher them. How was he keeping up with it all? He had Jillian and Logan's photos taped to the side of one monitor, and they reflected in his overly large glasses.

"I have a new clue." I showed him Brinda's drawing, which he glanced at for a millisecond before returning to the monitors.

I leaned against his desk, studying the drawing. "The brown triangle could be a mountain. And the gold circle might be a ring. What do you think?"

No response.

"Try looking at places in the mountains," I said. "Maybe they'll drive by a jewelry store. Or a gold mine."

His fingers blurred over the keyboards, but still he said nothing.

"You're having no luck scanning traffic cams and surveillance videos," I said. "I know this drawing is a long shot, but at least it's a new direction."

He didn't respond, just continued to scan the monitors. For a length of a heartbeat, his gaze rested on Jillian's photo and his fingers slowed, then he resumed his usual breakneck pace.

"I'm sure Jillian will be grateful for your help," I said.

His face turned red. "Brown triangle. Gold circle. I'll look."

"You'll call me when you find them?"

But he had sunk into his search again, and his answer was only a grunt. So I left, not sure he'd remember that I had been there.

A few mornings later, a series of rapid, high-pitched beeps woke me from my dream of silver knives and Nightmare Eyes. I jolted awake, heart in my throat, instincts telling me to run: Dennis Connelly found us again.

*No.* I was safe. No more running. Dennis Connelly was a friend, and my parents were the villains. The Nightmare Eyes weren't real. Marmalade was curled up next to me, Mac was lying on the floor, and Tristan was across the hall.

I was safe.

My heart rate revved up again when I recognized the beeping as the ringtone I'd assigned to Aaron Jacobs. Bolting upright, I grabbed my phone from the nightstand and scrambled to answer it. "Aaron! Do you have a lead?"

Marmalade mewed next to me as my door pushed open, and Tristan rushed in, on alert.

"I found her," Aaron said. "Them. I found them."

Joy, elation, euphoria shot into every cell of my body, lighting me up, making me weightless, and I flew out of bed. "Where are they?"

"In Colorado. A mountain town called Ringgold."

"That's Brinda's drawing," I exclaimed. Oh beautiful, glorious Brinda.

*Ringgold, Colorado,* I flashed to Tristan, who whirled around and ran to his room to dress.

"You did it, Aaron. You did it." Holding the phone to my ear with my shoulder, I shed my pajama pants and pulled on a pair of jeans. "Thank you, thank you, thank you."

"I–I concentrated on places in the mountains, like you told me to," Aaron said. "Yesterday I thought I s-saw them on a security cam at a used car lot in Colorado. They bought a blue 2006 Camry. From there I followed them on traffic cams until they stopped for the night at a motel." With each word, his voice became bolder, more confident.

"Why didn't you call me yesterday?"

"I wasn't sure it was them. But now I have visual confirmation. It's them. Her hair is red now. L–light red."

"What's the name of the motel?" I said. We'd have to get out there right away. I was shaking, so excited that I almost dropped the phone.

"They left it already," he said, "But I picked up their trail again. I'm driving up a mountain, a few cars behind them."

"Wait." This time I did drop my phone, then scrambled to hold it to my ear again. "You're already in Colorado? You went there without me?"

"I flew out last night while they were at the motel. D–don't be mad. I just...I...I want..."

My legs folded like they were made of paper and I sank to the bed. "You want to bring Jillian back here yourself," I said. "You want to be her hero."

For a long time, the only sound coming through my phone was the hum of the engine of Aaron's car. Then: "Yeah."

I could understand that. Tristan would do the same thing to be *my* hero. "I'm not mad," I half-lied. "But Aaron, Jillian and Logan won't trust anyone but me, so I'm flying out there. Don't let them notice you until I get there. I'll tell Jillian, first thing, that you were the one who found her, okay? I'll tell her how smart and nice and amazing you are."

"O-okay," he said.

"Once we land, I'll call you and you'll tell us exactly where you are. We'll catch up to you, and then we'll bring them home."

"All right."

"Aaron," I said. "Don't let them out of your sight."

"I won't."

I disconnected, then darted to Tristan's room. He was sitting at his computer, looking at a map of Ringgold. "Can we get that charter plane again? That'll be fastest," I said.

He slowly swiveled in his chair to face me. "Tessa, you can't go. You can't leave Lilybrook."

"What do you mean? Aaron's already in Colorado. He's driving right behind them. We have to go get them."

"You can't leave Lilybrook," he said, scraping his hand through his hair. "My mother's dream, remember?"

"But Jillian and Logan have already been found," I said. "They're on a road on a mountain. There won't be a silver room."

"We don't know that." His expression was stone.

"Is this because Aaron found them and you didn't?"

The stone crumbled, just a little, then recomposed itself. "No. This is because I need to keep you safe."

Anger swept through my body, setting my nerves ablaze. I wanted to throw my phone at him, but it was the only way I had to get ahold of

Aaron. "I just want my brother and sister," I snapped. "I don't care who finds them."

"It's okay. I figured out what to do." He rose and walked over to me, slowly, the way a patient parent would approach a child throwing a tantrum. "I'll call Aaron back and tell him there's been a change of plans. Once Jillian and Logan stop somewhere, Aaron will set his phone to video chat and show it to them. Then you will video chat with them so they know you're alive and safe, and you can tell them it's okay to come back here with Aaron."

Usually my blood burned with shame, but this time it boiled with rage. "That's ridiculous, Tristan! I need to get out there. Right now."

"No. Not when I can't depend on my premonitions to keep you safe. It's too risky."

"I'm not risking anything," I said.

"You're risking your life." He opened his arms for me. "Just stay here. By the end of the day today, they will be here with you, and we won't have to worry about my mother's dream anymore."

I pushed his arms away, then stomped back to the guest room, slamming my door on him when he tried to follow me in.

I sat on my bed with Marmalade, phone in my hands, and waited for Aaron to call.

And waited.

And waited.

I left my room only to brush my teeth and do my hair, so when I did video chat with Jillian and Logan, they would believe me that I was safe and happy.

Well, that I was safe. I was *not* happy. Especially not with my overprotective boyfriend who had more faith in his mother's defunct dream than he had in me.

I waited some more.

Hours later, a phone rang, but it wasn't mine. It was only the Connellys' landline.

After a minute, someone knocked on my door. "Tessa? It's Dennis. That was John Kellan on the phone," he said. "Honey, something's happened. We have to get to the APR."

# CHAPTER TWENTY-EIGHT

*I*N THE APR'S boardroom, Kellan leaned on the glossy table and glowered at me as I shivered in a chair across from him. Tristan sat next to me, as close as he could get. Dennis paced the room, stroking his chin, looking more and more devastated as he listened in on Kellan's thoughts. Various investigators, guards, and Lab employees crowded into the room, rumbling with shock and distress.

The Nightmare Eyes had returned, burning into me from above, and on the table, a letter opener glittered and glimmered, sparkled and glowed.

"Please," I begged. "What happened? Are Jillian and Logan okay? Is Aaron okay?"

"Tessa, honey, there was an accident," Dennis said.

"That was no accident," Kellan snapped. He placed a laptop on the table and connected it to a projector aimed at a big screen on the wall. "The people driving in the car behind Aaron recorded the whole thing on their phone," he said. "The idiots posted it on YouTube."

As the video buffered, more employees squeezed into the room. Nathan, lip curled, pushed his way to the front of the crowd while

Kellan shouted instructions. "Bring me someone from the Techno department. I need them to wipe this video from the internet."

Everyone hushed as the video started. Shaky and blurry, it showed fluffy white clouds in the distance over gold mountains. The cameraman was a passenger in a car that drove on an ill-paved road, about halfway up a mountain. Ahead of them was a gray sedan.

"That's Aaron's rental car," Kellan said. "Up ahead of him, in the blue Camry," he said, pointing to a blue car further up the road, "are the targets. Jillian and Logan Carson."

The camera was focused on the scenery, but I was focused on the blue car as it jostled and bumped its way up the mountain road. The image was too small and too blurry to see the occupants inside. The camera lazily shifted to the side window, to record the mountain's steep cliffs. Then, offscreen, the driver exclaimed, "Hey. Hey! That car's going off the road!"

The view rotated back to the windshield, just in time to capture Aaron's gray sedan swerving off the road and crashing through the guardrail. It hovered in place, dozens of feet in the air.

"Do you see that?" the cameraman shouted. "It's floating! How's it doing that?"

A blurry Aaron, eyes bulging behind his overly large glasses, pounded at the window. "Look!" the cameraman shouted. "The guy's trying to get out!"

Then the sedan, with Aaron in it, simply…

Dropped.

"Oh my God! Oh my God!" The driver screeched to a stop. Still holding the camera, the passenger ran out to the side of the road. He recorded the sedan as it hit the mountainside, then tumbled, tumbled, tumbled, crumpling and breaking, glass spraying, one door flying off beyond the camera's range, before finally coming to a stop against a boulder.

Then it exploded in a ball of fire.

Yelling and cursing with dismay, the cameraman turned the view to the side of the road. "911! Call 911!"

The camera's view pivoted, landing on Jillian and Logan, who also stood on the side of the road, their blue car parked at an angle to the side. Jillian, her hair dyed a light red and cut to her shoulders, sobbed into her hands. Logan, his arm around Jillian, watched calmly. "We did the right thing," he said, his voice muffled but icy. "I've always said we should fight instead of run. This time we did. And we won. If he sends anyone else after us, we'll kill them too. We have no other choice."

He turned to the guy holding the camera and snatched it from him. "You hear that, Dennis Connelly?" His brown eyes wild and enraged, he snarled directly into the camera lens. "You didn't think we'd notice that guy tailing us? Keep sending your people after us, Connelly, and we'll keep killing them. Or how about next time you come after us yourself? I cannot wait to kill you." He shoved the camera back to its owner. "Go ahead and post that video online," he said. "Let him see it. Let *everyone* see it."

The cameraman continued to record Logan as he led a weeping Jillian to their car and placed her inside. Then, tires screeching, they sped off up the mountain, passing a metal sign that read *Caution: Dangerous Curves Ahead.*

The sign reflected the sun, and it flashed silver. Brilliant, blinding silver.

The video ended, and in the silence the fog whooshed in, but only I could see it.

Well, the Nightmare Eyes did too.

Trembling, Tristan took me under his arm. "Aaron's dead?" he asked, his voice trembling too.

"He's alive," Kellan said, and the crowd slumped with relief. "But barely. He was thrown out of the car, but was hit by debris from the explosion. He was airlifted to the nearest hospital. Broken bones, lacerations, cerebral contusions, burns over forty percent of his body."

Broken bones. Lacerations. Burns. My brother and sister had done that to Aaron. They used their psychokinesis to push his car over the cliff. They tried to kill him.

All Aaron wanted was to be Jillian's hero.

The fog thickened, darkened, making me dizzy and woozy. I put my head to my knees. "Tristan, I'm going to—"

He was already placing a wastebasket under me, and I vomited into it.

Tristan and Dennis moved in, flanking me on either side, as I sniffled and wiped my mouth. The crowd, Nathan included, had watched as I heaved and retched into the wastebasket. Their expressions were not compassionate. My siblings tried to kill the son of the APR's executive director.

Dennis rubbed his chin. "What's your next step, Kellan? I think you should call off the investigation for a few weeks. Let the kids calm down."

"A few weeks?" I cried. "No. Please."

"Oh, no," Kellan said. "We did it your way for eight years, Dennis. Your kinder, gentler way of doing things got us nowhere while the Kitteridge Killers roamed the country, murdering everyone. Now their kids are doing the same thing."

He nodded to a small group of investigators with red badges hanging around their necks. "You, you, and you," he said, pointing to two women and a man. "Drop everything else you're doing. You're on my team now, and this case is our top priority. I'm tired of those Carsons killing people, especially *our* people. I'm not going to risk another murder."

Kellan turned to Dennis, a silent message flying between them.

Dennis turned white. "No," he said. "You can't. Kellan, they're just kids."

"Those *kids* are becoming more and more unstable. Just like their mother," Kellan said. "First they assaulted that motel manager in Tennessee, and now they used their psionic powers with the intent to kill. My order is completely justified, and Beverly Jacobs will support it."

"What order is that?" Tristan asked.

Kellan's gaze swept to me, landing for just a moment, before he turned to the investigators. "When you find those Carson kids," he said, "shoot to kill."

# CHAPTER TWENTY-NINE

*I* BLINKED, UNABLE to believe what I'd just heard. John Kellan had just ordered my siblings to be killed. Not found and brought back safely to me, not captured, not tranquilized. Killed. He wanted them dead.

Kellan shrugged into his black APR jacket and shoved a hat on his head. "I need to go tell Beverly Jacobs what the Carson kids did to her son," he muttered. The APR employees parted as he left the boardroom.

"Wait! Please! You can't kill them," I cried, jumping up from the chair and pushing through the crowd, Tristan close behind.

Someone grabbed my arm, preventing me from running after Kellan. "Let me go!" I turned to see that the person holding me back was Nathan Gallagher.

"Get your hands off her, Gallagher," Tristan growled, then stood back with a gasp. "It's you, isn't it? You're blocking my premonitions. That's why they haven't been working right. I thought it was my fault. I thought there was something wrong with me. But it's not me. It's you."

Nathan froze for one second, then his lip curled. "She's Killers' Spawn, Connelly. How can you be in love with that?"

Tristan roared, then flew at Nathan. Dreadlocks sailing, Nathan leapt upon him with both hands.

Dennis shouted, and Nathan's brother Cole rushed in. As they tried to pull the boys apart, I slipped from the room and caught up with Kellan in the hall.

"They thought Aaron was trying to kill them," I cried, grabbing the sleeve of his jacket. "It was self-defense. They don't know the truth. Kellan. M-Mr. Kellan. Please."

He pulled his jacket from my hand, then strode away without a word. I rushed after him again, but this time it was Dennis who held me back. "Let him go, Tessa."

"But he's going to kill my brother and sister."

"The board will never allow it," he said. "The APR doesn't kill people, Tessa. Unless…"

"Unless what?"

"Unless our lives are in jeopardy. Then we're allowed to use deadly force. It's been our policy since—"

"Since my parents killed Nathan and Melanie's dads." I sank against the wall. "And tried to kill you."

Dennis sighed. "Yes."

My siblings had vowed, on camera, that they would kill every person who came after them. And they had the motivation and the means to do it.

The APR employees filtered from the boardroom, rumbling amongst each other. Cole dragged Nathan out by the arm. They wore the same enraged expression. Nathan's anger was aimed at me, but Cole's was aimed at Nathan. "You're a safeguard," he yelled. "You're supposed to protect people, not hurt them." He shoved Nathan into a private office.

Tristan came staggering out, his lip bloody and swollen. I regained my legs and ran over, then gently touched his lip. "Are you okay?"

He grabbed me and drew me in. "I'm so sorry I didn't believe you. You told me he hated you, and I defended him. I thought I knew him." He glared at the office where Cole had brought Nathan, a muscle pulsing in his jaw.

I stopped him before he could burst into that office and attack Nathan again. "Tristan, we have to leave," I said. "We have to go to Colorado. Now. We have to find Jillian and Logan before Kellan does."

Sucking in air, he put me under one arm and wiped the blood from his lip with his other. "I'm sorry, Tessa," he said, taking another gulp of air. "But you can't leave Lilybrook."

"You—" I stopped, frozen, mouth agape. "Even now? But Nathan won't block your premonitions about me anymore. He wouldn't dare. They'll work now. You have to let me leave."

"My premonitions have nothing to do with it," he said. "My mom's dream is still a threat."

"But I'm the only one Jillian and Logan will trust. I'm the only one they won't hurt." I looked back at the crowd for support. They looked back at me, Killers' Spawn, and they were unmoved.

Dennis included. "We can't risk *three* dead Carson kids." He put a hand on my shoulder. "I'll go with Kellan to talk to Beverly Jacobs. I'll try to convince her to call off the shoot-to-kill order. Aaron is her son, but she's a rational person. At this point, that's about all we can do. Except hope that Jillian and Logan stay hidden long enough for us to figure something else out."

He glanced at Tristan. "Stay away from Nathan," he said. "Let Cole and the board deal with him."

With a sympathetic squeeze of my shoulder, he rushed away to catch up with Kellan.

Unbidden but welcomed, the fog rolled in to numb me as Tristan and I walked outside to his car. He kept me tight under his arm. He stood tall, chest thrust out, full of confidence now that he could depend on his warning premonitions again.

He drove us back to the Connellys' house. It would have been so easy for him to turn left onto Main Street, then left onto the highway, then west to Colorado. My yellow getaway bag was still in the trunk of his car.

But no. He turned right onto Main Street, then right onto his street, then parked on his driveway and led me inside. "We just have to wait, and hope," he said. "You stay in Lilybrook where it's safe. My dad and I will deal with Kellan. I'll fix everything. I promise."

I nodded, but I was tired of waiting. And hope, I'd learned, was useless. Hope wouldn't save my brother and sister. Promises wouldn't save them either.

Only action would save them. And Tristan, in his desperate attempt to keep me safe from Deirdre's dream of tiny houses with silver-walled rooms, refused to let me take action.

I wasn't going to hope. I couldn't just sit back and let Tristan *fix* things for me anymore. I didn't care about staying safe. I didn't care about Deirdre's dream. The only thing I cared about was Jillian and Logan.

With Marmalade on my lap, I watched as Tristan opened his laptop and do some more research. I nodded at his reassurances that he would fix this for me, that all I had to do was stay here in Lilybrook where it was safe.

But none of it sank in.

My getaway bag was in the trunk of Tristan's car.

That one was useless.

But I had another getaway bag, a denim bag I'd used for eight years while my family was on the run. Jillian and Logan had it now. They'd taken it with them when our parents sent them away that last night in Twelve Lakes.

I knew how to find my brother and sister. But there was only one person who could help me, and I had ruined her life.

Tristan didn't go to Heron University the next day. He was going to the APR, to try to convince Kellan to withdraw his shoot-to-kill order.

I, on the other hand, told Tristan I *wanted* to go to school.

"I can't leave Lilybrook anyway," I said. "And there's nothing I can do about Kellan. If I try to convince him to change his mind, it'll just make him more determined not to." I wrapped my arms around his chest. "I may as well go to school. I know you'll fix this for me."

Placated, he lifted my chin and kissed me tenderly. "I will," he said. "I promise."

I even let Deirdre drive me to school.

Instead of heading to my first period art class, I waited for Melanie Brunswick at her locker. She paused in her steps when she saw me, then continued forward. Her hair was down and she wore her usual Doc Martens with black tights and a black skirt.

We stared at each other awkwardly. We both had reasons not to trust the other. My parents murdered her dad. Tristan broke up with her to be with me. Her best friend was Winter Milbourne, who hated me. And her uncle had just issued a shoot-to-kill order on my brother and sister.

But she was the only person who could help me save their lives.

"Melanie," I said, thrusting out my chin, "I need your help."

"Me?" she said, opening her violet eyes wide. "Do you want me to talk to my uncle? He'd never listen to me."

"No. Don't talk to your uncle," I said, then leaned in closer. "You find lost things, right? That's your psionic ability?"

"Shh." She looked over her shoulder at the other students in the hall, then softly said, "Yes."

"How do you do it?"

She stepped closer to me. "I just need to know what you're missing," she said. "Then I see the item in my head. It works best with items you have an emotional connection to. Like jewelry. So if you lost your earring, I could tell you if it fell off at a restaurant or if it's in a drawer somewhere. If you only lost a tube of lipstick, I probably couldn't find it."

Perfect. I had a huge emotional connection to my missing item—a connection that meant life or death.

"I lost a bag," I said. It was my getaway bag, but I didn't call it that because I didn't want her to know I was looking for Jillian and Logan. Her uncle would read her mind, or Winter, and they would thwart my plan. "Can you find it for me?"

"What does it look like?" she asked.

"It's a denim bag with a shoulder strap," I said. The hallway was becoming crowded as more students stopped at their lockers or made their way to their first period class. "Light blue. Scuffed and worn. It has a zipper across the top."

"Is there anything inside?"

"Not much. A pair of jeans, a sweater, jogging clothes, a hairbrush, a toothbrush," I said. "And a book. *Anne of Green Gables.*" Tristan had given it to me in Twelve Lakes. He'd even signed an inscription inside the front cover. But Melanie didn't need to know that.

"A denim bag with a shoulder strap. Clothes and a book inside," she repeated. "Okay. I'll look." She closed her eyes.

I stood still. Bit my lips to stay quiet. Let her concentrate. A few feet away, a boy slammed his locker shut, and I shushed him.

Melanie tilted her head, furrowed her brow. "There is no bag."

"Yes, there is," I said. "I saw it a few weeks ago." I saw it in a vision in the motel room in Tennessee. Jillian was going through it, crying and reminiscing.

She only shrugged. "It must not exist anymore. Otherwise I would see it."

"Why wouldn't it exist anymore?" I asked. "How can something just cease to exist?"

Then I realized my siblings must have burned it. While my family was on the run, we'd always burned our things. Maybe Jillian and Logan had gotten tired of lugging my getaway bag around and burned it. I almost crumpled with disappointment.

"The book still exists though," Melanie said. "I can sense the book."

I almost leapt with joy. "*Anne of Green Gables?* Where is it?"

"It's inside a bag. Not *your* bag. A different bag."

"Where is *that* bag?" I asked.

"I don't know. It's dark inside the bag. But it's moving fast. And there's a humming."

"Like the trunk of a car?"

Her face scrunched up. "No, it's definitely not in a trunk. Too small and square. And it's up too high to be in a trunk."

"A small, moving, humming square that's up high," I said. "What does that mean?"

She opened her eyes and shrugged. "That's what I saw. I don't know what it is. Sorry."

"I guess it doesn't matter what it's inside of," I said with a sigh. "What I need to know is *where* it is. A town. I'll even take a state."

"It doesn't work like that," she said. "All I can do is see its surroundings. I wouldn't know what town it's in." She looked down at her boots. "I'm sorry. I guess I'm not very good."

Frustrated, I rubbed my fingertips into my eyes. "No, you're amazing, Melanie. You've already been a big help." Whatever that small, humming square was, it was moving. Which meant that Jillian and Logan were on the move too. "Will you keep looking? Once the book gets taken out of that square, you can describe its surroundings to me and I'll take it from there."

Hesitantly, she gave me one nod.

"Thanks, Melanie. Call me the moment you see it."

The warning bell rang for first period and she looked nervously down the hall. "I don't want to get in trouble."

"You won't. But call *me*," I said. "Not Tristan." I ripped a piece of paper from my notebook and scribbled my phone number on it.

She tucked my phone number in a textbook and rushed away, probably thinking I didn't want her to call Tristan so she could win him back. But that wasn't it at all. I didn't want her to call Tristan because if he knew what I was planning to do, he would try to stop me.

# CHAPTER THIRTY

N ART CLASS the next morning, Mr. Vargas assigned us to do a self-portrait using oil pastels. I accidentally drew the Nightmare Eyes instead. I threw my paper away before anyone saw it and told Mr. Vargas that I'd try again tomorrow.

It had been an entire day since I'd asked Melanie to find my *Anne of Green Gables* book, and she still hadn't found it. Every time I passed her in the hall, she shook her head. I kept my phone in my back pocket, but it never rang, except once, when Tristan triumphantly called to tell me I was about to trip over my shoelace on my way to chemistry.

My book was still inside that small, moving, humming square, and every minute that passed, my stomach knotted tighter with anxiety and worry. Dennis had reported this morning that Beverly Jacobs would support the shoot-to-kill order, but only if innocent lives were at risk. That was good news, but knowing Kellan, he wouldn't wait to make that judgment. He would kill them the moment he saw them.

I stopped at my locker before Spanish to grab my textbook, when Melanie came rushing up to me.

"It's on fire," she said, slightly out of breath.

"What's on fire?"

"Your book. It's on fire."

I clamped my hand over my mouth. "Inside that moving square?"

"It's not inside that square anymore. It's outside. On fire."

Why would Jillian and Logan have kept my book this whole time, only to burn it now?

It didn't matter why. For the first time since they went missing, I knew what my brother and sister were doing now, this very moment. Not in the past. Not in the future. *Now.* I knew what they were doing, but I still didn't know where they were.

"Do you know where it's burning?" I asked, trying to be casual, trying not to get my hopes up. "Like in a field, maybe?"

She tilted her head and closed her eyes. "It's in a garbage can. Red. Near a brick building."

I bounced on my toes with excitement. This was it. I was going to find my brother and sister today. "Do you see a road sign near that building? Anything that would identify its location?"

She scrunched her face in concentration. Then she exhaled, shoulders slumped. "It's gone."

I stopped bouncing, my heels dropping heavily to the floor. "What do you mean, gone?"

"The vision. It's gone."

"How can it just be gone like that?"

"Because it burned up," she said, shrugging. "It doesn't exist anymore, just like your bag. There's nothing left for me to see. I'm sorry, Tessa. I know you wanted your stuff, but it's all gone." She started to walk away.

"Wait," I said. "We can't just give up because the vision is gone. Did you remember seeing any landmarks?" I prompted her. "Describe the building to me."

She closed her eyes again, squeezed them tight. "Well, the building was brick. There was a sign over the door."

"Do you remember what it said?"

"Something Coin-Op Laundry. Lano Coin-Op Laundry? Something like that."

I whipped out my phone and typed Lano Coin-Op Laundry into the browser. "There are no results for Lano Coin-Op," I said, "but there's a Lako."

"Lako," she said, nodding with her eyes still closed. "Yes, that was it."

There was no website for Lako Coin-Op Laundry, only an old yellowpages.com listing. The business was marked closed, but there was an address. 56 Boynes Street. Woodmoor, North Dakota.

I entered the address into my Google Earth app and held my breath as it zoomed in on a building surrounded by an empty asphalt parking lot. The trees at the edge of the lot were in full bloom. It was winter now, so the image had been captured a while ago.

Heart pounding, I showed my phone to Melanie. "Is this the building in your vision?"

"Yeah, that's it!" she exclaimed.

I couldn't help it: I threw my arms around her and squeezed her tight. Jillian and Logan were in Woodmoor, North Dakota, this very moment.

Melanie Brunswick found my brother and sister.

# CHAPTER THIRTY-ONE

SIX HOURS LATER, I shivered beneath a blue North Dakota sky as I stood next to a dented red garbage can, behind the abandoned building that used to be Lako Coin-Op Laundry. Unlike the Google Earth image on my phone, icy wind blew snow across the cracked asphalt parking lot.

Inside the garbage can, the ashes of my *Anne of Green Gables* book were cold.

After Melanie gave me Jillian and Logan's location, instead of going to Spanish class, I'd slipped out of school. Took a cab to the Lilybrook airfield. Hired a charter plane—the same plane Tristan and I had taken to Tennessee, not the APR's plane, of course—to an airfield a few miles outside Woodmoor, North Dakota. The disinterested pilot had asked no questions. Then I took another cab here, to 56 Boynes Street. Lako Coin-Op Laundry.

To pay for all of this, I swiped the cash Tristan kept in his desk. He would forgive me when I returned to Lilybrook with Jillian and Logan.

If I didn't bleed to death inside a little silver-walled house first.

But I was not inside a little house with silver walls. I was outside, in a frigid empty parking lot, behind an abandoned laundromat. No house.

No silver. Just wind, asphalt, brick, and concrete.

And the Nightmare Eyes. They had accompanied me the whole way here. I couldn't escape them. No matter how far away I went, I'd never escape the guilt and shame of being Killers' Spawn.

But soon I'd have Jillian and Logan back. I was only six hours behind them. Now I just had to follow their path.

I glanced at the cab driver, who was waiting for me in his dirty white cab. He was lighting a cigarette and watching me from under his ungroomed eyebrows. He'd asked why I wanted to go to this place, and I'd told him I'd lost something here. True. I lost my brother and sister.

I took a breath, preparing myself to lift the fog. Should I do this without Tristan? I left my phone in my locker at school, on purpose, because I didn't want him to call and find out I'd left Lilybrook. But maybe that was a mistake. His premonitions were working again, but without my phone, he wouldn't be able to warn me before I lifted the fog too high, or brought it in too low.

Didn't matter. I'd come out here, risking bleeding to death inside a little house with silver walls, to find them. I could certainly risk lifting the fog to find them too.

Clutching Jillian's ballet shoe and Logan's sheet music for strength, I steeled myself against the wind.

Took a breath. Held it.

Concentrated.

Raised the fog.

Just half an inch.

I only had to lift it a teeny bit more before I saw Jillian and Logan.

It was easy. Not many people had ever been to this isolated parking lot behind this deserted building. Wisps of long-gone customers carrying baskets of laundry. A flurry of skateboarding kids doing tricks, one of whom fell and got a concussion. A runaway dog.

And two lonely and frightened teenagers, standing over a dented red garbage can, burning their dead sister's favorite book.

"Logan! What are you doing? Give it back!"

"I can't believe you've been carrying this book around this whole time. Why didn't you tell me?"

"We have nothing of Mom and Dad's. We burned everything else of Tessa's after Tennessee. I just want one thing to remember her by. She loved this book."

"We have to burn the book too. We can't take any more chances. Dennis Connelly keeps finding us."

"Don't you dare, Logan. This book is all we have left of her. And what if another psychic can sense something from it?"

"Lady Elke couldn't sense anything from it. She said Tessa was in art class drawing nightmare eyes. What does that even mean? Tessa's dead."

"That psychic was obviously a fake. We'll find one who's legitimate."

"Did you ever even open this book?"

"No. I don't need to read it. I just want to keep it."

"Look. Right here, inside the cover. This book was a gift from Tristan Walker. He signed a dedication to her. *To Sarah, and rainy days. -Tristan.*"

"Oh my God."

"That dedication is completely insincere. He was tricking her the whole time. He knew her real name was Tessa all along. She's dead because of Tristan Walker. Do you want to keep something *he* gave her?"

"No. Get rid of it. Destroy it. Set it on fire. Burn it to ashes."

"Give me the lighter."

The vision shattered when someone grabbed me from behind and growled into my ear, "Did you really think you'd get away with this?"

# CHAPTER THIRTY-TWO

TRONG, WARM, STURDY arms. Clean, fresh, soapy scent.

But I knew it was Tristan by his low, angry voice.

Was I relieved or disappointed?

Both. Relieved because I knew that this was not the start of Deirdre's dream, that I was safe.

Disappointed because I knew he would force me to go back to Lilybrook before I found Jillian and Logan. "Let me go, Tristan." I struggled, but he crushed me tight against his chest. He didn't hold me in a desperate hug. He held me so I wouldn't run away again.

"How could you?" he said. "How could you leave Lilybrook and come here all by yourself?"

"Because you would have stopped me."

"Yes, I would have stopped you. I would have come out here myself, so you could stay home, where it's safe."

I pushed out of his arms and threw my own arms wide. "Look around, Tristan. Do you see a little house with silver walls anywhere?"

"No. But you still shouldn't have come," he said, fuming.

I crossed my arms, shielding myself from the wind. Next to my cab was a blue car with a Woodmoor Auto Rental sticker in the window. "How did you find me so fast?" I'd only been here, behind the Coin-Op, for twenty minutes, tops. He must have been only twenty minutes behind me the whole time.

"I asked Ember to keep an eye on you at school, to make sure you were safe and to make sure Nathan wasn't bothering you. When she didn't see you before your Spanish class, she texted me. I tried calling you, but you didn't answer your phone."

He took my hoodie between his fingers. "This sweatshirt," he said, "is technically mine. So the next person I called was Melanie, to ask her to find it. And she told me that just a few minutes prior to that, she found your *Anne of Green Gables* book for you, but it was burning. I figured it out from there."

Something shuffled in the shadows, then stepped out. Melanie, shaking like a baby bird, her black hair spilling out from under her knit beret. "I'm sorry," she said. "I know you told me not to say anything to Tristan, but when he asked…I just can't lie to him."

I, clearly, was very good at lying to Tristan. Another strike against me; another reason he should be with Melanie.

What had they talked about during the flight out here? Or had she straddled his lap and kissed him the whole time, the same way I had kissed him when we flew to Tennessee?

"You didn't have to bring her with you," I muttered.

"Yes, I did," Tristan said. The anger still hadn't left his tone. "I couldn't risk her telling her uncle. Kellan would be out here in a second."

Melanie shuffled in her Doc Martens, then sniffled. Was she crying? She gave me a resentful glance through her tears.

Tristan seized my arm. "I'm taking you home. Let's go."

Perking up, Melanie nodded eagerly.

"We can't go back," I said. "I have a new lead. The best one yet."

With a dubious raise of his eyebrows, he said, "What is it?"

"Before they came here, they saw a psychic named Lady Elke. They gave her my book and she told them I was alive, that I was drawing—" I stopped myself before I said Nightmare Eyes. I didn't want Melanie to know my secret shame and grief had manifested itself into Nightmare Eyes that I never remembered drawing. I didn't want her to know the Nightmare Eyes were an almost constant presence, burning down on me, crushing me from all sides.

"She told them I was in art class," I said. "They didn't believe her, so they left and burned my book. But I *was* in art class. She knew exactly where I was this morning. She'll know where they are now."

Tristan raked his hands through his hair, then gave a long, reluctant sigh. "Then we'd better find this Lady Elke."

# CHAPTER THIRTY-THREE

*S*EE, *TRISTAN?* I flashed to him. *No silver walls here.*

I was squeezed between Tristan and Melanie, pressed shoulder to shoulder, on a dirty loveseat inside a run-down house. Its walls were covered with faded wallpaper and a cracked, dusty mirror. Cigarette smoke hung in the air like fog, clogging my lungs. But there was not a silver thing in sight.

We had found the psychic who'd told Jillian and Logan that I was alive and drawing Nightmare Eyes, and we were now sitting in her house. Tristan didn't have her in his database, and an internet search on our phones had revealed nothing. We found a listing for her in a coffee-stained Yellow Pages at a pancake place located across the street from the Lako Coin-Op Laundry. Lady Elke lived the next town over in Aldana, a town even smaller than Woodmoor. Her advertisement in the phonebook showed a sketch of a beautiful young woman wearing a jeweled turban and gazing dreamily into a crystal ball that looked amazingly similar to the one Brinda Lakhani had drawn.

Lady Elke in person was nothing like that sketch. She was in her fifties, and despite the cold February weather, she wore cutoff jeans and a yellowed tank top, both of which were several sizes too small. Her right eyelid was sunken and closed, as if she was missing her eye, and a thin white scar ran from her right cheekbone, over her eyelid, and disappeared into her scalp. Her remaining eye was the color of moss. Dark roots belied her frizzy blond hair. She sat across from us in a threadbare easy chair that at one time might have been white. Now it was just a dingy gray.

In addition to the crystal ball, Brinda had drawn a picture of a four-legged animal with one eye. I'd thought it was a deer. One of the psychics Tristan contacted had said it was a horse. Now I knew it was an elk. For Lady Elke.

Lady Elke had so far ignored Tristan and Melanie. She stared at me as her single eye gradually narrowed. Her lip curled up a little, like she smelled something bad. Her hands shook as she drew a puff from her cigarette, then released the smoke from the side of her mouth.

She used her cigarette to point to me. "You're the girl who was in that art class this morning," she said, like she was accusing me of something.

"Yes, ma'am," I replied. In contrast to Lady Elke's low, gravelly voice, mine seemed high and squeaky. I gave her a smile, but she didn't smile back.

"I told them two kids that you was alive. I told them, but they didn't believe me."

"I know," I said. "I'm sorry."

Lady Elke frowned. "You three is like me," she said. "You see things. Visions."

I glanced at Tristan. He nodded cautiously, so Melanie and I did too.

"Then what do you need me for?" she asked. Her single eye darted back and forth between us.

"We need you because you can see things that we can't." I pulled Jillian's ballet shoe and Logan's sheet music from my bag.

Lady Elke curled her lip again. She didn't seem to mind Tristan and Melanie; her looks of disgust were clearly directed at me. She'd look at me, then her eyes would flick up at the ceiling, then down to me again. The back of my neck started to burn, to prickle.

"I'll do it for fifty bucks," Lady Elke said. "No. Seventy-five."

Tristan reached into his wallet, withdrew a bill and placed on the table. She saw the bill was a hundred, and her face softened into a smile. "Let me get you some tea," she said, her voice now pleasant and sweet. She tucked the hundred inside her tank top, then swayed out of the room.

*That woman does not like me,* I flashed to Tristan.

*I don't like her either,* he said. Out loud, he called to her. "We're in a hurry."

"It won't take long," she chimed from the kitchen. "It's all part of the service."

Lady Elke had left the room, but her abhorrence for me lingered behind.

A vision appeared through the fog, one that instantly made me forgive Lady Elke's crude attitude. "Her ex-husband beat her," I whispered. "With a wrench. Right here in this room. That's how she lost her eye."

"Oh." Tristan shuddered. "Now I just feel bad for her," he said. Melanie and I nodded in agreement.

Melanie kept looking across me, setting her wide violet gaze on Tristan. He sat straight up, face tight, keeping his hands on his lap instead of putting his arm around me like he usually did. Was he sitting like that so he wouldn't make Melanie jealous? Or because he was still mad at me for leaving Lilybrook?

We were sitting on the same couch that Jillian and Logan had sat upon just a few hours ago. I could feel their presence, and I wanted more. I could simply lift the fog to have a vision of them, but I didn't want to make Tristan even angrier with me than he already was. "Tristan," I asked, "do you see anything happening if I lift the fog right now?"

He stiffened. "No. But be careful. Not too high. If I tell you to bring it back in, do it."

I touched his arm. "I will."

He still didn't put his arm around me, but at least he didn't shrink from my touch. "Go ahead. Lift the fog."

I took a breath, then carefully raised the fog. And there they were, right there, as if they were sitting next to me. Jillian and Logan, as easy as that. Jillian's hair was dyed brown again and cut to the length of her chin. Her gray eyes were duller than I remembered. Logan was wearing a black ski cap pulled down low over his forehead. With his gaunt features and distrusting glances, he looked almost menacing.

*Show me,* I instructed the visions.

She and Logan sit in a dusty living room on a loveseat that perhaps was once white with metallic gold flowers, but is now gray with dirt. The smoky, dusty air clogs her throat.

Lady Elke had offered them hot tea, and she is in the kitchen boiling the water. Logan mutters, "This is the worst place yet, Jillian."

"Be nice," she says. "Maybe she can help us."

Logan scoffs. "I don't see how."

"We can't keep running from place to place anymore," she says. "It's too dangerous. Maybe that's why Dennis Connelly keeps figuring out where we are. We're too exposed. We need to stop and find a place to stay."

"You want to stay here?"

"Maybe. It's remote. I don't care where we stay as long as it's safe. Please, Logan. Just give her a chance. If she does anything suspicious, we'll run. Or fight."

Logan purses his lips. "Fine."

Lady Elke returns with two mugs. They each take one, and she tries not to grimace at the dirty-dishwater taste.

Lady Elke takes a long drag on her cigarette and studies them. "You have a secret," she says.

Her heart flip-flops. They have many secrets. Their entire existence is a secret. Does Lady Elke know they are hiding? Does she know about their psychic abilities? Does she know their family was murdered? Does she know they pushed that guy off the cliff?

"You lost your family," Lady Elke says.

Another flip-flop. Logan puts his hand on her arm to remind her: don't confirm or deny anything. Trust no one.

"Do you have something of theirs?" Lady Elke asks. "I can contact them."

Logan rolls his eyes. "We don't have anything."

"Wait." She reaches into her getaway bag and pulls out Tessa's *Anne of Green Gables* book. "We have this."

Logan frowns. "Why do you still have that?"

"I just do."

Lady Elke takes the book and holds it to her chest. She twists her lips and looks up to the water-stained ceiling like she's thinking hard.

"This girl ain't dead," she declares. "She's in art class. She's drawing nightmare eyes."

Her heart stops flip-flopping and plummets into her stomach. Lady Elke is a fake, just like all the other so-called psychics they've seen. She avoids Logan's "told-ya-so" expression.

"She's looking for you," Lady Elke continues. "She needs to find you first."

"Okay," she sighs. "Thank you for your time." She reaches for the book, but Lady Elke grips it tightly in both hands.

"But there's more," she says. "Everything you think you know is wrong."

"We're done," Logan says, and stands up. He tosses some money on the dirty coffee table.

She snatches the book from Lady Elke, and they walk out the door.


I rose from my space between Tristan and Melanie, following the images of Jillian and Logan outside. Ignoring the cold wind, I stood on Lady Elke's rickety, cluttered front porch. Distantly, I felt Tristan behind me, on alert.

His blue rental car sat on the gravel driveway, and as I lifted the fog, it was replaced by a small white RV. Jillian and Logan were leaning against it, hunched over. Tired. Defeated. Crestfallen.


"You okay?" he asks. He sees Jillian is upset, but she held it together in there, so he decides not to mention the book. For now.

"Yeah, I'm okay. Just disappointed."

"For a moment I thought she might be legit," he says. "I mean, everyone has secrets. But when she said we lost our family? Wow. I got chills."

Jillian nods. "Me too. But look at us. We *look* like orphans."

"You're right, though," he says. "We need to stop running. We'll look for someone to help us. Maybe someone will give us a place to stay." He pulls a key from his pocket and tosses it to her. "Your turn to drive."

They climb into the RV. The front door of the house opens, and Lady Elke comes out. She waves at them to stop.

Jillian sighs impatiently and rolls the window down.

"That girl. She feels eyes everywhere," Lady Elke says. "They're black. They're from her nightmares. She feels them watching her."

Of course this one-eyed woman would be obsessed with eyes.

"Right now, in art class?" he says, sarcasm dripping like poison from his voice. "That's why she's drawing them?"

"Yes! Exactly," Lady Elke says. "She can't escape them."

He loses his patience with the crazy woman, and silently commands the RV to drive away. It jerks to a start and pulls out.

She runs after them, shouting something about two girls named Lily and Brooke, but her words get lost as the RV rumbles away, kicking up gravel and dirt.


"Tessa, she's ready," Tristan said from behind me.

I called in the fog, blinked, and looked up at him. "She was so accurate that Jillian and Logan thought she was a fake."

Tristan snorted at the irony. "Any other clues?"

"They're driving an RV," I said. "That moving square where Melanie saw my book? That was probably a box in the RV, or a cabinet. And they're looking for a place to stay now instead of driving around aimlessly."

"That's good," Tristan said.

"Maybe. We saw them a lot while they were on the road. It might be harder for us to find them once they settle somewhere."

"But if Lady Elke can tell us where they are right now," he said, "we should be able to catch up to them before that happens. Let's get back in there and get that reading."

# CHAPTER THIRTY-FOUR

*J* SAT BACK on the dirty loveseat, making sure to sit between Tristan and Melanie again. Lady Elke's lip curled up at the sight of me. Tristan handed the sheet music and ballet shoe to her again.

Without releasing the cigarette from between her fingers, Lady Elke grabbed the items. She held them to her chest and twisted her lips, then looked up to the ceiling in deep concentration. "These people ain't dead," she said.

"We know," Tristan replied. Still, I felt relieved to hear it.

"It's them kids who was here this morning," she said.

"Yes," Tristan said, offering no more information. "Where are they?"

"He's driving. She's playing with her charm bracelet."

I tapped my foot anxiously. Logan was driving. Jillian was fiddling with her charm bracelet. But knowing what they were doing didn't answer our question. "Where?" That's all that mattered: where.

Lady Elke closed her eyes. "He doesn't like this new car. It's too small. The RV had more space."

*They got rid of the RV,* Tristan flashed to me. "What are they driving now?" he asked Lady Elke.

She licked her lips. "It's shiny."

"Lady Elke, I need you to tell us where they are," I said, trying to be patient. "The name of a town."

"I don't see *where*. I only see *what*."

"Well then," Tristan said, "what do you see around them? Street signs? Buildings?"

"It glitters and glimmers."

"The sun?" he asked.

"Sparkles and glows."

I brought my shaking hands to my mouth. "Tristan…"

He exhaled with frustration, then tried a new question. "Are they driving toward the sun, which would mean they're heading west? Or away from it, which means they're driving east?"

"Everything is sparkling," Lady Elke breathed. "It's so bright."

"No, *where* is the sun, in relation to their car? North, south, east, or west?"

"Silver." Lady Elke's single-eyed gaze wandered around the room. "All those faces. All those people."

"My nightmare," I said, nerve endings igniting with alarm. "Tristan, she's seeing my nightmare."

"The eyes." Lady Elke shook her head, as if she was trying to shake my nightmare from her head.

Tristan went rigid. *Tessa, get out of here. Take Melanie with you, and get out of here now.*

Tristan told me to get out of here; he was having a warning premonition, but I couldn't leave. I couldn't move.

"Melanie," he whispered. "Get out of here. Run."

"Where should I go?" she whimpered. "What do I do?"

"Outside! Go. Now."

Melanie squealed and darted from the house. But Lady Elke didn't spare her a glance. Her one eye glared at me, weighed me down. I was frozen in her gaze. The Nightmare Eyes too, burned into me, trapping me, holding me prisoner.

Tristan stood, pulling me up with him, and backed toward the door. "You stay away from her."

"You need to pay, Tessa," she rumbled, her voice heavy with rage. "You need to bleed. You need to spill your tainted blood." She giggled with hysteria as her eye rolled in its socket.

She knew my name was Tessa. She knew my blood was tainted. And was—was her eye black? *Tristan do you see her eye it's black it's Nightmare black…*

"How did she do that?" he yelled. "Tessa, *run!*" He grabbed me around the middle with one arm and ran outside, dragging me with him. Once I was out of Lake Elke's sight, I was able to move again. Able to breathe.

Melanie was waiting just off the porch, scrunched down behind a post. "Is it over?" she quivered.

"Ye—" Tristan's eyes widened as another premonition struck him. "No!"

We needed to run, we needed to hide, but there was nowhere to go. I spied something across the yard—a weathered, crumbling shed. "There! Go!"

I grabbed Melanie's hand, dragging her as I ran with Tristan to the shed. He forced the door open, and I glanced behind me. Lady Elke came lurching out of her house, barefoot in her cutoff shorts and stained tank top, clutching something long and silver and shiny in her hand. A knife.

Of course it was a knife. Not quite the same as the one in my nightmares, but the blade was just as long. Just as silver. Just as sharp.

Lady Elke stopped in her tracks, gulping in air. Looking for me. The knife reflected a ray from the setting sun.

She spied me in the shed's doorway and howled with rage. Tristan dove with Melanie and me inside, then slammed the door shut behind us.

The wooden shed was old and corroding; sunlight streamed in through the dirty windows and several holes that had rotted through the roof and walls. One ray landed on me like a spotlight. Wind blew through the holes with a constant echoey whistle.

"Tristan," Melanie cried. "What should I do?"

"Get back there and hide," he whispered, and pointed to the back of the shed.

Shaking, whimpering, she squeezed herself into a dark space next to a rusty snowblower. Grunting, I pushed a lawn mower in front of her to hide her better. Tristan held the door shut with one hand as he strained to reach the tools that hung on the walls. Shovels, hammers, screwdrivers. Rakes, hoes, garden shears. Saws, circular blades, a chain saw blade, hedge clippers. The setting sun reflected on the tools' smooth blades, making them glimmer and glitter, sparkle and glow, illuminating the walls with silver.

Lady Elke flew at the shed, crashing into it with such intensity the walls shook. "Tessa!" she screamed. "Killers' Spawn!"

This was it. This was Deirdre's dream.

A little house with silver walls.

And soon, the silver will change to red. Red with blood.

"Spawn! Killers' Spawn!" Lady Elke pounded on the shed. "You need to spill your filthy-dirty-tainted-foul blood! You need to bleed. You need to bleeeeeeeed."

I was going to bleed to death in this little house with silver walls, and since I had led Tristan and Melanie here, they were going to die too.

# CHAPTER THIRTY-FIVE

"KILLERS' SPAWN," LADY Elke howled outside the shed. "You need to bleed! You need to bleeeeeeeed!"

The door jerked as she threw herself at it. The entire structure rattled and swayed, creaking and screeching, screaming for me because I could not.

The shed wouldn't hold for long.

Keeping the door pulled closed with one hand, Tristan reached again for the tools hanging on the wall. His fingertips knocked a pickaxe to the floor. He dragged it over with his foot, then grabbed it. He raised it in his clutched fist, ready to fight.

"Tessa," he whispered. "Get back there with Melanie."

"No." I wasn't going to hide and let Tristan fight for me. I was *not* Melanie. Shaking, I took the hedge clippers from a hook and held them up like a dagger.

"Tessa!" Tristan hissed. "Go hide!"

I planted my feet, drew a breath for courage, and tightened my grip on the hedge clippers.

Panting and wheezing, Lady Elke rattled the shed, pounding on it. It creaked and shook, causing the sunrays to dance merrily, making the walls so silver-bright I was blinded. Terror sang in my ears, time moved in tiny increments.

And then Lady Elke stopped screaming. Stopped pounding. The shed stopped rattling.

In the silence I whispered, "Where did she—"

Tristan's eyes flew open wide. "Tessa she's coming you need to hide NOW!"

From outside, an agonized shriek howled over running footsteps, and the door burst open, sending Tristan crashing to the floor. The shed flooded with light. Melanie screamed.

Lady Elke's single eye swirled maniacally in its socket, until it landed on me. The silver walls gleamed blindingly bright, forcing my vision to narrow, narrow, narrow, focusing it on that black Nightmare Eye. Dark as a starless night and black as a cavern of coal, it held me frozen.

Distantly I heard Tristan shouting, but I remained frozen, unable to move, unable to look away from the vengeful, gleeful, triumphant Nightmare Eye.

"Tainted Tessa, tarnished Tessa," Lady Elke cackled. With both hands, she raised the knife over her head.

Then she collapsed with a thud.

# CHAPTER THIRTY-SIX

"**G**OTTA ADMIT, I might not have stopped her if it was just you two trapped in this shed," John Kellan said to Tristan and me. Victorious, he stood with one booted foot on Lady Elke's crumpled form as he slid his tranq gun back into its holster. "But I wasn't about to let this woman kill my niece."

"U-Uncle Johnny?" Melanie whimpered from her hiding spot in the back of the shed.

Brushing past me, Kellan tromped over Tristan to push the lawn mower away and help her up. "I tracked you all the way here through your phone, sweetheart," he cooed.

Cheeks soaked with tears, she wouldn't look at either of us as Kellan gently guided her from the shed.

"Melanie," Tristan croaked from the floor. "Mel, I'm sorry."

Two guards in black APR jackets stood outside. Kellan cocked his head at Lady Elke. "Get that woman and transport her to the Underground."

They pushed me aside as they lifted her, one by her shoulders, the other by her knees, and carried her out. Her head fell back, and her one eye stared out into nothing.

Her mossy green eye.

That woman tried to kill me today. I'd grown up thinking that Dennis Connelly wanted to kill me, but he was only trying to rescue me. When Kellan abducted me from Twelve Lakes, I had believed he was going to kill me, but that was just a ruse to get my parents to surrender. Even my mother, who had once flown me against the wall in a fit of sleepless rage and who had sliced open my stomach in a fit of panicked terror, had never wanted to *kill* me.

But Lady Elke, she wanted to kill me. It wasn't a lie. It wasn't an act. Lady Elke had looked into my mind and saw my shame and grief and guilt, and it was so strong, so deep, that she'd fed upon it. It made her eye turn Nightmare black. It made her want to spill my tainted, tarnished, Killers' Spawn blood.

I dropped the hedge clippers, then slumped to my knees as my muscles lost their strength and all energy drained from me.

Lady Elke's knife had dropped when she collapsed, and from his place on the floor, Tristan angrily shoved it away with the heel of his shoe. With a huge exhale, he sank back to the floor. He scraped his hands in his hair, then stayed like that, his arms hiding his face from my view.

"Tristan," I whispered. "Are you okay?"

It took him a long time to answer. "You almost got us all killed, Tessa."

"I know. I'm sorry."

"This was what my mother dreamed about," he said. "Brinda drew it too."

"I know."

"This shed is the little house. The tools are the walls of silver."

"Yes."

He sat up, leaning on his elbows. "You *knew* this would happen if you left Lilybrook, and you did it anyway. You didn't tell anyone you got a lead. You sneaked out of town. You flew out to some godforsaken place in the middle of nowhere, and then not only did you almost get yourself killed, you almost got Melanie and me killed too."

I crawled over to him, crawled through the tools and junk and dirt. "Tristan, I'm sorry." I put my hand on his arm, but he flinched.

"All I've ever wanted to do is keep you safe, Tessa." Slowly, he stood, the setting sun making his shadow fall over me. "But I can't. I failed you again. I am always going to fail you."

Then he turned, and walked out.

# CHAPTER THIRTY-SEVEN

THE WIND HOWLED as I knelt in the dirt of Lady Elke's cluttered shed, watching Tristan leave. His shadow stretching long, he trudged across the littered yard without looking back.

All he'd ever wanted to do was keep me safe, but he couldn't. He thought he had failed me, that he would always fail me.

But I was the one who had failed him.

On shaking legs, I forced myself up and out of the shed, away from that little house with silver walls. I shuffled across the yard to the gravel driveway, where Tristan stood with his hands shoved into his pockets, head down, as Kellan lectured him. He wouldn't lift his head to look at me.

A black rental car sat next to Tristan's blue one. Melanie sat in the back of the black car, huddling under a blanket. She wouldn't look at me either.

I needed to get Jillian's ballet slipper and Logan's sheet music back. They weren't anywhere in the yard, so I pushed against the wind to Lady Elke's house and slipped inside. Silent, shadowed, and empty. Kellan's guards must have already headed back to the APR with her. I found the ballet shoe and sheet music on the kitchen floor. Above them, a drawer was open, and it was full of silver. Utensils, ladles, spatulas. And knives. Lots of knives. They glittered and glimmered, sparkled and glowed.

I slammed the drawer shut.

Then I tucked the ballet shoe and the sheet music into the pocket of Tristan's hoodie and went back outside. Time to face Tristan.

He was still standing at the car with Kellan. "She had a vision of the nightmare Tessa has every night, and then she made it come true," he said as I approached. "Her eye turned black, just like in Tessa's nightmare. She said Tessa was tarnished. Tainted. She wanted to make her pay for what her parents did."

I nodded. I couldn't disagree. That was exactly what had happened. "What's going to happen to her?" I asked Kellan.

"That woman is obviously an extremely wise and gifted psychic," he said, "but she tried to kill my niece. We can't risk her losing control like that again. She's headed for the Underground."

"Please don't neutralize her," I begged. "She can find my brother and sister. She was about to tell us where they were."

Kellan snorted. "All inmates are neutralized, Miss Carson. I can't do anything about it."

Frustration and despair roared in my ears. Once again, I'd come so close to finding Jillian and Logan, and they'd slipped away. "That's not fair," I said. "Nothing you do is fair. Our lives were in jeopardy today, but you didn't shoot to kill. You only tranquilized her. If you find my brother and sister, you don't have to kill them. Tranquilize them if you have to, but don't kill them. Please."

He stared at me, speechless. I stared back, knowing my point was valid. *Hypocrite,* I shouted at him silently.

Then the cool hardness returned to his face. "I am not a hypocrite. I didn't use deadly force on that woman because I had a clean shot from behind." He walked around the car to the driver's side. "Your brother and sister used their psychokinesis to fly Aaron Jacobs' car off a cliff. They can kill with the power of their minds, just like your mother. They are far more dangerous than a crazy old psychic with a knife. Make no mistake—if I feel my life, my agents' lives, or the lives of any innocent bystanders are in jeopardy, I *will* shoot to kill."

Now I was the one left speechless. And hopeless. Tristan just shook his head. "You're right, Tessa," he muttered, "but you'll never change his mind."

Kellan slid into the car. "I'm flying Melanie home. You two are on your own. Take a different plane, drive back, don't come back at all, I don't care. I don't want either of you anywhere near my niece."

He slammed the door shut and peeled off, leaving us alone under the darkening sky.

Behind us, Lady Elke's house stood empty. The shed sat off to the side, the door off its hinges, walls dented and sagging. As we watched, it moaned, creaked, and finally collapsed in on itself in a cacophony of screaming wood and clanging metal. The clatter echoed, and from far away, a dog howled.

"The little house with silver walls is gone now," I said. "Your mom's dream happened. I survived."

"Barely," Tristan mumbled. He kept his head down and leaned against the car.

"Tristan, I'm sorry." I pressed into his chest, but he didn't put his arms around me. "I don't mean to make you feel like a failure."

"I'm trying to keep you safe." His gaze, cold as the wind that whipped at my cheeks, was fixed on a brown patch of dirt on the ground. "But I can't. Even when my premonitions work and you don't ignore them, I still can't keep you safe." He whirled around, kicking the car's back tire. "Kellan had to save you today. *Kellan.*" He said his name like it tasted bad in his mouth.

"I did a stupid, reckless, irresponsible thing today," I said. "But it's not your job to keep me safe."

He looked at me then, just a glimpse, then back to the dirt. He swallowed hard, then whispered, "You fell in love with me because I made you feel safe."

The pain in his voice and the wounded look on his face made something break inside me. Being a hero was how he defined himself, and I'd taken that from him.

"I don't love you because of your warning premonitions," I said. "I love you because your eyes are so incredibly blue and because your hair turns gold in the sun. Because you have broad shoulders and strong arms and you let me wear your hoodies every day. And that's only the little things. You're kind, and smart, and supportive, and respectful. All you have to do to make me feel safe is put your arms around me. That's why I love you, Tristan."

He said nothing. Just stood there, stiff, and stared at that patch of dirt.

I'd hurt him so much that not even my expression of love could make it better.

"You're not failing me," I said. "You could never fail me. But I failed you. I came into your life and I ruined it. You gave up so much for me. You lost Melanie because of me. You lost Nathan because of me. You almost lost your life, so many times, because of me. And my parents..." My heart pumped my tainted, tarnished blood through my veins. "I'm Killers' Spawn, Tristan. I don't deserve your love."

At that, he melted. The anger in his eyes, the tightness in his face, the tension in his shoulders.

"Lady Elke saw your nightmare and called you Killers' Spawn," he murmured, taking a lock of my hair in his fingers. "She got that from you."

I nodded, and now *I* stared at the patch of dirt on the ground.

"Tainted blood. Tarnished blood. She got all of that from you. Is that how you really feel? Is that why you think you don't deserve my love?"

Shame and despair crawled up into my throat and blocked my words, and I could only nod.

Now, finally, *finally,* he put his arms around me, pulled me close. "You have wildflower eyes. Your hair is the color of honey. You slide your hands into your sleeves. You pick the green peppers from your salad. You wear my hoodies every day. And that's only the little things. You stand up to Kellan and the Lab Brats. You'll do *anything* to find your brother and sister. You've been through so much, but you get up every morning and you fight. You're amazing, Tessa. You more than deserve my love. You are my heart. You are my soul."

"But my parents—"

He kissed me. It tasted like love.

"I don't care about your parents," he said. "I only care about us. You and me."

"Us. You and me," I repeated, and for just a moment, my heart stopped pumping my killers' blood through my veins, and instead it echoed in rhythm: *Thump. Thump-th-thump.*

Even the Nightmare Eyes dimmed.

We stayed like that, me pressed against his chest and breathing him in, and him holding me tight, until the sky turned dark and it was just the two of us, under the stars.

# CHAPTER THIRTY-EIGHT

"*H*ow dare you."

Those were the words Deirdre used to greet me when Tristan and I returned to the Connellys' house as the sun rose the next morning. She stood in the foyer, hair a mess of copper, arms crossed, lips curved down.

"I gave you one rule to follow, Tessa. One. Stay in Lilybrook," she said. "And what did you do, the first chance you had? You left Lilybrook."

So this was it. I'd disregarded Deirdre's premonition. Disobeyed her orders. I'd left town, and in doing so, I almost got her son killed. Dennis and Tristan had already risked their lives for me, and now Tristan had to do it again. Tristan and I had finally reconciled, but Deirdre was going to tell me to leave, to get out and never come back, just like my mother had done.

"How dare you make me worry like that?" She grabbed both Tristan and me in a hug so tight I could barely breathe. "I was frantic."

"I—" I mumbled into her chest. "You're not kicking me out?"

"Kick you out?" she said, still holding me tight. "Tessa, no. I'm upset that you deceived us, but I understand how desperate you are to find your siblings. But honey, you cannot leave Lilybrook again. We can't risk my dream happening."

"Mom, it did happen," Tristan chuckled. "Your dream came true."

"What? How? Are you okay? Are you hurt?" She released us, then put her hands on my shoulders and looked me up and down. "Kellan told us a crazy woman tried to attack you with a knife. He didn't say anything about a little house with silver walls."

As Tristan and I gave Deirdre a sanitized version of yesterday's events, Dennis and Ember came downstairs. They listened breathlessly, Deirdre and Ember with their hands over their mouths in shock the whole time. "That lady had a vision of your nightmare and attacked you?" Ember asked, her face white.

Miserably, I nodded, and Dennis frowned.

When we got to the part about Lady Elke barging through the shed's door, Ember squeezed Lyric so tight that he hissed and bolted away, and Deirdre grabbed me again, crushing me to her chest.

When we finished, Dennis rubbed his chin. "So the shed was the little house," he concluded. "The tools on the wall were the silver."

"The *tools* were the silver?" Deirdre furrowed her brow. "Well, I'm just relieved it's over. Now we need to get you to stop having that nightmare, Tessa. It's a lot more serious than I thought."

I nodded. There was nothing I wanted more than to stop having my nightmare. Except for finding Jillian and Logan and bringing them back here, safe. And now that I no longer had to worry about Deirdre's dream of little houses with silver walls, I was free to leave Lilybrook to get them.

That afternoon, I held tight to Tristan's hand as I rang the doorbell to Aaron Jacobs' house. In my other hand, I held a bouquet of balloons in all different colors, each of them printed with *Get Well Soon*.

The healers who had flown out to Ringgold, Colorado to treat Aaron after his plunge off the cliff had worked fast, stealthily healing him enough to transport him back to Lilybrook within a few days. Now he was back home with his parents and a rotating crew of APR healers and physicians on hand to treat him.

Mrs. Jacobs answered the door. When she saw me, a little wrinkle formed between her eyebrows. That was the only wrinkly thing about her. Her chin-length hair was polished and glossy, and her slacks and blouse were perfectly pressed. I resisted the urge to smooth my hair.

"Mrs. Jacobs," I said, gathering my courage. "We came to see Aaron. And to talk to you. Please."

She regarded us for a moment, then let us in. Everything in her house was immaculate. White and cream with straight lines and right angles. Not a speck of dust. It smelled like Lysol. My mother would love it here.

"I heard about your little escapade to North Dakota," Mrs. Jacobs said. "That was a very reckless thing to do, Tessa."

"Yes, ma'am," I said. "I know. I'm sorry."

"I'm sure you're grateful that John Kellan was able to rescue you."

Tristan stiffened beside me, and I squeezed his hand to calm him. This was not a good time for him to get hotheaded about Kellan. "Yes, ma'am. We're very grateful."

But my humility wasn't good enough for her, because she continued, her expression hard and immobile as granite. "The Carson family has brought a lot of trouble and heartache to this town."

At her words, the Nightmare Eyes appeared and burned down on me from above. "Yes, we have," I said. "What I did was wrong. And my parents…there's no excuse for what they did. But my brother and sister didn't mean to hurt Aaron. It was self-defense."

The wrinkle between her brows deepened by a millimeter. "I am well aware of the situation. I saw the video. I read the reports. I talked to Aaron."

"Does that mean you'll repeal Kellan's shoot to-kill-order?" Tristan asked.

She paused for a moment, then spoke directly to me. "Your parents killed two of our agents, Tessa. If those agents had been allowed to use deadly force at that time, they'd be alive today, and so would all of the innocent people your parents killed while your family was on the run for eight years." Her face remained motionless, except for a tiny, defiant lift of her chin. "I stand by my decision. John Kellan is allowed to use deadly force if the situation calls for it."

She was motionless, but I was crumbling. "Mrs. Jacobs, Kellan will use deadly force whether the situation calls for it or not. He doesn't care about them. All he cares about is vengeance."

Another miniscule movement: her eyebrow raised.

I thought I'd convinced her, that my plea had softened her granite resolve, but her eyebrow lowered back into place and she said, "This discussion is over, Tessa."

Tristan put his arm around me. *I knew it would be useless to appeal to her,* he said silently. *She said the same thing to my dad. We'll just have to find another way.*

Mrs. Jacobs glanced up at the balloons we'd brought. "It's almost time for Aaron's meds. If you'd still like to see him, you have to do it now. Come with me."

My heart sinking, we followed her to Aaron's bedroom, which was dominated by several computers, stacks of video games, and a large flat-screen TV. The overhead lights of his bedroom were turned off, but sunlight streamed through the slats in the blinds, revealing a swollen white figure on the bed. A cotton sheet covered him up to his chest, which was wrapped in bandages, as were both arms. His face was turned away, toward the window. Only his eyes and lips were left uncovered.

*He looks even worse than I thought he would,* I flashed to Tristan. *He's just a pile of white bandages.*

*He's still a thousand times better than if he didn't have psionic healers working on him.*

"You have two minutes," Mrs. Jacobs said, then left.

"Hi, Aaron." The cheer in my voice was forced. "Welcome back." I tied the balloons to the handle on his nightstand drawer. Aaron didn't acknowledge me or the balloons. He didn't move.

Underneath all of Aaron's bandages were lacerations and burns. The healers were able to heal his lacerations, but most of his burns were so bad that he would always be scarred.

Above me, the Nightmare Eyes burned through my blood. But no matter how much I burned, it was nothing compared to the burns that Aaron was suffering. No matter how much I hated the scars my mother had carved into my belly, they were nothing compared to the burn scars Aaron would have on over forty percent of his body.

My brother and sister had done this to him.

But so had I.

*I* had given him that final clue to Ringgold, Colorado. And *I* had encouraged his crush on Jillian, used it to motivate him to find her.

A lump formed in my throat and I had to give up the cheerful act. "Aaron?" I choked. "Aaron, I am so, so sorry."

No reply. The only thing that moved were his eyelashes, down, then up.

"Jillian and Logan, they didn't know you were trying to help them," I said. "If they knew, they never would have..." I couldn't finish the sentence.

No reply. Just another blink as he looked out the window.

"When—*if,*" I corrected myself, because I was losing faith that there would be a when, "If I find Jillian, I'll tell her how smart you are. How talented. I'll bring her to meet you and—"

Aaron flinched, then exhaled, muttering something. Five syllables.

"What was that?" I asked.

"You…" he inhaled. "Are…" he stopped, recovered, then dragged in another breath. "Killers' …Spawn."

A vise clamped around my heart as Tristan went rigid. "Hey, man. That's not fair."

"Aaron, please." My heart shred into tiny pieces. "I'm sorry. I'm so sorry."

Slowly, Aaron turned his head to face me, and I was one hundred percent certain that when I looked at his eyes, they would be Nightmare black.

But they weren't. They were still brown.

Aaron wasn't feeding on my nightmare, on my shame and grief and despair.

Aaron hated me on his own accord. And for some reason, that was even worse.

"Here's a used car dealership in Warrenville," I said, and called out its phone number to Tristan.

Back in the Connellys' guest room, I sat on the bed with Tristan's laptop on my knees. Tristan dialed the number, then paced the room with his phone to his ear. Mac lay at my feet, thumping his tail occasionally, and Marmalade perched in her spot on top of the bookcase. The only good thing that happened today was finding out that the APR's board of directors had put Nathan on probation for blocking Tristan's premonitions, and he would be fired if he bothered me, or Tristan, ever again. But my blood still burned from Aaron's rebuke as I clicked on another car dealership's website.

Before Lady Elke had fed upon my nightmare and gone crazy, she told us that Jillian and Logan were driving in a new car. "He doesn't like this new car," she'd said. "It's too small. The RV had more space."

So, soon after their visit to Lady Elke, my siblings had gotten rid of their RV and purchased a different car. It was a tiny lead. We didn't know what kind of car, or what color, or if they'd bought it at a dealership or through a private sale. But our appeal to Beverly Jacobs had failed, so that tiny lead was our only hope of finding Jillian and Logan before Kellan did. Now Tristan and I were contacting car dealerships in North Dakota one by one, asking if they recalled two teenagers buying a car with cash.

There was a soft knock on my door frame: Deirdre, her copper hair falling over a sweatshirt painted with little upside-down handprints. In childish writing it read, Best Teacher Hands Down!

"Tessa, can I talk to you?" she asked. "Alone?"

I shot Tristan a message—*what's this about?*—but he just shrugged. He gathered his notes and laptop, and kissed me before departing to his room. Mac padded after him, and Marmalade jumped onto the bed and mewed.

Deirdre sat next to me, and I tried not to stiffen when she tucked a lock of hair behind my ear. But she must have noticed, because she sighed and pulled away. "When you got back from North Dakota this morning, you asked if I was going to kick you out. Do you really think I would do that?"

"I did for a second," I admitted.

She took my chin in her hand and made me look at her. "You will always have a home here, Tessa. Always."

"But—"

"When you find Jillian and Logan, they will have a home here too."

"But our parents—"

"Your parents tried to kill Dennis. They wanted to kill Tristan. They killed a lot of people, and hurt many more."

I pulled away, hung my head, but she grabbed my chin again. "Your *parents* did those things," she said. "Not you."

Logically, I knew that. I understood that. But they were my parents. Their blood pumped through my veins with every beat of my heart. Shame and grief, hurt and despair built up inside me, growing bigger and bigger, heavier and heavier, until it burst out of me with a sob. "I'm just so…" The next word ripped itself from my throat. "…*ashamed.*"

"That shame is what's causing your nightmare," Deirdre said. "A nightmare so strong that some crazy psychic with a knife fed upon it."

"But what can I do?" I cried. "How do I get rid of it? I can't change who my parents are. I can't change what they did. I can't change the past."

Deirdre sighed. "Oh, Tessa. Sometimes I think the person your parents hurt the most, was you."

I lost it then. Sobs tore from my throat, one after another, and I couldn't see past my tears. I covered my face with my hands and cried, and through my sobs, I told her everything. She already knew it, but I told her anyway. How every word from my parents' mouths had been a lie. How my entire childhood had been a lie. How they forced my brother and sister and me to live in constant fear. How my mother had flown me into the wall. How she'd sliced me open. How the scars on my stomach were nothing compared to the scars on my soul. How, just as I was ready to accept my mother back into my life, she rejected me when I told her I was living with Tristan. And most of all, how on that last night in Twelve Lakes, my parents had instructed Jillian and Logan to run away instead of telling them the truth, costing me the only two people in the world who could possibly understand how it felt to be so betrayed by the people we had trusted the most.

Deirdre didn't tell me to stop crying. She didn't ask questions. She just listened.

I continued to cry, and with each sob, each tear, I felt lighter, and my blood became cooler. When I finally stopped, exhausted, she wiped my tears. "You can't change the past," she said, "but you can let go of it. And Tessa, you *can* change who your parents are."

That was enough to make me sob one last time.

I lay down, and slowly, put my head on her plump lap. She rested her hand on my head for a moment, then ran her fingers through my hair.

My parents committed those crimes, not me. They'd hurt me just as much as they'd hurt everyone else. Maybe even more. Deirdre understood that. So did Tristan. And Dennis, and Ember.

I lost so much, but I gained something too. A new family. I started with Tristan, and then I added Dennis, Deirdre, and Ember. Once I found Jillian and Logan, my new family would be complete.

I fell asleep with my head on Deirdre's lap as she stroked my hair. And when the Nightmare Eyes made their appearance in my dreams that night, they weren't quite as black.

# CHAPTER THIRTY-NINE

ENNIS AND DEIRDRE insisted that Tristan and I return to school the next day. We'd both missed a lot of school lately, they said, and until there was a lead in the search for Jillian and Logan, they expected us both to go to class every day. Dennis promised he'd continue our efforts to contact car dealerships in North Dakota and call us if he got a hit.

I didn't protest—there was something I needed to do at school. Someone I needed to talk to.

I waited by Melanie's locker before first period, but she never showed up. In the foreign language hallway before my Spanish class, I asked Ember if she knew where Melanie was. She informed me that Melanie hadn't been to school since our trip to North Dakota. She'd also quit Lyre, Ember's band. Poor Melanie was traumatized. I whipped out my phone and texted her my apology, six times throughout the day, but she never replied.

Nathan ignored me all day too. He would lose his job at the APR if he bothered me, so he didn't even look at me.

Deirdre had also insisted that after school, instead of going home, I go straight to the APR and meet her in her preschool classroom. She wanted me to start sketching a mural to paint on the classroom walls. She was babysitting me, keeping me from getting into more trouble. But I didn't mind. If I was at the APR, I could keep my eye on Kellan to see if he'd gotten any leads on Jillian and Logan.

And also, hanging out with Deirdre sounded kind of nice.

The preschoolers were gone for the day by the time I got there, so Deirdre sat at one of the short round tables with her curriculum planner, while I took a pencil to the wall near the window. I would paint a mural of a garden, I decided. An oversized flower garden. Soon the walls were covered with my pencil sketches of gigantic wildflowers, an enormous rainbow, and whimsical trees. And a pair of Nightmare Eyes, which I quickly turned into two giant sunflowers before they overpowered me.

"Hey, Deirdre?" I said as the Nightmare Eyes burned into me anyway. "Would you mind if I took a break? Maybe I'll go upstairs and visit Brinda. I want to see if she'll make any more drawings for me."

"Sure, honey. When you get back, we can swing by Hawthorne's to pick up dinner." Humming contentedly, Deirdre resumed her project, and I left the classroom. I passed the lunchroom, where Kellan was sitting at a table near the door, peeling an apple. Good. He was here, which meant he didn't have a lead on Jillian and Logan. I slipped away before he noticed me.

Upstairs, Brinda and her dad welcomed me to the playroom. Brinda spun around, showing off her new pink dress, which I admired with a silent clap.

She gestured to her table, inviting me to sit and have tea. I sipped my invisible beverage, then placed Jillian's ballet slipper and Logan's sheet music on the table, hoping Brinda could squeeze one more prediction from them.

She didn't look at them. Instead, she stared at me. Her gaze grew unfocused as Mr. Lakhani lifted the pail of crayons. She dug through them and pulled one out.

Silver.

She covered the entire paper with silver, solid and shiny, and it reflected the lights from above.

*But Deirdre's dream of a silver-walled house already happened*, I wanted to tell her. *It's over. I survived.* But I couldn't speak in here.

She pointed to the paper and then to me, tilting her head.

Oh, she was asking if her drawing had happened already. I nodded yes, then smiled to show her I was okay.

Brinda wiped her forehead with her hand, miming a relieved expression. Then she tore the silver paper in two.

I nudged the ballet slipper and sheet music closer to her. *One more premonition,* I pleaded silently. *Just one.*

She glanced at the items and shook her head, then offered me a plastic chocolate chip cookie. Trying not to be too disappointed, I took the cookie and pretended to take a bite.

Brinda sipped her tea, and her gaze landed on the ballet shoe and sheet music again. But after a millisecond, she turned away to pour more tea into her father's cup.

Mr. Lakhani took a pretend sip of the tea. I took another pretend bite of the cookie.

Brinda's gaze returned to the shoe and sheet music. This time they lingered for a full two seconds before she looked away.

*Come on, Brinda*, I pleaded silently. *One more prediction. You can do it.*

She daintily dabbed her mouth with a napkin, then looked at the ballet shoe and sheet music again.

Her gaze stuck, then very slowly, her eyes glazed over.

*Yes.* This was it. Brinda was going to have one more premonition for me.

Mr. Lakhani raised the crayon bucket. She withdrew two crayons:

one pink and one blue. With the pink, she drew a starburst at the top of the paper. With the blue, she drew a long wavy line underneath the star.

She placed the ballet shoe and sheet music on top of the drawing, and with clear eyes and a definitive nod, slid it over to me.

A year ago, Brinda drew twelve lakes, and my family went to Twelve Lakes, Illinois.

A couple weeks ago, Brinda drew a gold ring, and Jillian and Logan went to Ringgold, Colorado.

Today she drew a pink starburst and a wavy blue line.

A pink starburst. A wavy blue line.

I froze for a moment, then started shaking as hope, joy, elation zipped up my spine and into every nerve ending. I knew where I would find Jillian and Logan.

I whipped out my phone and did a quick internet search.

I gave Brinda a handful of stickers and the world's tightest hug, waved 'bye to her dad, and left the playroom with the ballet shoe, the sheet music, and the drawing of the pink starburst and wavy blue line. Down on the main floor, instead of going back to Deirdre's classroom, I went to the lunchroom.

Kellan was still there, using his index finger and thumb to pop a cherry tomato into his mouth. His apple was gone, but the peel was on his paper plate, coiled up like a red snake about to strike.

I skidded to a stop. Shoved Brinda's drawing behind my back.

"Whatcha got there?" Kellan said.

"N-nothing," I said. *Brinda's drawing,* I thought.

"A drawing from Brinda?"

"No." *Yes.*

Kellan unfolded himself from the plastic chair and sidled to the doorway, blocking my exit. "What did she draw?"

"Nothing." *Pink starburst. Wavy blue line,* I thought. *A star. A river.* "Meaningless scribbles."

He took a step toward me. "None of Brinda's drawings are meaningless."

*A star. A river,* I thought again. "This one is." *Star River.*

"If it's so meaningless, why do you have it?"

"Because—" *Because Brinda drew Star River.* "Because Brinda gave it to me as a present." *Star River I looked it up on my phone it's a town in Texas Jillian and Logan are going to Star River Texas.*

Then I gasped. "I—you aren't reading my mind, are you?" I made pleading, innocent doe eyes at him. "Please, Mr. Kellan. Please don't." *Star River.* "Because this drawing—it doesn't mean anything."

His lip twitched through his red beard. "I am not reading your mind. I don't have time for this anyway. I'm late for something." He pivoted on his heel and marched out.

*Star River,* I shouted silently after him, as loud as I could. *Star River, Texas!* I pushed the words at him as he dashed triumphantly down the hallway at a speed just slower than a sprint. *Star River!*

He pulled his phone from his pocket as he rounded the corner. To look up information on Star River, no doubt.

Kellan was going to go to Star River, Texas.

Good. That was exactly where I wanted him to go.

Because that pink starburst wasn't a star. It was a water lily.

That wavy blue line wasn't a river. It was a brook.

While Kellan was hundreds of miles away in Star River to lie in wait for Jillian and Logan... Jillian and Logan would be coming to Lilybrook.

Less than an hour later, Tristan and I stood at his bedroom window, looking out at the sunset. In the distance, a little plane coursed past a white cloud. Tristan raised his childhood binoculars to his eyes.

"Is that it?" I asked.

"That's it." He handed me the binoculars to look for myself. I adjusted them, and… yes, there it was: a white plane, marked with NWSL in navy along the side. The APR's plane was heading south, flying John Kellan and his team to a tiny impoverished town in Texas called Star River.

"Kellan moves fast," I said.

"When he wants to." Tristan stroked my cheek with his thumb. "You did good, Clockwise. You used Kellan's telepathy against him."

I twisted around so I faced him, then stood on tiptoe to kiss the soft spot on his neck, right under his ear. "Did you write the email?"

"All I have to do is hit send." Holding me against him with one arm, he reached over to his computer and pressed the enter key. "Done. If any of the psychics in my database get a visit from Jillian and Logan, they'll send them to Lilybrook."

*If a teenage brother and sister come see you,* the email read, *tell them to go to Lilybrook, Wisconsin. Tell them they'll be safe here, and there are people who can help them.*

"I just hope it works," I said.

"It will. It may not happen with the first psychic they visit, but it will happen."

"They need to get here fast, before Kellan realizes I tricked him. He'll realize something's wrong when we don't show up in Star River ourselves."

"I'll take care of Kellan." Dennis came in, carrying a battered leather suitcase. Deirdre stood behind him, her hand flittering nervously to her throat.

"I'm going to Star River too," Dennis continued. "I'll tell Kellan that Deirdre refused to let you two go, so I came instead, to make sure he doesn't harm Jillian and Logan when they get there. Heath Van der Sande is coming as my safeguard. It's standard APR procedure, and Kellan won't be able to get into my mind to read the truth." He met my gaze. "We'll stay as long as it takes, Tessa."

"You're okay with this, Mom?" Tristan asked. "Dad going on a case? It could be dangerous. It could be stressful on his heart."

"It was her idea," Dennis said.

Deirdre gave a resigned sigh. "Retirement made your father bored and miserable." With an open palm, she placed her hand on his chest, right over his heart. "I'd rather he be happy. Happiness is good for his heart."

Dennis put his arm around her and kissed the top of her frizzy head. Tristan strode across his room. "Thanks, Dad." As the Connellys hugged each other goodbye, I stayed back. Then I remembered that I was part of this family too.

I leapt across the bedroom and tried to wrap my arms around Tristan, Dennis, and Deirdre at the same time. It didn't work, so they opened their arms for me, and hugged me too.

# CHAPTER FORTY

THE PLAN WAS to act like we were waiting for word from Star River that Jillian and Logan had arrived. To act nervous. Anxious. Afraid.

I didn't have to act.

It had been five days since Dennis and Kellan left for Star River. Tristan kept in contact with our network of psychics around the country, and Dennis kept in contact with us. His messages were short: "Nothing today," or "No activity." The negative messages were good: it meant Kellan hadn't caught on to our subterfuge.

To keep up appearances, Tristan and I went to school, and Deirdre went to work. Every day after school, though, Tristan and I camped out at Hawthorne's in a booth at the front window until the diner closed at midnight. Main Street's wooden *Welcome to Lilybrook - a Friendly Place to Live* sign was visible from where we sat. If—*when*—Jillian and Logan came to Lilybrook, they would drive past that sign.

Through visions, I had gotten to know the previous inhabitants of this booth very well. Bernie Jessup and Mandy Klein shared a sundae here in 1973. A kindergarten soccer team in yellow uniforms celebrated a victory here in 1995. Two weeks ago, while Tristan and I were driving back to Lilybrook from Lady Elke's, Nathan Gallagher and Winter Milbourne had occupied this booth after leaving the APR. Nathan had just been put on probation for blocking Tristan's premonitions. Then they'd heard what had happened in Lady Elke's shed that day, and they were furious that we'd dragged Melanie along.

I smothered that last vision with fog and stared outside, willing Jillian and Logan to drive past the wooden sign.

So far, two psychics—one in Wyoming and one in Minnesota—had contacted Tristan. They had both been visited by Jillian and Logan, and they both had directed them to Lilybrook.

Every day, we waited. Every day, they didn't come.

But they *would* come. Brinda Lakhani had predicted it. I carried her drawing of a pink lily over a blue brook with me, wherever I went, along with Jillian's ballet shoe and Logan's sheet music.

They *will* come. I repeated that to myself with every step I took, with every breath, every heartbeat. They *will* come.

My reflection shone in the window at Hawthorne's that Saturday evening. Tristan and I had been here since seven that morning, eleven hours straight, trying to study, but mostly watching for Jillian and Logan. His criminal justice textbook was open on the table, but he hadn't turned the page in over an hour. My geometry homework had turned into doodles of starbursts and wavy lines, replicas of Brinda's drawings. His pork chops had gone cold, and I couldn't take yet another bite of blueberry pie.

As I stared outside, Nathan Gallagher appeared in the window. Faint, ghostly. I blinked, then realized the image was just a reflection in the glass, and he was here, inside the diner, walking past our table.

He paused in his steps, looking down his narrow nose at us.

Tristan went rigid, his hands curling into fists. "Get out of here, Gallagher," he rumbled. "You know you'll get fired if you bother her.

Looks to me like you're bothering her."

Nathan gave him an innocent shrug and held up a to-go bag. "Just picking up some food," he said, and lumbered away.

With a shaky sigh, Tristan put his arm around me. "I never thought he and I would end up like this."

"I'm sorry you lost your best friend because of me," I said.

"His loss." He brushed my hair aside to kiss my neck. I leaned against him. "Tired?" he asked.

I nodded. "Tired of waiting. Tired of wondering. Tired of worrying."

"You won't have to wait much longer," he said, his breath warm on my neck. I closed my eyes and sank into him, bending my neck to give him more access. "Jillian and Logan are on their way to Lilybrook…" he dotted kisses under my ear. "…and Kellan is hundreds of miles away where he can't hurt—"

He cut himself off, and I opened my eyes. Had Nathan come back?

No. Beverly Jacobs was standing at a table by our booth. The executive director of the APR. Aaron's mother. Her clothes were ironed, her hair was smooth. But her brows were lowered and pulled together, making deep wrinkles across her forehead. Her lips were pressed tight together, forming deep lines around her mouth.

Mrs. Jacobs was furious.

And she was staring straight at us.

# CHAPTER FORTY-ONE

RISTAN AND I swept everything into our bags and fled from the restaurant. "Did she hear us?" I cried. "What if she figured out what we're doing?"

"I'm calling my dad," Tristan whipped his phone from his pocket. "He'll have to intercept any message she tries to get to Kellan."

As he held the phone to his ear, a white sedan rumbled past. Out of habit, even in our rush, I looked at it. Thousands of vehicles had driven down Main Street over the past week, the majority of them Lilybrook residents. By this point, I was used to disappointment, and expected it.

The sedan pulled into a parking spot near the *Welcome to Lilybrook* sign. The setting sun reflected on its windshield, obscuring my view, but I could see that there were two people inside. Young. A boy and a girl.

Hope flooded my chest, a flash flood of hope, and I stopped short. "Tristan."

"Is it them?" he asked.

"I don't know," I said, barely able to speak. Oh please, oh please, oh please.

Both car doors opened, and they climbed out. Still shadowed, just silhouettes.

Jillian and Logan? No. I couldn't let myself believe it was them. I couldn't believe it until I actually saw them as more than shadows.

Tristan shoved his phone back in his pocket, and we crept a little closer.

Oh please, oh please, oh please…

They stepped into the fading sunlight. Both weary, disheveled, and much too thin.

The girl's hair was a stringy dull brown, cut to the length of her chin.

Jillian.

The boy's dark hair brushed past the collar of his jacket.

Logan.

The flood of hope turned into a tidal wave of joy. "It's them," I cried. "They're here. In Lilybrook. They came." They were here, really here, not visions of the past, not premonitions of the future. They were now. Here. In Lilybrook. Safe. Jillian and Logan. Jillian and Logan!

I pulled Tristan down by his collar. Kissed him, hard. *This is it,* I said. *We found them. Us. You and me.*

He kissed me back, just as hard. *Now go get them, Clockwise. Go get your brother and sister.*

I wanted to run to them. I wanted to fly to them. But if I scared them, they would flee again. I forced myself to walk, slowly, in the shadows. Surely they could hear my steps as I approached. Surely they could hear my heart pounding.

Finally, I was close enough to hear what they were saying.

"This is it, Logan," Jillian said. She gestured to the sign. "*Lilybrook, Wisconsin. A Friendly Place to Live.*"

"It's got to be a trap." Logan, speaking in his low voice. So different, so clear, from how it sounded in my visions.

"It's not a trap. Two different psychics told us to come here." Jillian's voice was higher, hopeful. "They said we'd be safe here. There are people here who can help us. We just have to find them."

I took one more step, out of the shadows. "One of the people who can help you is standing right here."

Our gazes locked. Jillian's gray eyes, Logan's brown eyes.

"T—Tessa?" Jillian stammered.

Logan backed up, pulling Jillian with him. "It can't be." On guard, he scanned the street.

"It's me," I said, palms up. "I've been trying to find you. Don't be scared. What those psychics told you was true. You're safe here."

Jillian squeezed her eyes shut, then opened them again. "But—but I saw them… I *saw* them kill—"

"They didn't kill me. Mom and Dad are alive too."

Finally Logan's gaze landed on me again. Just as I was about to raise my hoodie and expose the scars on my stomach, he exhaled, "It's really you. Tessa."

That's when I lost it. Nodding and sobbing, I ran to them, stumbling in my rush, and threw my arms around both of them at once. I squeezed. Breathed them in. They were solid. Real. Now.

Relief and elation filled me up and I couldn't contain it; I was bursting with it, overflowing with it, and I wanted to share this incredible feeling with Tristan, the person I loved most in the world. He was hiding in the shadows, out of sight, and I shot him a message: *I wish I could share this with you.*

*You are, Clockwise.*

Finally, when our joyful sobs lessened to happy tears, I released my siblings and stepped back to look at them. I'd seen them in visions a few times, but seeing them in person was like switching from standard to high def. Each strand of hair. Each eyelash. Logan had stubble on his chin now. Jillian had flecks of blue in her gray eyes that I'd never noticed before. Awed, I reached out to touch them again, as they did to me.

Jillian finally pulled away. "Where are Mom and Dad?"

I sniffled one more time, my heart shattering at what I had to tell them. "There's so much you need to know. But it's getting dark. Come with me, and I'll tell you everything."

# CHAPTER FORTY-TWO

I BROUGHT THEM to the Connellys'.

Dennis was still in Star River, keeping up the charade. We didn't know if Beverly Jacobs had overheard us at Hawthorne's, and we didn't want Kellan to return to Lilybrook until we were sure Jillian and Logan would be safe.

Deirdre, Ember, and the animals stayed upstairs, as we'd predetermined as part of the plan. And as much as I wanted Tristan to help me tell my siblings the truth, I thought it'd be better if he stayed hidden until they had a chance to digest the information. Now he hovered at the top of the stairs, out of sight, but close by.

It was just the three of us. Jillian, Logan, and me. I sat between them on the couch and held their hands in mine, unwilling to let go. They sat stiffly, on guard, like their bodies didn't remember how to relax. Their gazes darted to the exits, to the clutter, to the family photos on the walls, and to the exits again.

"Is that Tristan Walker in those pictures?" Jillian said, her voice trembling.

"That's Tristan, yes," I said. I couldn't tell them about the Connelly part. Not yet.

"But how—"

"I live here with Tristan and his family."

Logan sat up even straighter. "Where are Mom and Dad." A demand, not a question. "Tell us what's happening, T—" He cut himself off and glanced at the doorway again.

"*Tessa*," I finished for him. "You can use my real name. Everyone knows who I am."

"Tessa," he said, softly this time, like he was testing it. He glanced at the doorway, and when no one burst through to attack, he added, "Please."

I squeezed their hands. Closed my eyes. Took a breath.

Licked my lips, swallowed.

But I couldn't say it.

Our parents murdered people. Our parents had lied to us, they ruined our childhoods, they made us Killers' Spawn. How could I tell them that? How could I give them that burden to carry for the rest of their lives?

But we were together now. I was no longer alone. As much as Tristan sympathized, he would never understand. Even if he was an empath like Cole, he would never fully understand. No one would understand, except for Jillian and Logan.

So maybe, by telling them the truth, all of that grief and despair and shame would be divided up three ways, and it would be lessened for each of us.

*You can do this, Tessa.* Tristan told me from his place at the top of the stairs. *I had to tell* you *the truth, and it was hard for me too. But I did it, and you can too.*

Tristan understood more than I thought he did.

*God, I love you,* I told him.

*I love you too, Clockwise. I'll be right here the whole time.*

*Us,* I said.

*You and me.*

Knowing Tristan was supporting me, I closed my eyes. Took a breath.

Licked my lips, swallowed.

Then I said it. "Dennis Connelly isn't the killer," I began. "Our parents are."

The sun rose long before I finished telling my siblings about our parents, and Tristan, and Dennis Connelly, and the APR, and the Underground, and Kellan, and Aaron Jacobs, and my new psionic abilities.

I held their hands the whole time, except when I wiped away tears. Their tears, and mine.

Now, his muscles tight and his jaw set, Logan had the green evidence binder open on his lap, absorbing the information with his hypercognition—swiping his palm over the pages. With each turn of the page, his face became grayer. I couldn't watch as he stared at the photos of our parents' victims. Would he dream about them now? Would his dreams be invaded by Nightmare Eyes now, too?

"No. *No,*" Jillian said. The entire room buzzed and vibrated. On the mantle, the mosaic vase I'd made in art class toppled over. "I don't believe it. None of what you're saying is true."

"I wish it wasn't," I said. "But it is." I was repeating the arguments I had with Tristan when we were in the Underground, only this time, I was reciting his words, and Jillian and Logan were the ones stuck in denial.

"They're tricking you, Tessa," she said. "You said this town is full of—what did you call them—*psionic* people? Maybe they're controlling your mind. Projecting ideas into your head and making you believe them."

Memories of our father's eyes turning Nightmare black, and the old man at Union Station, and a knife-wielding Lady Elke floated to the surface, but I shoved them back as Marmalade padded into the room on her tiny paws. She tapped Jillian's leg and mewed. Jillian blinked her puffy eyes, and the room stopped vibrating.

*I had Ember send Marmalade to you,* Tristan said from upstairs. *Thought it would help if they saw that we're not torturing you or anything like that.*

My heart swelled again. *Thank you, Tristan.*

"This is Marmalade," I said, scooping her up and nuzzling her neck. "She's my little Marma-lady. Tristan's sister gave her to me for my birthday."

Jillian sniffled. "You have a kitten?"

I placed Marmalade on her lap. "I also have a bedroom and a painting studio. I painted a mural at school."

"You go to school?"

"Of course."

But Jillian's expression hardened again. "No. No. They did something to you. I don't know how, and I don't know why, but there's no way what you're saying can be true."

Logan tapped the binder. "This entire binder could be false. Made up."

"I once thought the binder was made up too," I said. "And then I proved that it wasn't."

"How?" he asked.

"I'll show you." I ran my finger over Jillian's gold bracelet, the one her boyfriend Gavin had given her. I played with the heart charm and lifted the fog.

"You took this off once," I said.

"I—"

"Six weeks ago. In the desert. Along a stretch of highway somewhere in…" I raised the fog a little higher. "Arizona."

"How did you…"

"It was right after you found out Gavin was dead. You and Logan were about to burn my getaway bag. There was no reason to keep lugging it around, and he thought that going through it every day was making things worse. You also took off this bracelet and threw it in the pile. You'd convinced yourself that if you weren't wearing the bracelet, you wouldn't think about Gavin all the time, and then it wouldn't hurt so much."

She raised her hand to her mouth.

"But the moment you took it off," I continued, "you felt empty without it. Logan was about to light the match. You wanted one thing to remember me by, so you swiped my *Anne of Green Gables* book from the pile when he wasn't looking. You also took back the bracelet. While Logan burned everything else, you hid my book in your getaway bag and put the bracelet back on."

"How do you know that?" Logan said. "We were in the middle of the desert. No one was around."

"Maybe one of those APR people has remote vision, like Dad," Jillian said. "Someone was watching us." She craned her neck and looked up over her shoulder, as if she felt the Nightmare Eyes burning into her too.

"If that was true," I said, "it would have been a lot easier to find you."

"Then how can you possibly know what I did with Gavin's bracelet?"

"The same way I proved that Mom and Dad are guilty," I said. "I'm psionic. I'm retrocognitive. I always have been, but it was suppressed by a mental fog until recently. I had a vision of your past when I touched your bracelet. I had a vision—lots of visions—of Mom and Dad when I touched their wedding rings. I saw it all. They're guilty. They lied to us about Dennis Connelly. They lied to us about everything."

"B-but that means…" She sank back and buried her face in her hands. "That means they killed Gavin." Her voice was very small.

I knew the devastation she was feeling, that all-consuming ache that makes you feel hollow and heavy at the same time. I pulled her in and held her tight, and let her cry.

*Tessa watch out!* Tristan shouted in my head.

Jillian sobbed, and with it, the glass in all the picture frames shattered and shot through the air like bullets.

Marmalade darted off my lap, and Tristan flew into the room.

Logan jumped up, arms splayed wide. The coffee table tipped over, forming a barrier between Tristan and me. "Get away from us, Tristan."

Tristan raised his hands innocently. "I just want to make sure everyone's okay."

"Logan," I said. "Tristan is my boyfriend. He loves me. He wouldn't hurt me. Or you. He almost died trying to find you."

Logan eyed Tristan up and down. "Doesn't matter. Tristan *Connelly* doesn't come near you until we see Mom and Dad. Take us to them. Now."

# CHAPTER FORTY-THREE

OM RELUCTANTLY APPROVED my appearance in the Underground's visiting room because I brought her two coveted gifts: Jillian and Logan. She even sobbed a thank you.

The warden wouldn't let them hug. "No touching," he grunted, as usual. Four guards stood against the wall with their tranq guns loaded, and Tristan remained on the do-not-allow list. He waited just outside.

The stainless steel table glittered and glowed in the gray cinderblock room. Jillian, Logan and I huddled on one side of it, and Mom was shackled to her chair on the other.

"This is where they're keeping you?" Jillian whimpered. She peered from behind her limp brown hair at the knobless door, the intrusive security cameras, the scowling guards. "They took away your PK?"

Mom looked at her hands, chained to her waist. "They took everything away."

"Tell us Tessa's wrong, Mom," Logan said, sitting straight on his metal chair. With white knuckles, he clutched the green evidence binder. It trembled in his grip, like he was trying very hard not to rip it apart. "Tell us everything in this binder is false. Tell us you didn't cut those scars into Tessa's stomach. Tell us you didn't kill all those people. Tell us you didn't lie to us our entire lives."

Jillian sniffled. "Tell us you didn't kill Gavin."

A tear trailed down Mom's cheek as she shook her head.

*She's going to lie to them*, I flashed to Tristan.

*You need to convince her to tell them the truth. Otherwise—*

"Mom," I said. "Tell them the truth." The lies were awful. The truth was agonizing. But they still needed to know it.

"We attacked the manager of a motel because we thought he was there to kill us," Logan said. "We threw some guy's car off a cliff. Mom. Please tell us we didn't hurt innocent people."

"This is a trick, isn't it," Jillian said. "A trap. They brainwashed Tessa. Or they threatened her. They made her lure us down here too, that's it, isn't it? There's no way a single word of what she told us can be true. Mom, what are they doing to you down here? Are they experimenting on you? Are they hurting you? Where's Dad? Why aren't you with him?"

Jillian continued, words tumbling from her mouth, faster and faster, higher and higher. The air hummed and buzzed.

"Mom, look what you're doing to her," I said. "You're making it worse for them. Tell them the truth. You *owe* them the truth."

Mom opened her mouth, but closed it again. She wouldn't look at me. Her anguished gaze fluttered to the guards, then to the door, then locked onto Jillian's identical gray eyes.

My sister calmed. She gave a tiny little nod.

Then the door started to rumble.

"Jillian," I whispered. "Are you doing that?"

The locked door trembled. Buckled.

"Jillian," I hissed. "Stop it. Don't." *Tristan she's breaking our mother out you need to stop her.*

Mr. Milbourne shouted, and the guards pulled their guns, each aiming at one of us: Jillian, Logan, my mother, and me.

*Tristan!* I cried.

Logan flicked his hand at each of the guards, and the barrels of their guns bent up with a screech and Mom's shackles fell off with a clatter. The table slid across the floor, barricading the guards against the wall.

The door exploded open with a tremendous boom, and I screamed for the first time since I was unconscious in the Underground. "Tristan!"

Jillian grabbed my arm with an unyielding grip and pulled me from the chair. "Go. Run!"

"Mom," I cried as Jillian dragged me to the door. "Tell them the truth. Do you really want this kind of life for us again? Running and aliases and never being safe?"

The guards shouted and struggled, but using only his open palm, Logan used the table to hold them against the back wall. He backed toward the door. "Mom, get up! Let's go!"

Underneath all the screaming and screeching and shouting, there was a whisper, just one word, one syllable. It came from our mother, and it made everything fall silent:

"No."

Jillian froze. "Mom?"

Mom was staring longingly at the door, and even though her shackles had fallen away, she hadn't moved from her chair. "Everything Tessa told you is true," she said. "She wasn't brainwashed or threatened. This isn't a trick or a trap. Your dad and I are guilty."

Logan's hand dropped to his side.

The table dropped to the floor.

Jillian dropped her grip on my arm.

She dropped to her knees.

Now they knew. They knew the truth. They knew our parents were killers. They knew their entire lives had been a lie.

The guards brushed themselves off, and from down the hall came the echoed sound of rushing, booted footsteps. A new guard rushed into the visitors' room, his beady eyes barely visible under his large forehead, muscles so large that his black T-shirt strained against them.

"Jillian, Logan, come to me," Mom said, calmly, from the chair. She patted her lap. "Babydoll, you too."

My siblings and I knelt around our mother. Jillian buried her face in her lap. Logan's chin was thrust out like he was trying not to cry. I brought in the fog to numb the pain. I took their hands, attempting to comfort them.

Mom smoothed Jillian's hair. "Your dad and I did some horrible things. We hurt a lot of people, and I regret it. I regret every single moment." She inhaled a shaky breath. "Most of all, I regret hurting you. I only wanted to keep our family together. But you three are together now, and that's what's important."

Jillian sobbed. I expected the table and everything else that wasn't bolted down to start vibrating, but nothing did.

"I'm going to stay here with your father," Mom said. "Maybe, one day, he'll wake up, and they'll let me be with him. I'll be okay as long as we have each other, even if it's here. But you three, I want you to leave this place. Leave this town and never come back. Not because I don't love you, but because I do." She cupped my cheek with her hand, and something inside me broke free. "I want you to go live the life I should have given you a long time ago. A normal life. A peaceful life. A happy life."

Mr. Milbourne came at her with handcuffs, and she wiped her tears before meekly offering her wrists to him. She sniffled one last time as he locked them on.

Mom looked to Logan. "Kiss me goodbye?"

With tight lips, he stared hard at an invisible spot on the floor and shook his head.

She sighed resignedly. "Jillian?"

Jillian covered her face in her hands and gave an aching, breathless sob, then turned away, too devastated to make anything tremble except for herself. I put my arms around my grieving sister.

"Babydoll?" Mom quivered.

I patted Jillian and murmured that I would be right back, then obediently hugged our mother. Kissed her cheek. She was setting us free. It didn't change anything. It didn't negate her lifetime of lies. It didn't bring back the people she'd killed. But maybe she hadn't rejected me during my last visit, when she told me to leave and never come back. Maybe, for the first time in her life, she had been trying to do the right thing: to be a good mother.

"You're the strong one now, Tessa," she whispered in my ear. "Take care of your brother and sister."

"I will," I said. "I promise."

She kissed my cheek one last time, and Mr. Milbourne took her away.

# CHAPTER FORTY-FOUR

*I* HELPED JILLIAN and Logan up from the concrete floor of the Underground's visiting room, and the enormous, beady-eyed guard escorted us through the exit that used to be a locked door before Jillian blew it up. My siblings went without protest, their gazes blank. I was a little stunned too, but they had been assaulted with so much new, agonizing information in the past few hours, no wonder they were in shock.

Now Tristan and I would bring them home. Deirdre would set up cots for them, and while they slept, Dennis would come back from Star River. Then together, we would help them heal.

But Tristan wasn't there, waiting outside the door.

"Tristan?" My voice echoed down the dim and musty hallway.

"He's in Milbourne's office," the guard said. "I'm supposed to bring you there."

"Is he okay?" I asked as we followed him. "Did he get hurt when the door exploded?" But as I said it, I knew the answer. Something like that wouldn't happen to Tristan. He'd get a warning premonition first.

"Some guards brought him there when things got out of hand in the visiting room," he said, and ushered Jillian, Logan, and me in.

Tristan sat across from the warden's streamlined desk. Knees wide, head down. When we came in, he lifted his head. "Tessa—"

That's when I saw his arms were behind his back, handcuffed to the chair.

A smirking Nathan Gallagher was standing on the other side of the office, and next to him was John Kellan.

I pushed my siblings behind me.

*How did Kellan get here?* I flashed to Tristan. *He's supposed to be in Star River. Was it Beverly Jacobs? She called him after she saw us at Hawthorne's, didn't she?*

*It was Nathan.* Tristan shook his head with disgust. *He saw your doodles on your geometry homework at Hawthorne's and figured it out. And then he safeguarded Kellan when he got to the Underground.* He tugged at the handcuffs. *He sneaked up on me and I never saw him coming.* "I'm sorry," he said aloud. "I can't stop this from happening."

"Stop what from happening?" Jillian asked, her voice high with panic.

Kellan approached us, drawing something from his jacket. A gun? A real gun?

"I can't shoot to kill unless someone's life is in jeopardy," he said, reading my mind. "Fortunately for them, and no thanks to you, we are able to take them into custody without incident." He pulled two pairs of handcuffs from his jacket and let them dangle from his fingers.

Jillian whimpered, and Logan stiffened. "Custody?" he asked. "Tessa, what is he talking about?"

"Don't bother trying to use your PK, hotshot," Kellan warned him, and gestured to the hulking guard in the doorway. "This guy's inhibiting it."

"But they know the truth now," I said. "They won't hurt anyone. I'm taking them home."

"They're not going anywhere," he said. "Not after what they did to Aaron Jacobs. Jillian and Logan Carson are dangerous criminals. I may not be able to shoot to kill, but I can incarcerate them. They're staying right here in the Underground."

He grabbed Jillian and she screamed, and the guard grabbed Logan's arm in one meaty hand.

"Take them off," Jillian cried as Kellan handcuffed her. "Please. Please!" She closed her eyes and held her breath, the way she activated her PK when she was little, but the chains didn't fall away. Logan tried to fight, but the guard easily apprehended him, too. They struggled powerlessly, screaming and shouting, as Nathan and the guard dragged them toward the door.

"We need to take them for their first round of neutralization," Kellan said.

Tristan wrestled fruitlessly against his own restraints. *Tessa, I'm sorry, I can't help, there's nothing I can do….*

I'd promised my mother I would take care of Jillian and Logan. I could not let Kellan neutralize them and toss them into tiny gray cells. I raced to the doorway, throwing my arms wide to block their exit. "No!"

But I was a hummingbird trying to stop a stampede of elephants. Tristan shouted a warning a millisecond before Kellan pushed me aside, and I stumbled to the floor.

He glowered down at me. "You sent me across the country when you knew the targets were coming here." He swung his pointed finger at me, then at Tristan. "You both impeded my investigation. So did Dennis. I should arrest all three of you for obstruction of justice."

"You will do no such thing," a voice echoed from down the hall. Beverly Jacobs strode over to us, her gold Executive Director badge pinned to her starched white shirt, her face hard and still as ice.

"It's not justice you're seeking, John," she said. "It's vengeance. You want the Carsons to suffer, and they have. We've all suffered. Let the kids go."

"They're psychokinetic, Beverly," Kellan said. "They're dangerous."

Mrs. Jacobs raised one eyebrow a fraction of an inch. "Are you saying all psychokinetics are dangerous? *I'm* not dangerous." She gave the smallest of glances to Jillian and Logan's handcuffs, and they broke apart and fell to the floor with a metallic clang. She did the same for Tristan.

"Even the friendliest dog will bite when threatened, John," she said. "Jillian and Logan Carson were dangerous because they were being pursued. I stand by our policy to use deadly force if innocent lives are at risk. But they are no longer being pursued. They are no longer a threat. Under no circumstances will you neutralize or incarcerate them."

"But they tried to kill Aaron," Kellan said, his mouth agape behind his red beard. "Your *son*."

"There you go again with the vengeance," she said. "What they did to Aaron was a regrettable but warranted act of self-defense." She glanced at her watch. "I need to go home now to take care of him. He's in a lot of pain today."

Jillian gave a soft cry and covered her mouth with her hand. "The boy from the car? He's your son?" she whimpered. "Please, please, ma'am, please tell him we're sorry."

Mrs. Jacobs gave her a tiny nod. There was no warmth in that nod, no softening of her features. It was simply an acknowledgment of their shared distress.

Tristan put me under his arm. "Come on, guys," he said wearily. "Let's go home."

Now Kellan and Nathan were the helpless ones. They could do nothing but watch us walk away.

"It's not over, Spawn," Nathan shouted as we turned the corner. "Now there's three of you infesting my town."

# CHAPTER FORTY-FIVE

E WENT HOME, and slept for a long time. We'd all been awake for too long. So much had happened since we last slept. I got my brother and sister back. They learned some agonizing truths. Our mother sent us away in an act of love. They were apprehended in an act of revenge, then freed in an act of magnanimity.

And through it all, Tristan was there. Supporting me. Loving me.

Jillian and Logan slept on the cots Dennis and Deirdre set up for them in the family room. I wasn't ready to leave them, not even to sleep in my room right upstairs, so I curled up on the couch with Marmalade. Tristan reclined on the La-Z-Boy, close enough that we could reach out and hold hands. I woke up later, in the darkness, when he squeezed onto the couch with me.

*You okay?* he asked, entwining his fingers in mine. *About your mom?*

*Yeah,* I replied silently, and sighed aloud. *She did the right thing. For the first time in her life.*

Logan stirred in his sleep, muttering, and Jillian whimpered.

*What about them?* he asked. *Think they'll be okay?*

*Eventually.*

My brother and sister were just starting to grieve. They might even have their own versions of the Nightmare Eyes. And Tristan and I, along with Dennis, Deirdre, and Ember, would help them through it.

*Thank you for helping me find them,* I said. *I couldn't have done it without you.*

*I'm sorry I couldn't stop Kellan today. And Nathan…*

I deflected his regret with a kiss. *You helped me get my brother and sister back. That's what's important.*

Marmalade purred. I scratched her behind her ears, then snuggled into Tristan. I put my head on his shoulder and fell back to sleep.

Jillian seemed better when she woke up later that day. Still devastated, but she managed a small smile when Deirdre offered her a bowl of ramen noodles and a PB&J for lunch. She liked Marmalade a lot, and held her on her lap. She kept looking at Ember's hair, which was purple today. She brought her hand up to her own brown hair. "I can go back to blond now," she murmured.

Ember showed her pink electric guitar to Logan. With her cheeks flushed almost the same shade, she asked him to demonstrate the music prowess I'd bragged about. "Tessa said you can play any instrument," she said. "Will you show me? I also have a classical guitar if you'd rather play that."

Logan just shook his head.

They kept staring at Dennis, who was tired and pale from his trip to Star River and chasing Kellan back home, but was patiently trying to build their trust. It would take longer than a few hours to erase eight years of fear.

Neither of them wanted to visit our father. He wouldn't send them away—even if he was conscious, he wouldn't send them away, I was sure—but it would also take longer than a few hours to erase their heartache over his crimes and lies and betrayal.

They both stiffened instinctively whenever we used their real names. I made sure to say them a lot so they'd get used to it. I showed them my paintings and demonstrated my retrocognition a few times. They were very impressed, and I was very proud.

I offered to bring them to school to show them my fruit mural and to Hawthorne's to have a slice of blueberry pie. Tristan offered to show them around Lilybrook and give them a tour of the APR, but they declined it all. "You don't have to hide anymore," I reminded them, but I didn't push it. They needed time to get used to the idea.

The next morning was a school day, but except for Ember, Dennis and Deirdre didn't make us go. Instead, they allowed us to continue our reunion at home. Dennis and Deirdre went to buy two beds to replace the cots.

Jillian and Logan didn't come downstairs after taking their showers, so I went upstairs to find them. They were in my room. Jillian was rubbing Marmalade's chin, then she stood at the mirror over the dresser to brush her hair, which she had already dyed back to blond. Another night's sleep had done wonders for her: no longer huddled into herself, she'd regained her confident ballerina posture with shoulders back and chin up. Logan was kneeling, tying his worn sneakers.

Their scuffed getaway bags hovered in the air behind him, his packed neatly and zipped up, hers unzipped with toiletries sticking out and one red sleeve dangling from the top. The duffle bag full of cash sat open on my bed.

Instantly alarmed, I asked, "What are you doing?"

"We're leaving," Logan said, standing up and putting his ski cap on.

"You don't have to leave," I said. "Dennis and Deirdre *want* you to stay. They're out buying beds for you right now."

"We're not just leaving this house, Tessa," he said. "We're leaving this town."

"Why would you want to leave?" I said. "There's people like us here. Psionic people. You don't have to hide. You can use your real names. For the first time in your lives, you're safe. Everything is fine now."

"*Nothing* is fine now, Tessa," Jillian said. Her ballet slipper shot into the air and stuffed itself into a pocket of her bag. "Mom told us to leave this town, and we don't want to be anywhere near her or Dad anyway. That man, Kellan, is here. And that other guy, the one with the dreadlocks who said we're infesting his town. And… that boy we hurt is here too. Aaron. I can't… If I ever see him, I won't be able to…" She looked at me, and her face crumpled with pain and guilt.

Like a match, Jillian's guilt ignited the Nightmare Eyes. *Killers' Spawn,* they taunted silently as my blood started to burn. *Tainted blood. Tarnished blood.*

"We're not living here," Jillian continued. "We can't. We *won't*. We need to go somewhere far away, where no one knows who we are. It's the only way we can get past what happened."

"You can't leave. I just got you back." I crossed my arms and blocked the doorway. "I won't let you leave."

"We're not leaving *you*," Logan said. "We wouldn't leave you behind."

Jillian flicked her fingers at my closet door, and it swung itself open. My jeans floated out. My sneakers. Sweaters from Deirdre that I'd never worn. Hoodies from Tristan that I wore every day. "Tessa, of course you're coming with us," she said. "How could you even consider *not* coming with us?"

Us. The word hung in the air like a bubble about to burst.

*Us* was Tristan and me.

Tristan came upstairs with a frown. "Tessa, I just had a premonition that—" He saw the getaway bags and my clothes hovering behind me, and shook his head. "You guys don't have to leave."

"Yes we do," Jillian said. "We're not going to live in a place where we did so much to hurt so many people. Not in this house, not in this town."

*Tainted blood,* the Nightmare Eyes sang to me. *Tarnished blood.*

"It doesn't have to be that way," Tristan said. "We'll figure it out. We'll do anything you want."

"What we want," Logan said, "is to leave. Don't try to stop us. You wouldn't be able to, anyway." He turned to me. "Are you going to pack your things, Tess, or do you need me to do it for you?"

"Tessa," Tristan said. "Tell them to unpack, because no one is going anywhere."

I tried to speak, to protest, but the Nightmare Eyes, dark as a starless night and black as a cavern of coal, held me frozen and rendered me mute. Inside my veins, my blood burned. *Tainted blood, tarnished blood.*

Jillian stood straight, her chin jutting out defiantly. "We are leaving, and Tessa is coming with us. She belongs with us."

No. I belonged with Tristan. We belonged together.

But I also belonged with Jillian and Logan.

Jillian came over and smoothed my hair. "Tristan's your boyfriend, Babydoll. I understand that. It was nice of his family to take you in for a while, but like that lady said, everyone has suffered because of us. Not just Tristan's family. This entire town went through eight years of turmoil and misery, because of us! And it's not going to end, for anybody, unless we leave. No one wants us here."

"Tristan wants us here," I said, forcing the words past the Nightmare Eyes. "*I* want us here."

"It'll be hard at first," Jillian cooed, "for both of you. But you'll see. Once we're far away from this place, Tristan will be happier, his family will be happier, everyone will be happier. You want Tristan to be happy, don't you? Leaving is the right thing to do."

The Nightmare Eyes burned from above, agreeing with Jillian.

Logan floated the last of my belongings into my bag. It zipped itself up.

"Wait," Tristan cried, growing desperate. "You don't have to leave right this minute. Let's just talk about it some more."

"There's no point in stalling," Logan said. The room started vibrating, a low rumble. Marmalade leapt off the dresser and hid under the bed. "All you'll do is try to convince us to stay, but there's nothing anyone can do or say to make us change our mind. We're leaving. Now." The rumbling got louder, and the dresser drawers rattled.

"No." Tristan strode over and pulled me to him, wrapping his arms around me. "You're staying here. All of you."

"Tristan, let her go," Logan said, "or I swear to God I'll rip—" He stopped, then adjusted his words, his voice low and menacing. "I could, but I'm not going to hurt you. But if you don't let her go right now, I'll take her away from you myself, and lock you up somewhere you won't get out of until we are long gone." The closet door slammed itself shut, enforcing Logan's warning.

Tristan tightened his hold on me. "Try it."

Jillian put her hand up. "Logan, there's no need for threats," she said, calmly, serenely. The room stopped vibrating. She approached me, still in Tristan's arms, and cupped my cheeks. "Babydoll, we've caused everyone so much pain. But you can make it stop. You can end it. You don't belong here. You know it, and deep down, Tristan knows it."

The Nightmare Eyes knew it too.

"You belong with Logan and me," Jillian said. "We're your family.

We're your only family."

That wasn't true. I had another family. The Connellys.

But I still had to choose.

Jillian and Logan, or Tristan, Dennis, Deirdre, and Ember.

I looked up at Tristan, to my siblings, and back to Tristan.

The Nightmare Eyes watched. *Killers' Spawn*, they taunted, high and invisible, but condemning and unforgiving. My tainted, tarnished blood coursed through my veins, scorching me, scalding me, scarring me.

There was only one choice to make.

# CHAPTER FORTY-SIX

 CHOSE JILLIAN and Logan.

# CHAPTER FORTY-SEVEN

Y BROTHER AND sister stood by the open front door, getaway bags in hand, as I sat with Tristan on the couch in the family room. He scraped his hand through his hair. "Where are you going to go?" His voice was tight, strained, like it hurt to say every word.

"We haven't decided yet." I'd wrapped myself in the thickest fog possible, but it wasn't enough to numb my heartache, or to extinguish the fire in my blood. My lungs were rocks, and I could barely speak. "Maybe back home to Virginia. Maybe we'll go somewhere south. Jillian likes the warmer states."

It took him a long time to speak again. "You said you were never running again."

"I'm not running," I said. "I'm not hiding either. No more aliases. We're using our real names." I was wearing a soft white sweater that Deirdre had purchased for me, not one of Tristan's hoodies, and I was leaving my phone behind. Not that it would make a difference. If Tristan wanted to find us, he could. He wouldn't even need the APR's help. "Please don't look for us. Not even if you have a warning premonition about me. You'll be too far to stop anything from happening anyway. It'll be easier that way."

He just shook his head. "Not for me."

"We left the money upstairs in the duffle bag," I said. "We took a little. Just enough to last us a few days. We'll pay it back as soon as we can. We don't want any of that money. We want you to return it to the victims." I swallowed hard. "The victims' families, anyway."

"What will you do for money?"

"Our mother used to clean motels in exchange for a room. We can do the same thing. I can cook at a diner." But if I cooked, I'd be around all those silver sparkling knives. "Or I could be a waitress."

His head was down, and he wouldn't look at me. "You're making a mistake."

"They're my brother and sister, Tristan. I have to stay with them." They were Killers' Spawn, like me.

*Killers' Spawn*, the Nightmare Eyes echoed.

But the Nightmare Eyes were right. No matter how much Tristan loved me, he never would have blood that burned through his veins like a disease. But maybe, hopefully, once we started a new, normal life somewhere else, the Nightmare Eyes would fade and my blood wouldn't burn so much.

Marmalade padded over, then climbed onto my lap and mewed.

"What about Marmalade?" Tristan asked. "Are you leaving her too?"

"She's coming with me." Ember would have taken good care of her, I knew, but Marmalade was *my* kitten. She'd already been abandoned by her mother, and I couldn't abandon her too. And Jillian wanted her. Marmalade soothed her.

Tristan took Marmalade and stood, pulling me up with him. "Fine. Then I'm coming too. We can take my car. I'll go pack right now."

I wanted him to come with me. I wanted to say yes, come with me, keep your arm around my shoulders and crawl into bed with me and chase my nightmares away and kiss me, kiss me, kiss me.

Instead, I looked around the Connelly's cluttered family room, at the art projects and sports trophies and the dozens of family photos on the walls. The fog was thick, but the Nightmare Eyes burned it away to show me the visions:

Tristan and the Lab Brats cheering at the annual Connelly Superbowl party. Three years ago.

Tristan, coming back from a college tour, exclaiming how much fun it'll be to live in the dorms. Two years ago.

Tristan bursting into the house, proudly announcing that he was chosen to be a junior agent at the APR, the first step in his career plan to become executive director. Eighteen months ago.

Tristan kissing Melanie as she looks up at him like he's her knight in shining armor, the night before he left for his first mission in a little town called Twelve Lakes. One year ago.

Tristan, stretching his arms around the back of the couch, sighing contentedly, happy with his life. Ten years ago, five years ago, two years ago, one year ago.

I couldn't take that away from him. If he came with me, he'd be giving up everything that made him happy. If he stayed, he'd keep his family. He could become an investigator for the APR. He'd get Melanie back. He could easily slay her dragons, and he would finally feel like a hero again.

I had to do to him what my mother had done to me: set him free, so he could be happy.

"You can't come, Tristan. You need to stay here."

He hung his head, and when he spoke, his voice was strangled and aching and raw. "What about us? You and me?"

My heart echoed in rhythm: *Thump. Thump-th-thump.*

But that was the last time. Because there could be no more *us*. There could be no more *you and me*.

My heart was bound in barbed wire and it squeezed, squeezed, squeezed.

I took his face between my palms. Stroked his stubble. Ran my fingers through his tousled hair. Stared into his blue eyes, imprinting them into my mind, so when I slept, I would dream of them instead of the Nightmare Eyes.

"I love you, Tristan." I brought him down and kissed him one last time, his warm lips and soft breath—

But he pushed away. "No. I won't just sit here and let *us* end. We belong together, Tessa. You can leave, but I'm coming with you. Give me five minutes to grab my things. Wait for me. Five minutes."

"Tristan…" I started to protest, to argue, to tell him *us* was over. But the words wouldn't come.

I closed my eyes. Took a breath.

Licked my lips, swallowed.

But I still couldn't say it.

So instead I said, "Okay. Five minutes."

He lit up, kissed me hard, then sprinted upstairs.

As soon as he was out of sight, I grabbed a notepad and pen from the coffee table. I could have written a million words, but I needed only eight.

*Tristan,*

*I love you.*

*I'm sorry.*

*Goodbye.*

*~Tessa*

I took off my promise ring, placed it on the note, and scooped up Marmalade. Then Jillian, Logan, and I slipped out the front door.

# CHAPTER FORTY-EIGHT

HE WHITE SEDAN that Jillian and Logan had driven here was purchased with money our parents had stolen, so we didn't want it. We drove it to the bus depot on Main Street and left it in the parking lot. Someone, Tristan probably, would find it and turn it in to the APR.

The Nightmare Eyes hovered over me like a storm cloud as we stood in the shiny Plexiglas bus shelter. Jillian and Logan wanted to leave Lilybrook so we could forget everything, but *I* could never forget. The scars on my stomach were a permanent reminder of my parents, and I would never allow myself to forget Tristan—I owed him that much.

Lilybrook was quiet on this cold weekday morning; almost everyone was at home or work or school or yoga class. Very few cars drove down Main Street, and except for a pair of speed walkers in matching Under Armour, there were no pedestrians. The only thing my siblings and I wanted to see coming down the street was the bus. We had a twenty-minute wait, so I kept Marmalade warm inside my jacket.

A vehicle rolled down the street and pulled into the parking lot, but it was just a Jeep. The door opened, and Cole Gallagher stepped out in his black APR jacket.

Great. We hadn't even made it out of town before they sent someone after us.

Jillian and Logan went rigid out of habit, and I went rigid out of determination. Tristan could beg, Dennis could demand, Deirdre could cry. We were still leaving Lilybrook. Our mother wanted us to leave. Except for the Connellys, no one wanted us here. Tristan, eventually, would be happier without me. No matter how much it hurt, no matter how my lungs ached so much that they felt like rocks, no matter how many tears I had to blink away before they fell, leaving was the right thing to do.

Cole lifted his cell phone to his ear. "I found them, Deirdre. At the bus depot on Main Street. No problem. I'll tell them." He snapped the phone shut and pocketed it as he jogged over.

"You're not bringing us back, Cole," I said.

"That's not why—" He flinched. "Wow, you're upset. Just hit me hard." He put his hand on his chest and took a shallow breath. "It's like my lungs are rocks."

The knowledge that Cole felt my anguish made a tear fall, and I swiped it away. "I'll be fine."

Jillian put her arm around me. "She may be upset now, but she understands why we have to leave."

"Please tell Deirdre and Dennis that I'm sorry," I said. God, after everything they'd done for me, I hadn't even left them a note. "And tell them I said thank you. For everything."

Cole sighed and rubbed the back of his neck, his brows drawn together over his tawny brown eyes. "Tessa, I don't know how to tell you this…"

"What is it?" Something was wrong. He looked too distraught for something not to be wrong. "Is Tristan okay?"

"It's Dennis," Cole said. "He was still tired from the trip to Star River, and when he and Deirdre got back from buying the beds and learned you were gone, I don't know, maybe all of it was too much for him...."

Oh no. "Cole, what happened?" I cried. "What happened to Dennis?"

"He had a heart attack. It's bad, Tessa."

A heart attack. The fog swooped in and my legs lost their strength and I sank to the bench, and Cole was talking, each word fainter and fainter, disappearing down a tunnel as my periphery narrowed. "Deirdre says if you want to say goodbye, you'd better come now."

Say goodbye. I needed to say goodbye to Dennis. I'd left without saying goodbye, and now I had to say a real goodbye, a permanent goodbye, and it may be too late.

"Please," I begged my brother and sister. "Please let me say goodbye to him."

Perhaps out of respect for Dennis, or maybe because of the rasping sob that pushed its way from my throat, Jillian and Logan nodded grimly. They followed me as I stumbled through the fog, following Cole to his Jeep. They climbed into the back, and I held a squirming Marmalade against my chest and buckled myself in the passenger seat. "Hurry, Cole. Please."

Please don't let it be too late.

Cole pulled onto Main Street and sped off. I was going to see Tristan again, less than an hour after I'd left him. I could picture him in the APR's clinic, sitting at his father's bedside. Knees wide, head down, occasionally raking his hand through his hair. Devastated about his father. Devastated about me.

I watched through the fog as Cole turned off Main Street, onto a smaller, woodsy road that wound around Lilybrook Lake. "We should be there in less than ten minutes," he said.

My mother had given Dennis his first heart attack, and now I had given him his last. He went to Star River to help me. He came back and I'd left, breaking his heart, for real.

I really was Killers' Spawn.

Ten minutes had never seemed so long.

The Nightmare Eyes burned into me, yet I shivered. They hovered above me, dark as a starless night and black as a cavern of coal. I lowered the fog but they wouldn't go away. All I felt was my tainted blood pulsing through my veins.

Cole glanced sideways at me, my anguish mirrored on his face, but he didn't say anything. Agitated, Marmalade squeaked and jumped from my arms into the backseat.

As Cole raced around the lake, the Nightmare Eyes burned through the fog. Hating me, accusing me. I squeezed my eyes closed, certain that if I looked up, I would see the Nightmare Eyes glowering down at me, full of grief and despair and shame and fury. But behind my closed lids, all I saw were images of all the people my family had hurt. Aaron Jacobs, burned and scarred. The college professor I'd contacted for help back in Twelve Lakes. Gavin, the only boy my sister had ever loved. The waitress at a Georgia truck stop, the one my mother had killed with a heart attack. The politicians and businessmen my parents had blackmailed and killed. Timothy Brunswick and Kip Gallagher. And the loved ones they'd left behind. Melanie. Nathan and Cole. Kellan.

Now Dennis was dying, and he would leave behind Deirdre, and Ember, and Tristan.

So many victims. So much death. So much grief. So much pain.

It was too much. I pried my lids open again, but it did nothing to relieve the ache.

Behind me, Jillian and Logan jerked back and forth as we jostled down the poorly paved road.

Next to me, Cole swerved around a fallen branch. Why were we driving around the lake? The APR was the other way, wasn't it?

Above me, the Nightmare Eyes continued to glower and burn, dark as a starless night and black as a cavern of coal.

Black as a cavern of coal.

Black as a cavern of coal.

Black as a cavern of…

Cole.

No.

No, no, no, no, *no!*

No. Please.

But yes. My father. Lady Elke. They hadn't gotten the Nightmare Eyes from me. They'd gotten the Nightmare Eyes from Cole.

Slowly, I turned to see him watching me, his eyes black, deep, endless, eternal black, and filled with shame and grief and guilt and fury. "The Nightmare Eyes are yours?"

"No, Tessa. The Nightmare Eyes have always been yours," he said. "But I know exactly how you feel, so I took them and projected them into as many people as I could."

"Tessa?" Jillian said from the back. "What are Nightmare Eyes?"

Cole raised a tranq gun, and in the space between heartbeats he fired once at Jillian, once at Logan, and once at me.

I had just enough time to feel a sharp pinch in my neck and the instant spreading burn, and then the fog closed in, and there was nothing.

# CHAPTER FORTY-NINE

*F*OGGY.

Groggy.

Muscles deadened.

Pulled from the car.

Tossed roughly over a shoulder.

Heart pounding.

Breath gone.

Jillian and Logan. Where were they?

I put all my strength into lifting my eyelids. Through my lashes, I saw something orange dash by—Marmalade? In the distance, through a snarl of leafless trees, I saw a sliver of Lilybrook Lake, its blue water shimmering peacefully in the sun.

Arms dangling and useless, unable to move, I could only watch Cole's booted feet trudge down a dirt path strewn with dead leaves. Spring birds chirped somewhere above me in the trees.

His boots making a hollow echoey sound, Cole stepped onto a wooden porch, gray with rot, then carried me inside a cabin. A bright, glowing, luminous cabin. It glittered and glimmered, sparkled and glowed.

With silver.

Cole dropped me, and I landed on my shoulder and hip. It hurt. Not as much as it should have, but any amount of pain was good—the tranquilizer was wearing off already. I blinked, trying to see through the fog, through the fear, through the silver. Jillian and Logan were sprawled next to me, eyes closed, limbs splayed like discarded rag dolls. Jillian's blond hair covered her face. They weren't moving, but they were breathing.

"So this is why you wanted me to safeguard you?" a gruff voice said from the other side of the cabin. Though I couldn't see him, I knew it was Nathan.

"Thought I'd bring you a little present," Cole said. "Three presents, actually."

More silver flashed, and I looked up to see what made everything so bright and blinding.

All four walls of this little cabin were covered with mirrors. Small, large, round, square. Dozens of mirrors, covering every inch of wall. A sunbeam streamed from a single round window in the door. One mirror caught it and bounced it to another, and another, and another, making the place glow with silver.

*This* was Deirdre's premonition. It wasn't Lady Elke's shed. It was this cabin. Cole's mirror-lined cabin. I left Lilybrook for my brother and sister, and ended up in a little house with silver walls.

And in Deirdre's dream, after silver, came red.

"Cole, what's wrong with your eyes?" Nathan said. "How did they get so black?"

"I got them from *her*," he said. "She calls them Nightmare Eyes."

My fingers tingled, then my hands. I reached out to my brother and sister.

"You're awake," Cole noted. "Good." He nudged Jillian and Logan with his foot and tapped the gun at his waist. "I had to give these two an extra dose. Their PK makes them too powerful. But you, I want you awake for this."

My tongue heavy, I licked my lips. I tried to speak but it came out as a raspy huff of air.

He looked down at me with my Nightmare Eyes, his solemn calm more chilling than my father's crazed panic or Lady Elke's frenzied fury.

My arms and legs were tingling now, and I could move them enough to roll over and push myself up to my hands and knees. With my legs folded under me, I supported my torso by planting my hands flat on the floor. My head was heavy, but I lifted it. Nathan stood a few feet away, leaning against a wooden table with his arms crossed and glowering at me.

Tristan wouldn't even have a warning premonition about this. Not with Nathan here, blocking everything.

"You're feeling hopeless," Cole said. "Probably because Tristan will never know what happened to you, right?" He gazed into one of the mirrors, his eyes hard and cold and black. "I can see him right now, through the reflection on the TV screen in the Connellys' family room. He thinks you left Lilybrook already with your brother and sister. Dennis and Deirdre are there too. They're trying to comfort him, but he's despondent. Poor guy." He put his hand to his chest. "You broke his heart."

Dennis was okay. He was alive. Cole had lied about the heart attack. I hung my head, not because of the drug, but because of relief for Dennis, and remorse and regret for Tristan.

No one will know what happened to Jillian, Logan, and me. Everyone believed we got on a bus and left Lilybrook. I'd asked Tristan not to look for us. No one would even know that we were dead. And Nathan would safeguard any traces of evidence against himself and his brother.

All around me, silver glittered and glimmered, sparkled and glowed, taunting me. Slowly, incrementally, the silver grew brighter. It seemed to pulsate, vibrate, hum, sing at a pitch I couldn't quite hear. My reflection shone in the mirrors. So many mirrors. My face appeared disjointed, sliced into pieces.

I closed my eyes against it. But when my eyes were closed, all I saw were the Nightmare Eyes, glowering at me. I called in the fog to numb my heart-pounding fear, but it resisted. It lifted instead, showing me visions of this little house with silver walls.

Through the mirrors, he watches the events unfurl at the APR. The Kitteridge Killers, the people who'd murdered his father, the people who'd plunged a knife into his back as he tried to crawl away, have been captured. They're locked up forever, but that's not good enough. Two of their spawn have run off, but he watches as one of them decides to stay in Lilybrook. With the Connellys, no less.

Perfect.

Everywhere she goes, he watches her via reflective surfaces. Mirrors. Windows. Screens. The glass on his wristwatch. Silver crayon drawings. And knives. She feels shame, seeing those knives. Her guilt and grief burn through her blood. Her tainted, tarnished killers' blood.

He feels the girl's despair along with her. It burns through his blood too. Her shame festers within her, manifesting itself into a pair of glaring, gleeful black eyes. They invade her dreams, and in her waking hours, they follow her around like a shadow. Nightmare Eyes, she calls them.

He can use these Nightmare Eyes.

There are no reflective surfaces in Wendy Carson's cinder-block cell, but there are plenty in Andrew Carson's hospital-cell. He watches him every day through the reflection on the heart monitor, whispering to him, torturing him with threats against his darling Tessa Blessa. He tells him that she is going to pay the ultimate price for his sins. He tells him that he and his wife will finally know how it feels to have the life of someone they love snuffed out like the flame of a candle.

Nathan wants revenge. Retribution. Retaliation. Sending the Kitteridge Killers to prison isn't good enough. Nathan is dismayed that Tristan, his best friend, doesn't feel the same way as he does. Tristan is *in love* with the Spawn of the Kitteridge Killers. Tristan even broke up with Melanie, a fellow victim, to be with her.

He understands Nathan's pain because he feels it too. He can feel Nathan's sense of betrayal. He can feel Nathan's need for retribution along with his own, and it grows exponentially.

But Nathan's doing it wrong. He's being too obvious, bullying her and blocking Tristan from his premonitions. When things get bad for the Spawn—and things will get very, very bad—everyone will immediately suspect him. He needs to rein Nathan in.

He harnesses the Spawn's Nightmare Eyes and, using reflective surfaces, projects them into others. It only works with the weak ones. It almost worked on Aaron the computer geek with the concussion, but he wasn't quite weak enough. Her father with the brain hemorrhage, that trashy one-eyed psychic with the brain injury: they were weak. Vulnerable. Open. He makes their eyes turn black. The Nightmare Eyes are her grief and despair and shame, and he projects his own hatred and rage into them too. He makes them want to hurt her. He makes them want to kill her.

And all the while, he pretends to be her friend.

There has been a development. A good one.

The Spawn knows how to find the brother and sister, the other two spawn of the Kitteridge Killers.

They're coming here, to Lilybrook. Now he can have all three of them at once, and he and Nathan can do to them what their parents did to his father.

The fog fell like a curtain over the visions, and they disappeared.

Cole Gallagher. It had been him all along. I thought he'd been protecting me from Nathan, but he wanted revenge for his father's death as much as Nathan did. Maybe even more.

The Nightmare Eyes pulsated and my blood burned.

"I understand how you're feeling," Cole said. "The shame. The despair. The guilt. Your blood is burning. It's tarnished. Tainted. Killers' blood pumps through your veins with every beat of your heart. You *feel* it. I feel it too. That time in the Underground when you were so consumed with guilt and grief and shame that you tried to slice your wrists in the shower? That was the first time I watched you. I watched you through that little silver blade on the razor, and I felt your shame then, too."

"You did that?" Nathan asked me from across the room. "You really tried to kill yourself once?"

The Nightmare Eyes, both the invisible ones above me and the ones that had replaced Cole's brown eyes, glowered and burned through my blood, setting my soul ablaze with shame. I had created the Nightmare Eyes, and Cole was feeding on them. He felt my guilt and shame as if they were his own.

"What are you going to do with them?" Nathan asked Cole.

Cole pulled a corrugated box from the corner, and from it he withdrew a clear plastic bag with something long and slim inside, wrapped in bubble wrap and tape. I'd seen bags like that before; in the evidence room at the APR, when I'd tried to prove my parents were innocent.

I knew exactly which piece of evidence was in that bag. Terror shot through my limbs like an electric current, spurring my muscles to move, and I scooted between Cole and my unconscious siblings in a pathetic attempt to shield them from the object in his hands. "No," I croaked.

Cole slid the top open and pulled it out. He unwound the tape from around it, then unwrapped it from the bubble wrap, and held it up triumphantly.

Nathan sipped in air. "Is that—"

"Yes it is," Cole said. "This is the knife. *The* knife. I took it from the evidence room."

He gripped the black handle, and silver flashed again, this time from the long sharp blade of the knife my parents had used to kill Cole and Nathan's father.

Nathan looked from the knife to me and my siblings, and back again. "You're going to kill them with that knife?"

"No." Cole angled the blade so it caught the light. "*We* are."

# CHAPTER FIFTY

NEXT TO ME, Logan moaned and twitched his fingers. I didn't see Cole shoot him again; I only heard the whisper of the tranq bullet, then saw the thin needle sticking from his neck. Cole shot Jillian again, too. But he didn't shoot me. He wanted me awake. He wanted me to suffer. He wanted to tell my father how I'd suffered, the way his father had suffered as he died.

Nathan stared at me through the silver, his mouth slack, like he was anxiously, greedily, waiting to see my tarnished, tainted blood spill from my veins.

Cole reached into the corrugated box again and pulled out a green binder. The evidence binder. His eyes feverish and Nightmare black, he ripped out the pages, one by one, flinging them at me. They landed like a flurry of enormous snowflakes, the faces of every one of my parents' victims staring up at me, wounded and accusatory. He shouted their names as he flung each page at me.

The politicians and businessmen my parents had blackmailed or murdered or both, starting it all.

The Georgia waitress my mother killed with a heart attack because she'd spilled coffee on me.

The college professor my mother killed with an aneurysm because I'd contacted him, asking for help.

Gavin, the boy my mother killed because my sister loved him.

Aaron Jacobs, whom my siblings had scarred for life, and his mother, who was grieving.

So many pages. So many faces. So many eyes glaring and accusing me. "No more," I begged. "Please stop. Please." Yet Cole continued to tear page after page from the binder.

Mr. Milbourne, the warden, had a page because my mother had given him a heart attack during her escape attempt.

Dennis Connelly had a page, because my parents had tried to kill him, too.

Tristan had a page because my parents had tried to kill him twice.

Deirdre and Ember had a page because they'd almost lost both of them.

Timothy Brunswick and Kip Gallagher, innocent agents sent to our house to recruit my family to come work for the APR, had a page because that visit was their last.

Melanie Brunswick had a page because she'd lost her father, her mother had a page because she'd lost her husband, and John Kellan had a page because Timothy Brunswick was his brother-in-law and best friend, but he'd loved him like a brother.

Cole and Nathan and their mother each had a page for losing Kip Gallagher.

Everyone my parents had hurt, directly or indirectly, had a page in Cole's binder. And with each page, the Nightmare Eyes darkened and the silver blades brightened. I couldn't see past my shame, past my grief, past my guilt.

There were too many pages to count. All those pages. All those people. Their eyes crushed me, squeezed my heart, turned my lungs to stone. Despair crawled up my throat and lodged there. I was choking on it, couldn't get air past it. I closed my eyes, covered my face with my hands, but even with my eyes closed, I still saw the victims.

Too much. It was too much. My blood boiled, blazed, blistered. My parents' blood, my killers' blood, my tainted, tarnished blood. I had to get it out. I had to get it out of me, it hurt too much, it burned, it *burned,* and I had to stop it, I had to end it.

"Stop!" I shrieked. "Make it stop. Make the burning stop. Please."

Cole stopped shouting. Stopped ripping pages.

Breath shaky, I sniffled twice. Wiped my damp cheeks with the sleeve of my sweater. Cole and Nathan stood above me. Cole's eyes: hot black. Nathan's eyes: cold steel.

Cole picked up the knife. "It'll be over quickly. And then no more burning," he said. "No more grief. No more shame. No more Killers' Spawn."

Sobbing, I nodded. "Please."

As Nathan watched, Cole approached me with the knife, his boots tapping on the wood floor. The blade reflected the light, and it glowed, glimmered, glistened.

I took Jillian and Logan's limp hands in each of mine, and squeezed them even though they couldn't squeeze back. My only hope was that once I was dead, Cole would stop feeding upon my shame and grief. His emotion supply would be cut off at its source: me. Without those shameful, hateful feelings burning through his veins, he would spare my brother and sister.

My death would save Jillian and Logan.

I couldn't watch him as he knelt down. Blood burning, I stared at the papers strewn around me, at the dozens of victims.

There was a page missing.

I sniffled. "Where's my page?" I asked Cole.

"*Your* page?"

Trembling, I released Jillian and Logan, then lifted my sweater to reveal the five twisted scars on my belly. "My mother did this to me. She hurt me, too. My entire life was a lie because of my parents. I should have a page in your binder."

Above me, the Nightmare Eyes blinked. When they opened again, the blackness was dimmed. Just a little. Charcoal gray instead of solid black.

"Jillian and Logan too," I said. "They're victims too. We should each have a page."

With each word, the Nightmare Eyes faded, from charcoal to slate to ash.

I looked at the photos on the floor, one by one. Those people were still my parents' victims, but their eyes no longer glowered at me.

Above me, The Nightmare Eyes lightened to the color of smoke. I could see through it.

They lightened again, becoming the color of fog, the fog I used to keep the visions away.

They blinked, and this time, the lids stayed shut.

And then they disappeared.

The Nightmare Eyes were gone.

My blood cooled. The shame was still there, it would always be there, but now it was directed at my parents. It was no longer directed at myself.

For the first time in months, my lungs expanded, and I took a deep breath. No longer shackled by shame, I felt airy and light and free.

Cole and Nathan still had my siblings and me trapped in this cabin, and they still had the knife. But now that I was no longer feeling the incredible burning shame of the Nightmare Eyes, Cole should stop feeding on it.

I looked up, into Cole's eyes. They had returned to their usual tawny brown.

But they were full of fury.

He was no longer feeding on my shame, but he was feeding on Nathan's rage and desire for retribution, or his own, or both. A storm brewed behind his eyes, and, jaw clenching, neck cording, his face grew tight, and he opened his mouth and roared.

He dove, tackling me onto my back. Panting, he sat on my legs and grabbed the knife. I struggled, but couldn't get him off me.

Deirdre's premonition was about to come true. I looked at Jillian and Logan one last time. "I'm sorry," I choked to them. "I'm so sorry." At least they would be unconscious. At least their last moments wouldn't be filled with terror and pain.

Cole clutched the knife in both hands and raised it over his head. I covered my eyes with my hands, not wanting to see the knife plunging down.

*Tristan!* I screamed silently, knowing it was useless, that he would never hear me, but I said it anyway, because I wanted my last thoughts to be of him. *I love you Tristan I love you I love you I love you…*

"Stop!"

It was Nathan who'd shouted.

I uncovered my eyes. Was he trying to help me?

"Give me the knife," he said, hand outstretched. "I want to do it."

Once again, my hopes sank.

Cole snickered and climbed off of me. As he stood, I scrambled up and grabbed Jillian and Logan's hands, and fueled by fear and adrenaline and the desperation to live, I tried to drag them toward the door.

"No!" Cole whirled around with a roar, and plunged the knife into my stomach, right through one of my scars.

Hot pain exploded like a firebomb and spread through my limbs.

Cole pulled out the knife and held it up, and the blade was covered in blood.

I dropped Jillian and Logan's hands, then dropped to my knees.

Blood. My blood. Sticky. Thick. Red. Soaking through my sweater. Covering my hands. Pouring out of me.

So much blood.

An ocean of blood.

I was floating away in it.

The fog was closing in. Lower, thicker, closer.

I couldn't stop it.

# CHAPTER FIFTY-ONE

AS I LAY bleeding, dying, my mind played tricks on me. It gave me a show. Shadows dancing in the fog.

One of those shadows was Tristan. Bursting through the door. Shouting my name.

Cole howling. The knife sailing.

Nathan diving. Nathan screaming. Nathan plummeting.

Tristan and Cole, fists flying, slamming into walls, mirrors shattering with ear-splitting clatter. Broken glass falling like rain.

Jillian and Logan moaning.

Cole pinning Tristan on his back, gripping a jagged piece of mirror like a dagger.

And me. I was in the show too. Sliding a large piece of glass to Tristan.

Tristan, with a war cry, jabbing the glass into Cole's side with a mighty thrust, then scrambling out from under him and over to me.

Cole crawling, dragging, arms folding then straightening again, after Tristan.

Me, dizzy, woozy, using my last ounce of strength to crawl to the bloody knife on the floor and plunge it into Cole's…

Leg.

Because I may always be Killers' Spawn, but I will never be a killer.

Cole collapsed onto a pile of broken mirrors.

I collapsed into a puddle of my own blood.

The fog came. Swift. Thick. Dark. So dark.

Each beat of my heart pumped more blood from the slice in my stomach.

A shadow scrambled through the fog. Tristan. "Please, please, please, Tessa," he begged as he scrambled over Nathan, over Cole, over the broken mirrors. "Don't bleed out. Don't die."

He reached me, breathless, and pulled me from the puddle of blood and into his arms.

I tried to raise my arm to wipe away some blood from Tristan's lip, but couldn't. Tried to keep my eyes open, but couldn't. Tried to speak, but couldn't.

*Take care of Jillian and Logan,* I told him.

"I will," he choked.

I couldn't have much blood left. It would be over soon.

I braced myself for the Nightmare Eyes to appear, to triumphantly shove me into death.

They never came. The Nightmare Eyes had been mine, but I'd destroyed them. No more Nightmare Eyes.

But the fog was still there, looming, sinking, swooping, carrying me away in a tidal wave. The gray fog became tinged with pink, then soaked with red, then saturated with crimson.

*tristaniloveyou*

And as he howled with grief above me, the crimson fog flashed a blinding silver, then turned deep, endless, forever black.

# CHAPTER FIFTY-TWO

OFT.

Furry.

Mewling.

A rough tongue licking my cheek.

Funny the things the brain does as it shuts down. Mine brought Marmalade to me. My little Marma-lady.

She felt so real. Her tongue almost tickled.

Tristan's murmur: "You miss her, don't you, Marmalade?" Then a sigh. Then: "Don't worry, she'll come back to us. I know she will."

Marmalade stopped licking me and hopped off the bed.

*Don't go*, I cried out to her. I wanted my Marma-lady back.

Huh.

Marmalade had hopped off the bed.

Was I… yes. I was on a bed.

A soft bed. With blankets. And pillows. And Tristan, next to me.

But how…

No. It was just another trick of my brain. I was lying in Tristan's arms in Cole's hunting cabin by Lilybrook Lake. My blood was spilling. I was dying.

Deirdre's whisper: "Tristan, sweetheart, go to bed."

"I'm not leaving her."

"I'll stay. She won't be alone."

"I'm not leaving her."

"You need to sleep."

"I'm not leaving her."

"We don't know how long this will last."

"I'm not leaving her."

"They say she may never—"

"I am not leaving her."

# CHAPTER FIFTY-THREE

OG. EVERYWHERE. FOG outside, fog inside. But Tristan was here, somewhere. I could feel him beyond the miles and eons and eternity of fog. Waiting. Waiting for me.

Not waiting for me to die.

Waiting for me to live.

He didn't plead. Didn't squeeze my hand with desperation. He just held it, gently, sometimes raising it to his lips.

There was no anxiety in his grasp. No panic. Only patience.

And confidence. Faith.

He was waiting for me to fight off the fog, and live.

I'd fought off Cole and Nathan Gallagher. I'd destroyed the Nightmare Eyes. Now I had to battle the fog.

I struggled against it. It held me tight, and the more I struggled, the tighter its grasp became, the deeper it dragged me inside its never-ending nothingness.

Tethering me to the light, to life, was Tristan's calm, patient grip on my hand.

I couldn't fight the fog.

But I could run.

So I ran.

Slowly at first. Wobbly. Stumbling.

I ran through the fog, so cold that the air in my lungs turned to ice with each breath. The fog, dark and heavy, surrounded me on all sides, stretching to eternal lengths.

I ran.

With each step I ran faster, and with each step the fog became lighter.

I ran.

I ran to life.

I ran to love.

I ran to Jillian and Logan. I ran to Dennis and Deirdre and Ember. I ran to Tristan.

Faster and lighter. Faster and lighter.

My steps drummed out the beat: Left right, fast-er, light-er, fast-er, light-er, faster, lighter, faster, lighter, fasterlighterfasterlighter-fasterlighter—

The fog thinned, dispersed, dissolved, disintegrated, until it was just a mist, so thin I could barely feel it, and then with one giant leap, I burst through.

Into life.

Into love.

Into Tristan's arms.

I opened my eyes to see him at my bedside in my room, smiling gently down at me, not at all surprised that I'd woken up. "You did it, Clockwise," he whispered. "I knew you would."

I reached out my hand to caress his cheek. *You're my hero after all.*

He became my hero, not because he'd found me in the cabin, not because he'd saved me from Cole and Nathan, not because he'd saved me from the fog.

Tristan finally became my hero by having faith that I could save myself.

# CHAPTER FIFTY-FOUR

WHILE I'D BEEN lost in the fog, the Connellys' guest room had transformed into a hospital room; beeping medical machines lined the perimeter, and I was attached to tubes and an IV. But it was definitely the guest room—the celery-green walls, the white comforter with the little yellow flowers, the reading nook under the window. Marmalade purred at me from atop the bookcase, and Mac thumped his tail beside the bed.

The only thing missing was the Nightmare Eyes. And those were never coming back.

Tristan brushed my hair from my forehead. His own hair was tousled, the way I loved it. His eyes were so blue; I could see their brilliance even in the dark night.

*Jillian and Logan?* I asked, still too weak to speak aloud. *Where are they? Are they okay?*

"They're fine," he murmured, bringing my hand to his lips and kissing it. "They're here. Jillian's rooming with Ember, and Logan's been using my room. I'll go wake everyone up."

*Not yet.* I wanted to see Jillian and Logan and the Connellys, but I wanted to reunite with Tristan first. *Lay down with me.*

He lifted the covers and crawled into my bed, careful not to pull out any tubes. I was wearing a hospital-type gown, and he wore his Lilybrook High tennis hoodie and sweatpants. *Can I have your hoodie?* I asked him. I wanted his hoodie, not for modesty, but because I loved the way I felt when I wore them—safe and cozy and loved. I missed the way they smelled—like soap and masculinity and strength. Like Tristan.

He obliged, peeling off the hoodie and carefully helping me slide it on. The IV tube snaked out from the cuff, but it didn't bother me. I felt whole again. Stronger. Now Tristan wore just a white T-shirt, stretched tight over his chest. We lay back together, and I rested my head on his shoulder and ran my finger over his chin, exploring him again. *So scruffy.* I motioned to the IV. *How long was I in the fog?*

*A long time,* he said.

*What, like two days? Three?*

*Fifteen.*

"Fifteen *days?*" I said out loud, my voice raspy from lack of use.

"We've all been here the whole time. Jillian, Logan, my mom and dad, Ember, and me. It gets kind of crowded in here," he added with a chuckle.

"What happened to Cole and Nathan?" I asked. "Did they hurt you? What about Jillian and Logan? How did you find us in that cabin?"

"Your brother and sister are fine," he said. "They were groggy for a few hours, but they don't remember a thing. I had a cut on my hand from one of the mirrors. The healers took care of it." He held up his palm and flexed his fingers. "Not even a scar."

He caressed my cheek with his thumb. "You have a new scar, though. When Cole stabbed you, the blade nicked your kidney. The healers got to you just in time."

I lifted the covers, then Tristan's hoodie, and peered at my belly. I had a new scar there, a sixth, running down the side right next to one that my mother had given me. The new scar was just a short, thin white line. "A battle scar," I boasted. I'd survived. I could be proud of that scar. Not ashamed.

"And to answer everything else..." He held up his scar-free palm again. "I'll show you."

I raised my hand too, placing my palm on his. We laced our fingers together.

And, now fully in control of the fog, I raised it again.


"Okay," Tessa says. "Five minutes."

Tessa is leaving. Not running away. She's leaving Lilybrook with Jillian and Logan. But she finally relented to letting him come with. Thank God. He won't lose her after all. He kisses her hard in relief, then sprints upstairs to pack.

He'll call his parents from the road. They'll try to convince him to come back, to bring Tessa, Jillian and Logan back, but he will do what Tessa wants. Where she goes, he will go. They belong together.

It takes him four minutes and thirty seconds to throw his stuff in his bag. Phone. Laptop. All of his cash. Jeans. Shoes. Lots of hoodies so Tessa can wear them. He zips up his bag, pats Mac goodbye, jogs down the stairs with his bag in hand.

"I'm ready," he calls out. "Let's go." But no one answers. The front door is open. Jillian and Logan are gone.

And Tessa is gone too.


His chest empty and hollow, he sits slumped on the couch of the family room, holding the promise ring in his fingers. He reads her note, her eight-word note, for the hundredth time.

He knows he can find her. Easily. She said they are going to use their real names. But Tessa asked him not to look for her. She thinks he'll be happier without her.

She is wrong.

But he will do what she wants. He won't look for her, even though he feels like he was roundhouse-kicked in the gut.

His parents come home with two new beds loaded in the minivan, two beds that will never be used now. He tells them that Tessa, Jillian, and Logan left. They try to console him, they tell him they'll find her, there's no way they'll let the three Carson kids go off to live on their own. But their words don't help. Tessa left. She didn't want to stay.

Mac and Aria whine and paw at the front door. For a moment, the emptiness in his chest is replaced by hope. Have they come back? Did Tessa change her mind? He throws the door open, and his chest goes hollow again. The porch is empty.

He hears a tiny *mew,* looks down, and sees Tessa's little orange kitten. How did Marmalade get home? Did Tessa drop her off and leave again?

He scoops the kitten into his arms, looks up and down the street, but doesn't see the white sedan.

He goes back to the family room with Marmalade when a warning premonition slams into him like a speeding truck.

*Tessa.* She's on the floor of a small room. A silver room. Mirrors line the walls, and she's blinded by silver. Jillian and Logan lay near her, not moving.

He feels the blood drain from his face. *This* is his mother's dream. Tessa left Lilybrook because of her brother and sister, and ended up in a little house with silver walls. And after silver, comes red.

Tessa is going to die.

His pulse races; his heart is an engine in his chest. He must stop it from happening. He must find her. He must save her. But where is she? Where is this little house with mirrors lining the walls? Who had taken her?

Tessa's looking up at Nathan. Nathan, his best friend since childhood. Nathan, who hates Tessa simply because of her parents.

Nathan is going to kill Tessa, and her brother and sister.

Tessa's gaze swings to the other side of the mirror-lined room, and lands on Cole.

Cole is there too. But Cole is an ally, a friend. He must be trying to stop Nathan.

But wait. No. Cole is holding a knife. The knife from the evidence room. Cole is taunting her, tormenting her.

Cole is in on it too. He's going to help Nathan kill Tessa, Jillian, and Logan.

But how can he be seeing this? Nathan knows he'd have a warning premonition. He's blocked Tessa from him before. Why isn't he blocking him now?

Then he gets it.

Nathan is *purposely* not blocking the events unfurling in that little silver room. Nathan's not trying to kill Tessa. Nathan is letting him have a premonition about Tessa so he can come save her. Nathan, his best friend since childhood, is betraying his own brother so Tessa will live.

Cole is the enemy. Nathan is an ally.

He needs to find Tessa, fast, before Cole uses that knife.

But where is she? Where is this little house with silver walls?

In his arms, Marmalade mewls.

He needs to get Ember.


Tristan uncurled his hand from mine, and I lowered the fog, ending the visions. "So that's how I found you," he said.

"My hero," I sighed, and snuggled into him.

But he just chuckled. "Nathan was the real hero. And Ember. Even Marmalade. Ember looked into Marmalade's mind, and she showed

Ember where to find you."

"I still wouldn't have survived if you hadn't come when you did," I said.

"And *I* wouldn't have survived if you didn't slide that glass over to me when Cole had me pinned. And then you stabbed him in the leg when he came after me. You're a hero too, Clockwise. You're *my* hero."

I propped myself up on my elbow to study him. To be the hero he'd always thought himself to be, Tristan had wanted to keep me safe in an ivory tower while he slew all my dragons for me. But now he knew that he could not slay my dragons all by himself—and that I was never going to let him. Was he okay with that?

His face was open, his eyes clear. Our gazes locked in the brightening sunlight, and he grinned. A contented, serene, satisfied grin.

"We're heroes for each other," I said.

"I wouldn't have it any other way."

With the tip of my finger, I traced heart shapes on his chest. "What happened next?" I asked. "Did Cole get away?"

He put his arm around me and stroked my arm. "Nope. My dad and a bunch of agents from the APR were a few minutes behind me. They captured him when he tried to leave the cabin. Now he's locked up in the Underground. Forever. They'll make sure to keep him away from your parents," he added, before I could worry about that.

Cole would spend the rest of his life locked up with the very people he hated most, and unable to do anything about it.

"What about Nathan?" I asked. "He betrayed his own brother to help you find me. Why did he do it?"

Tristan gave a little shrug. "I think whatever you said in that cabin convinced him that you shouldn't have to suffer for what your parents did."

I'd convinced myself, too, at the same time.

"Can you text him and ask him to come over tomorrow?" I asked. "I want to thank him."

"I can't," he murmured.

"Why not?"

"Tess." The tightness had returned to his voice, and his body stiffened a little.

I knew, then, why Tristan couldn't text Nathan. My throat closed up, along with my lungs. "He's dead, isn't he?"

Tristan took a deep breath, held it, and finally let it out. "The knife, the one Cole threw at me when I burst in the cabin. Nathan dove in front of it to save me. It got him in the heart. He died instantly." He drew me in closer. "He was my best friend, Tessa, and he died for me. He died for *us*."

I bundled up all of my bad memories of Nathan Gallagher and pushed them deep into the fog. Nathan had died a hero; he died to save Tristan's life, and that was how I wanted to remember him.

Tristan slid his hand behind my head, caressed my cheek with his thumb and leaned in.

But just before he kissed me, I pulled away. "Stop. There's one thing you need to do before you can do that."

"Anything."

I held out my hand, palm down, and wiggled my fingers. "I'd like my promise ring back, please."

He laughed, then hopped out of the bed and strode to my bookcase. He took Marmalade from her top-shelf perch and brought her over. She was wearing a rhinestone-studded periwinkle collar now, and dangling from the collar was my band of pearls.

"She's been holding it for us," Tristan said as he unhooked it. Then he took my hand and slid the ring onto the fourth finger of my left hand. Where it belonged.

"*Now* you can kiss me," I said, giggling.

Grinning hungrily, he dove back under the covers, slid his hand back behind my head, but didn't pause long enough to caress my cheek. He just pressed his lips to mine, and I pressed my body to his, and we didn't part until the sun came up in the morning.

# CHAPTER FIFTY-FIVE

WHEN MARMALADE'S MEOWS woke me up again later that morning, Tristan was still next to me in bed, as I knew he would be. Waiting patiently for me to wake up, as he knew I would.

While I was asleep, I'd had no dreams. There were no more Nightmare Eyes.

I scratched Marmalade's chin then snuggled back into Tristan. He slipped out of the bed just before everyone came in. Dennis, Deirdre, Ember, Jillian, and Logan.

My family.

I didn't know whom to hug first.

Jillian, clearly back to her old self, solved that dilemma for me by pushing past everyone and tackling me. Her hair was still blond, and she was no longer gaunt. I noticed that she still wore the gold bracelet with the heart charm from Gavin.

Logan came next, dressed in pressed Dockers and a button-down shirt. His dark hair was short again, and combed conservatively.

Ember, her hair turquoise with purple tips, carried a little gray ball of fur. A bunny rabbit. "This," she said, "is Harmony. Tristan bought her for me."

"To thank her for helping me find you," Tristan said.

"And plus also," Ember said, "Lyre got back together. We won Battle of the Bands." She glanced at my brother. With a slight blush, she added, "Logan composed the song for us."

My brother shrugged. "I started with the notes on the sheet music you found in Twelve Lakes." Behind him, the sheet music floated in the air. "I decided to call it Long Journey's End."

I gasped, my lungs filling up with hope. "Does that mean…"

"We're staying," Jillian said. She smoothed a strand of my hair behind my ear. "Do you know Tristan stayed here with you this whole time?"

"He's never left me," I said, thinking about our time in the Underground together. I brought his hand to my lips and kissed it. "Not even once."

"I'm sorry we tried to take you away from him," Jillian said.

"But you were willing to leave for us," Logan said. "So, now, we're willing to stay for you."

Jillian and Logan were staying. Here, in Lilybrook, in this house, with me.

Deirdre came forward and squeezed me against her chest, smothering me. But in a good way. In the best way. She was Tristan's mother, my substitute mother, and the best mother in the world.

Dennis, looking vibrant and healthier than ever, patted my knee and kissed the top of my head. "Welcome back, honey."

I was more than back. I was home.

# CHAPTER FIFTY-SIX

THOUGH DENNIS KEPT Jillian and Logan updated on our father's condition while I was lost in the fog for fifteen days, they still weren't ready to visit him. I didn't blame them, but now that I had conquered my Nightmare Eyes, I wanted to see him again. As soon as Deirdre declared me healthy enough to leave the house, my dad's Underground hospital cell was the first place I went. Tristan came with me, of course. Now we stood at his bedside.

Still unconscious, still withered, still pale. He hadn't moved from the last time I was here over six weeks ago. He remained tethered to machines, which beeped evenly. Beep… beep… beep… My presence in his cell was no longer disturbing him, because Cole was no longer able to project his hatred into him.

"I found Jillian and Logan," I told his unconscious form. "They're fine. We're all living together. Us and the Connellys."

No response, as I'd expected. But I hoped that some small part of him heard, and understood.

I opened my bag and pulled out a small canvas, painted in sweeping shades of deep blues, and propped it on the table across from his bed. I'd painted it the night before, and even though I had a tube of black, I didn't paint the Nightmare Eyes.

"I painted this for you, Dad," I said. "It's the ocean. We used to go to the ocean all the time when Jillian, Logan, and I were little. Do you remember that? We were all so happy back then."

No response, except for the rhythmic beeping of the machines. He continued to breathe evenly. In, out. In, out.

I placed my hand over his, and at my touch, his breath caught. "Dad?" I whispered. "Are you awake?"

I waited, not daring to move, to breathe, to blink. "Dad?"

I leaned closer, and Tristan stiffened. Was he having a warning premonition? Was my dad about to grab, squeeze, break my wrist? Was he mad that I was living with Tristan and the Connellys?

Then Tristan shook his head—nothing bad was going to happen—and chuckled at himself. He was just being Tristan, always on guard, ready to save the day if anything bad did happen.

My dad breathed again. My hand still on his, I closed my eyes. I wanted to share my peace and happiness with him. I wasn't a projector, but I tried to project my contentment and serenity into him, as if they were drugs that would heal him.

"Wake up, Dad," I whispered.

His breath caught again, and I knew, one day soon perhaps, he would wake up.

The next person I wanted to visit was Lady Elke, but Mr. Milbourne reported to us that she was gone. The moment the APR learned that Cole had provoked her attack on Tristan, Melanie, and me, they released her. And just in time, too—they had been about to administer her final, permanent neutralization treatment. They'd offered her a job instead. But, distrustful and angry, she wanted nothing to do with it, and threatened to expose the APR. A mnemokinetic agent erased her memory of the entire experience, and she was sent back home to North Dakota. Her psychic powers would eventually regenerate, and she would find an anonymous, and substantial, deposit in her bank account: the APR's confidential restitution.

Lady Elke wasn't going to spend the rest of her life incarcerated and neutralized for a crime she did not commit. Good. She had been a victim, just like I had been. And now we were survivors.

But I wasn't ready to leave the Underground just yet. I had one more thing to do.

Mr. Milbourne, chomping his gum, shook his head before I could even speak. "Forget it. You're still on your mother's refusal list. She added your brother and sister to the list too."

"I didn't come to visit her," I told the warden. "I have something I'd like you to give to her."

From my bag I withdrew a canvas I'd painted of five flowers—one for each member of our family—and a letter written on a page torn from a spiral notebook:

*Mom,*

*I am so incredibly ashamed of all the horrible things you and Dad did. That shame made me feel tainted and tarnished and undeserving of anyone's love.*

*Tristan loved me anyway. Even when I pushed him away, he loved me. His love helped me let go of that shame. I'm ashamed of what you did, but I am no longer ashamed of myself.*

*Despite all that, Mom, I still love you, and somewhere deep down, Jillian and Logan do too. I know you love us. That's why you sent us away.*

*This is the last time I'll contact you. But if you ever want to see me again, just send a message, and I'll come.*

*Thank you for setting us free.*

*~Tessa*

Tristan and I went home for dinner, and as we walked up our driveway, a short figure in black stood at the door, about to ring the bell. Melanie Brunswick.

I hadn't seen her since Lady Elke's, huddling in the backseat of her uncle Kellan's rental car.

"Hey, Mel," Tristan called. There was affection in his tone, but it was more like he was saying hi to a good friend, not someone he had once been in love with. "I didn't realize Lyre had practice today. You can go on in. I'm sure Ember's waiting for you."

"We don't have practice until tomorrow," she said. "I came to talk to you."

"I'll go inside," I said. "Leave you two alone."

"No," Melanie said, "I came to talk to *you*, Tessa."

"Oh. *I'll* go inside then," Tristan said. Melanie gave him a sad smile as he passed her and went inside.

She and I stood in silence, each of us looking at our shoes.

Then at the same time, we each blurted, "I'm sorry."

"What are you sorry for?" she asked.

"For dragging you into the whole Lady Elke thing," I said.

"You were *amazing* at Lady Elke's," she said. "You sneaked out of Lilybrook on your own, flew all by yourself to another state. I would be way too scared to do that. And then, in the shed, you stayed at the door. You found a weapon. You were going to fight. I just hid in the back and cried. I could never do what you did."

"A few months ago, I would have hidden too," I said. "My whole life, all I did was run and hide. But I'm different now."

She cleared her throat. "You know how I knew it was truly over between Tristan and me?"

"How?"

"When we found you behind that laundromat in North Dakota, when he saw you standing there, alone. He just…melted. He has never looked at me the way he looks at you. Never. That's a big part of the reason it took me so long to recover from what happened at Lady Elke's. It wasn't all trauma. It was heartbreak."

"I'm sorry, Melanie."

"I'm okay now." She shuffled her boots, then wiped some invisible dust from her skirt. "Tristan was only with me because I needed him. But he's with you because he *wants* to be."

That was true. I didn't need Tristan. I wanted him. He wanted me.

"Anyway. I just came by to tell you that I'm sorry I held onto him for so long," she said. "He's yours, and I'm okay with that now. I want someone who wants me, not someone who's only with me because I need him."

"Thanks, Melanie." I gestured to the door. "Do you want to come in? It's cold out here."

"No," she said. "I'm going to Winter's house."

"Oh, please give her our condolences," I said. Nathan was her boyfriend, and he died saving us. "How is she?"

"She's the one who's heartbroken now."

"Does she know you came here?" I asked.

"Yeah. I told her that I'm going to be friends with both of you." She looked up from her boots and smiled.

Good for Melanie for standing up for herself. And good for me, because Melanie had just called me her friend.

The next day, Tristan and I returned to the APR, and this time I insisted Jillian and Logan accompany us. There was someone I wanted them to meet.

But first I had to make sure it was okay with him. Tristan and I had my siblings wait outside his office. They agreed, Jillian already starting to cry.

Aaron Jacobs sat at the back of the narrow Technokinetics office, facing the wall. The overhead light was off; the six computer monitors stacked on his desk emitted a faint glow. He was using only one keyboard this time, and his typing rate was slower now. Passionless. I could only see his profile in the dim room, but he could not completely conceal the rough, grooved skin that covered his face behind his oversized glasses. Burn scars.

I gripped Tristan's hand. This was going to be hard. It would be even harder for Jillian and Logan. Hardest of all for Aaron.

I cleared my throat. "Hi, Aaron."

He flinched, then hunched over, hiding his face behind his hand. The scars covered his hand and arm, too.

"My brother and sister are here," I said. "Can I bring them in?"

"No."

Tristan stepped forward. "They feel really bad about what happened. They want to say sorry, and thanks."

Aaron didn't move.

"I told Jillian about you," I said. "Not only how you found them, but how smart you are. How talented. How nice you are. She wants to meet you."

He turned so I could only see the back of his head. "No, she doesn't. She just feels sorry for me. I don't want to meet her anyway."

"Aaron?" The plea came from my sister, standing in the doorway. Her cheeks were streaked with tears. "It's Jillian. Can I talk to you?"

He practically dove into the darkest corner of the office. "Get out. Get out!"

"Please let me talk to you," she begged.

He kept his head turned away. "Just leave. All of you."

I put my hand on his shoulder, just for a moment. "Sorry, Aaron."

We slowly shuffled away.

# CHAPTER FIFTY-SEVEN

THE MENU FOR Sunday brunch: crepes with strawberries and bananas, fluffy egg-white omelets, and blueberry muffins with extra blueberries.

I rubbed my hands together and set to work. The cooking supplies Dennis and Deirdre had given me for my birthday were set out on the counter. I separated the eggs with my egg-separator. I mixed the batter with my mixing spoon. I heated the crepes to perfection on my pans. Tristan offered to help, but I wanted to do it all myself. I missed cooking.

"Smells great." Tristan came up behind me, rubbing my hip with one hand and popping a blueberry in his mouth with the other. "Can I help?"

"Nope, I got it." I needed to cut up the vegetables for the omelets. I reached for the knife, and stopped.

I couldn't do it. I could not touch that knife. Flashes of Cole standing over me, swiping the knife through the air...

I wrapped my hands around my stomach. I searched my mind for the Nightmare Eyes, but they were gone. I tried again, but I still couldn't make myself touch that long, shiny, sharp, blade.

"Um, actually, will you chop the veggies?" I asked Tristan. "I need to set the table."

"No prob." He kissed me, then grabbed the knife and began slicing the mushrooms. Relieved, I grabbed a stack of plates from the cabinet.

"Kids, help Tessa out and set the table," Deirdre said.

From his seat, Logan waved his hand at the fridge. The orange juice and milk floated across the kitchen and set themselves on the table.

"That's cheating," Ember pouted as she made three trips to bring seven glasses.

Jillian didn't even glance at the utensil drawer. It opened on its own, and seven forks and spoons glided through the air. Dennis ducked as a spoon zipped past him. "Sorry," Jillian mumbled. "Forgot that you're not used to things like that."

While we ate, Tristan teased Ember by pulling on her hair, and she stuck out her tongue at him, then grabbed the blueberry muffin from his hand. The animals scampered through the kitchen, except for Harmony the bunny, who ignored all of us. Dennis and Logan discussed internships at the APR. Tristan and I discussed the blood drive we were starting next week in memory of Nathan Gallagher. Ember, her cheeks pink, asked Logan if he'd please write another song for the band. Deirdre asked Jillian if she'd like to sign up for dance classes, and Jillian shyly replied yes.

I kept my eye on the knife, which remained on the counter, long, shiny, and sharp.

When we were done and the kitchen was clean—an easy task thanks to Jillian and Logan's PK—Deirdre shooed everyone away, ordering us to go study. We had a lot of schoolwork to make up.

We camped out in the family room with our textbooks and notes, Tristan next to me and giving me the occasional kiss. After a while, I took a break and lifted the fog, allowing visions of happy Connelly family moments to filter through. Jillian, Logan, and I would be part of those happy family moments from now on.

The heartless thing about the past is our inability to change it. It's too late to make any alterations.

We could not change the past. But we could take charge of our future.

Taking charge of our future meant we had a lot of work ahead of us. Jillian and Logan needed to recover from their ordeal, and they needed to get Aaron to forgive them. Tristan would try to get his job back at the APR. I would paint my murals, and maybe even use knives again.

But no matter what, my future would be spent in this cluttered, chaotic, happy home in Lilybrook, with Dennis and Deirdre, and Jillian and Logan and Ember, and two dogs, two cats, and one bunny rabbit. And with Tristan, my blue-eyed, broad-shouldered, perfectly heroic boyfriend.

My future would be spent surrounded by love.

Run. *Run.*

Muscles aching, lungs burning, heart bursting, I ran against the April wind down a path lined with trees just beginning to bud.

It felt fantastic.

Tristan was only a few feet ahead of me. For our first jog in Lilybrook, he'd taken me to a trail that wound around Lilybrook Park. As we had in Twelve Lakes, we ran in a clockwise direction. He was almost fully up to speed, but I was still a little weak from my long, fog-induced slumber.

But I was catching up to him.

He stopped, turned, and wiggled his blue baseball cap, which he wore backwards on his head. "If you catch me," he said, "I'll let you keep the hat." Then he shot off again.

That was all the inspiration I needed—the same challenge he'd issued once before, in Twelve Lakes. I'd beaten him then; I could beat him now.

I charged forward at full throttle, zooming past the budding wildflowers, feet pounding in rhythm. Left-right-left-right.

Within seconds I reached him. "Ha! Caught you!"

But he turned and caught me in his arms instead, and gave me a kiss. "Us," he said as he put the hat on my head. "You and me."

And my heart echoed in rhythm: *thump. Thump-th-thump.*

I wrapped my arms around his neck, and together, we stumbled to a tree just off the path and sank behind it.

By the time we came out from behind the tree, clothes disheveled, hair tangled, and lips tingling, we were too tired to finish our run. We headed home instead, hand-in-hand.

# ACKNOWLEDGMENTS

I started writing because sometimes I love a book so much that I never want it to end. I don't want to say goodbye to the characters. I realized that the only way I'd never have to say goodbye to characters I love would be to write them myself. Thus, Tessa, Tristan, Jillian, Logan, Ember, Dennis, and Deirdre (and yes, even Wendy, Andy, and Kellan) were created. I wrote their first book, *Deception So Deadly*, and I was having so much fun and I loved the characters so much that I continued their story in this book, *Deception So Dark*. And now that the *Deception So* series is continuing indefinitely, I may never have to say goodbye to my beloved characters. And neither will you!

Thank you to Erica O'Rourke and Heather Marshall for being the initial readers of *Deception So Dark*. You gave me indispensable advice and encouragement from the first word to the last.

Erica and Heather, along with Lynne Hartzer, Melonie Johnson, Melanie Bruce, and Sonali Dev, Portland Midwest: Thank you for your friendship, knowledge, and laughs. I feel a sisterhood with you that is unparalleled. You got me through a very dark time and helped me emerge victorious. #PortlandMidwest forever.

Thank you to Snowy Wings Publishing. You helped me love publishing, and writing, again.

Thank you to my cover artist, Lyssa Chiavari of Key of Heart

Designs. Once again, you have created a masterpiece.

Special thanks to Maya Rock for your critical eye and spot-on editorial notes.

Thanks to my friends who always ask how the writing is going and occasionally drag me back to the real world. Mary & Mike and Lisa & Rosie, I look forward to our Sunday Night Viewing Parties all week long. They are the only social event I won't decline in favor of staying home and writing.

Thanks to my unfailingly supportive parents, Judi & Richard and Chuck & Bonnie.

Thank you, always and forever, to my beautiful children. You amaze me every day.

Thanks to my husband, Glen. I couldn't have done this without you. You are my hero.

And finally, I want to thank you, my wonderful readers. It means the world to me that you care enough about Tessa and Tristan to read more of their story. Thank you for recommending my books to your friends, and especially for reviewing them online. Thank you for your emails, too. I cherish each and every one of them. It is truly an honor to be part of your lives.

# Q&A WITH AUTHOR CLARA KENSIE

**Why do I sometimes see the first two DECEPTION SO books online, broken up into six short parts with different titles and different covers?**

The first two books of the DECEPTION SO series were originally published by a different publisher. They decided to take the two books and turn them into a six-part serial titled *Run to You*. I eventually got my rights back to the series. I compiled the two books back to their original full lengths and returned their original titles. So, *Run to You Parts 1-3* is now the full-length *Deception So Deadly*, and *Run to You Parts 4-6* is now *Deception So Dark*. I commissioned gorgeous new covers and re-released the books through an amazing indie author co-op called Snowy Wings Publishing. The DECEPTION SO series is finally published the way it was meant to be. Best of all, I'm continuing the series with more books, starting with the never-before-published *Deception So Dangerous*!

**Were any of the events in the DECEPTION SO books based on things that happened to you in real life?**

No events, but some of the characters are based on people I know in real life. My husband is unfailingly supportive of all of my endeavors, the same way Tristan supports Tessa's. Melanie's seeking ability was inspired by my daughter's uncanny skill of finding lost things. Tessa has nightmares, and so do I. We both paint murals. I love to wear my husband's oversized hoodies the same way Tessa loves to wear Tristan's. Deirdre's dislike of housework and cooking comes directly from me. I even have a plaque hanging in my kitchen that reads, *Please excuse the noise and mess, we are busy making happy memories.*

**Of the new characters in Book Two, which one is your favorite?**

I love Aaron. Sweet, smart, wounded, love-struck Aaron.

**Will there be more books in the DECEPTION SO series?**

I'm thrilled to finally be able to say YES! Amazing things happen for Tessa and Tristan in DECEPTION SO #3: *Deception So Dangerous.* After that, I have books in mind for Jillian, Logan, Ember, Aaron, Melanie, some new characters you'll meet in Book Three, a few short stories and novellas, and even a prequel about a teenage Dennis and Deirdre (you'll never guess how they met!).

**How can I find out more about the DECEPTION SO series and learn about your next releases?**

There are lots of ways! You can visit my website at clarakensie.com; you can also sign up for my newsletter there and be the first to know all my latest news.

You can also like me on Facebook at facebook.com/authorclarakensie; and of course you can send me an email at clara@clarakensie.com!

# PLAYLIST FOR DECEPTION SO DEADLY

Listen on Spotify: spoti.fi/DeceptionSoDark

**"Wildflowers"** – Tom Petty and the Heartbreakers

**"Down in a Cold Dirty Well"** – Justin Nozuka

**"Bad Things"** – Jace Everett

**"Fireflies of Montreal"** – Laurena Segura

**"All Too Well"** – Taylor Swift

**"The Reason"** – Hoobastank

**"Candy Machine Gun"** – Haley Bonar

**"Silhouette Serenade"** – Vendetta Red

**"Open Season"** – High Highs

**"Dead Hearts"** – Stars

**"Do You Realize??"** – The Flaming Lips

**"The Adventure"** – Angels & Airwaves

**"Agenda Suicide"** – The Faint

**"Ghosts and Creatures"** – Telekinesis

**"Hold On, Hold On"** – Neko Case

**"Home"** – Phillip Phillips

**"Home Again"** – Michael Kiwanuka

**"Just a Game"** – Birdy

**"I Want You to Want Me"** – Cheap Trick

# ALSO BY CLARA KENSIE

*The Deception So Series*

Book One: Deception So Deadly

Book Three: Deception So Dangerous
(coming August 2018)

*Other Novels*

Aftermath

# ABOUT THE AUTHOR

Clara Kensie grew up near Chicago, reading every book she could find and using her diary to write stories about a girl with psychic powers who solved mysteries. She purposely did not hide her diary, hoping someone would read it and assume she was writing about herself. Since then, she's swapped her diary for a computer and admits her characters are fictional, but otherwise she hasn't changed one bit.

Today, Clara is an award-winning author of dark fiction for young adults. Her novel *Aftermath* (S&S/Simon Pulse), a dark, ripped-from-the-headlines contemporary in the tradition of *Room* and *The Lovely Bones*, is on Goodreads' list of Most Popular Books Published in November 2016, and Young Adult Books Central declared it a Top Ten Book of 2016. The first two books in her super-romantic psychic thriller Deception So series were an RT Book Review Editors' Pick for Best Books of 2014, and the first book in the series, *Deception So Deadly*, was a 2015 RITA® Award finalist for Best Young Adult Romance and the 2015 RITA® Award Winner for Best First Book. Clara is re-releasing the first two Deception So books and continuing the series with Snowy Wings Publishing.

Her favorite foods are guacamole and cookie dough. But not together. That would be gross.

Visit Clara online at www.clarakensie.com.